CON GAME

CON GAME

TERRY AMBROSE

CON GAME

This book is a work of fiction. Names, characters, places, and incidents are either products of the author's imagination or are used fictitiously.

CON GAME

Copyright © 2014 by Terry Ambrose

Cover and Book design by Kathy Ambrose
Cover type treatment by Monkey C Media

ISBN: 978-0-9859540-4-8

Printed in the United States of America.

ACKNOWLEDGMENTS

I'd like to thank the Rancho Bernardo Writers Group for their continued support and critiques. Each week, the group listened to five pages of the manuscript and provided valuable feedback on what worked and what didn't. The group included Peter Berkos, Mark Carlson, Lillian Herzberg, Debra Friend, Rosalie Kramer, Maryjane Roe, Morry Shechet, and Brae Wykoff. A special thank you goes out to my niece Brenna, who helped me with the dialogue for Lily. In the face of adults who were upset by the way Lily spoke, it was like, awesome, to get a teen's-eye view.

As always, my wife Kathy deserves huge kudos for her patience and support and for her design of the cover. Also, thanks go to Jennifer Thompson and Aleta at Monkey C Media for the text treatment on the cover—you really helped make it pop!

Along the way, there have certainly been others who have helped me and if I haven't mentioned you, please accept my apologies. I really need to keep better notes!

Other books by Terry Ambrose

McKenna Mysteries

PHOTO FINISH

KAUAI TEMPTATIONS

License to Lie Series

LICENSE TO LIE

CON GAME

Anthologies

LIFE'S SHORTS

AUTHOR'S NOTE

Con Game is the sequel to *License to Lie*. Even though this is a sequel and there are references to events that have brought Skip Cosgrove and Roxy Tanner to a turning point in their lives, you can read either book first. When I originally conceived the idea of this series, I wanted to bring together two characters with opposing views of the world. In this second book, each understands the other a bit more and they must decide whether they can live with that knowledge.

The premise behind *Con Game* from the beginning was that everyone has a breaking point. The question is, what do we do when we reach it?

Terry Ambrose
March 2014

CHAPTER 1

ROXY

I'm not particularly proud of my profession. When I was a little girl, I never said, "I want to grow up to be a con artist." But, here I was at a swanky Hollywood party, wearing a thousand-dollar sapphire-blue cocktail dress from Lela Rose, a pair of Jimmy Choo stilettos that set me back another half grand and a Victoria's Secret bra that gave me cleavage any hooker would be proud to display.

If I had a regular job—one where I wasn't trying to steal money from the moron in front of me—I'd slap him hard before telling him to look me in my baby blues. Instead, I knew what he expected, his reputation, and even what buttons to push. Go ahead, check out "the girls," Jack. His fun would cost him not six, but seven figures.

I leaned into him, smiling sweetly. "So, you're really an investment banker?"

Jack Welton gave the lapels of his tux a little tug of satisfaction as he puffed up his chest. "Honey, I deal with millions of dollars every day. I have clients who invest more money than you can dream of."

Believe me, Jack, I can dream. I glanced at the floor for a half second, then gazed into his eyes. "That's exciting."

He took a quick sip of his scotch, then spent two seconds checking out my neckline before he surveyed the room. Welton reached out; his fingers rested lightly on my arm. I sucked in a little breath for effect. He motioned toward the door with his head as his hand inched up my arm. He was so reassuring. "No one will know."

No one except your wife, asshole. Since Mrs. Welton was the majority shareholder in "his" company—the legitimate one—pissing her off could be fatal to the front for his other business, a massive stock scam. Welton's hand lingered a few inches above my elbow.

When my phone rang, I recognized the tone immediately. It was Skip. Was he calling to chew me out again? He hated what I did. The cons. The danger. The rush.

"Excuse me." I pulled the phone from my cocktail bag to shut off the ringer. Sorry Skip, I'm done. Work comes before stupid arguments. Or feelings. I slipped the phone back into my bag.

Shit. When I glanced up, Welton was surveying the room in search of other available women. I put my hand on the sleeve of his tux. "Are you, um, married?" The gentle caress, paired with the subtle promise of things to come, got his attention.

"What if I was?"

I winked. "The girls just want to have fun."

He leered at my cleavage again; I arched my back enough to give him a better look. Never mind the fact that my knock-em-dead dress had silk lining or that it accented my eyes perfectly. And forget the killer black stilettos. Jack only cared about where my neckline stopped. Oh Jack, I thought, drool is so unbecoming.

My source had told me how much the wife, Frederica Gurney-Welton, hated fundraisers. She almost always begged off of these things with a headache, being too tired, or some other excuse. With Frederica out of the picture, this jackass only cared about how fast he could get laid. He whispered, "I have a little apartment downtown."

What Jack the Ass didn't know was, I already knew about his apartment thanks to his last girlfriend. It was all I could do to not laugh at how naturally the nickname flowed. The woman who hired me gave it to him. Thanks to her, I had a little surprise waiting for Mr. Smooth at his apartment. He probably never gave breaking up with Anita a second thought, but she wanted revenge. Lots of it. That's where I came in.

Anita swore her motive for hiring me was to bring Welton to justice, to stop him from hurting innocent victims. The thing is, I learned a long time ago how even the purest of the pure can be fueled by greed when huge sums of money are in play. Her motives or the possible fallout from this job didn't matter to me. This was a job. A half mil. The bottom line? Jack's morality wasn't my concern.

Another man approached. Decked out in a fitted tux, he was, you might say, tall, dark and gorgeous. Slicked back hair with dark penetrating eyes. For him, I might be willing to—who knows?

"Hey, Jack!"

The two men shook hands. Immediately, Tall, Dark and Gorgeous flashed me a brilliant smile. "I'm Sam Oswald. Everyone calls me Oz."

"I'm delighted to meet you, Oz." Which I was. I put Welton on hold for a moment while I absorbed the musky scent of this new arrival's aftershave. The chemistry between us was what I needed to push my mark into the corner where I wanted him. I let Oz hold my hand a couple of seconds too long. Precisely long enough to make Welton bristle.

"Why haven't we met before?"

"Fate, I guess." It was my dad who taught me about contingency planning. Always have a backup, he'd said. Thank goodness Dad wasn't here to see how well his overachiever daughter learned how to use those lessons. I extracted a business card from my clutch. It was from an old con in which I'd pretended to run an escort service. "Call me." Welton peered at the card over Oz's shoulder—it looked like he might dump his load on the spot.

Oz eyed the card before he snatched it out of my hand. He stuffed it into his shirt pocket, then lowered his voice. He, too, couldn't keep his eyes where they belonged. "Are you, um, here on business?"

I turned to Welton. "Well?"

Oz said, "You lucky bastard. If you don't, I will."

Welton practically spit on himself when he blurted his answer. "Beat it."

"Guess I'm busy tonight." Now, it was Oz's turn to pine while I stroked Welton's arm.

Oz shook his head, a look of wonder on his face. "How'd you meet—never mind. God, I love Hollywood." He pulled out the card again, read it, and slipped it back into his pocket. "I'd really like to see you sometime."

He got the oh-so-genuine wink with the smile I'd perfected during my freshman year in high school. "Call me."

Before he walked away, he slapped Welton on the shoulder. "You lucky bastard. You goddamn lucky bastard."

If he only knew. Jack Welton wasn't going to come anywhere close to getting lucky tonight.

With Oz out of earshot, Welton said, "I thought you were a guest."

"I am." It took only a moment to catch the eye of our host, a distinguished, silver-haired Hollywood producer, across the room. He had no clue who I was, but when I smiled, he tipped his glass in acknowledgment. I gave Jack my full attention again. "I can play rough, too. Would you prefer that?"

Jack swallowed hard. "You know him? Personally?"

I reached out to rest my fingertips on Jack's arm before hitting him with the Southern drawl. "How do you like it, sugar?"

"How much?"

"A thousand."

"For the night?"

I shook my head. "Oh, Jack. You're funny. An hour. But, you're kind of cute, so for the night we'll just call it an even five." The room was filled with high society. Tuxes, cocktail dresses and evening gowns. Glamor and glitz. Boring conversations, fake laughs.

"Let's get out of here," he said.

The minute he took my arm, I could almost taste my regret.

CHAPTER 2

S K I P

Skip Cosgrove dropped his cell phone to the cold asphalt. He didn't want to die alone. Not now. Not next to some dumpster in a dark alley.

Roxy didn't even answer.

A horn blared a block away on the Coast Highway. The world felt hazy. Dammit. He was disconnecting.

How long would it take to bleed out?

He remembered lights from a car passing on the street. It may have been the only thing that saved him from his attacker. The rumble of a truck's diesel engine drowned out the traffic noise a block away.

Two figures outlined by white light ran toward him.

"Christ almighty," said the closer of the two.

"He alive?" It was the other. He stood, a frozen shadow against the light.

The closest one kneeled next to Skip, fingering his neck. The man's fingers shook so violently Skip doubted he could detect a pulse. "I ain't never seen so much blood. Call 9-1-1!"

"Already on it . . . yeah . . . we found a guy bleeding."

Skip closed his eyes. The world faded. In the background, he heard, "Hell if I know lady, the guy's layin' here in the alley bleeding to death when we shown up to haul away the trash."

"Christ, I got blood all over me."

"She said two minutes!"

Skip opened his eyes. The kneeling man had pulled away. He stood, wiping his hands on his chest. "I got this shit all over me, man. I'm gonna puke." Retching sounds mixed with the diesel's rumble.

Moments later, sirens wailed, at first, distant, then so intense their echoes vibrated off the walls. Flashing lights cast the alley into alternating bands of red, white and blue.

The pavement. It felt cold.

Someone rolled him over. Dirt and blood from the asphalt filled his mouth, dried his throat.

A woman yelled, "Head wound. I'll try to stop the bleeding."

Were these the EMTs?

"Can you hear me?" Another new voice. Afraid, but determined.

"BP dropping!" It was the woman.

Skip's arm stung with the prick of a needle. Cold coursed through his veins.

"1 . . . 2 . . . 3."

Strong hands hoisted him onto a soft surface. The world moved. A bright overhead light slid into view. He shut his eyes to block out the brightness. Tightness in his chest. Bile filled his throat. Everything so foggy. Before he died, he had to remember. There was something to do. Would they ask questions on the other side?

He felt something on his face. Cool air rushed into his lungs. Fragmented pictures popped into Skip's mind.

Joey Santino. A dingy bar. A meeting. Oncoming headlights on Coast Highway.

More sirens pierced the air. Disembodied voices barked. Was someone yelling at him? He couldn't tell.

Santino. He turned down this street.

The woman's insistent voice broke in. "C'mon mister, don't you give up on my shift."

There's only one street lamp. It's not enough light. There's too much risk.

A bright light shone in one of Skip's eyes, then the other.

Too many hidden shadows.

"BP seventy-two over forty-one."

Nothing here but danger. It even smells like it.

"Son-of-a-bitch is lucky he didn't bleed out."

A footstep. Behind him. The pain. White lightening shooting through his skull.

"Damn. Sixty-eight over forty."

"Your girlfriend's next. But first—"

"No! You will not die on my shift, goddammit!"

CHAPTER 3

ROXY

Welton and I stepped into the coolness of night. The air was fresh. Exactly what I needed to cleanse my senses. Here in the hills above L.A., the residents lived in multimillion-dollar homes, kept perfectly manicured yards, drove elegant cars and could peer down on the little people whenever they chose. I'd enjoyed my brief opportunity to rub shoulders with the rich and famous, but now it was time to do my job.

Goosebumps rose on my bare skin, but Welton didn't offer his coat. He made no move to comfort me. I was hired help. Nothing more. I knew it. He knew it.

"How'd you get here?" he asked.

"Limo." Cons often lived or died based on seemingly insignificant details. It was a fact of life. It was also a mistake I tried not to make.

"Can you—"

I cut the jerk off. "Not unless I'm going home alone. You don't have a car?"

"I told my driver to take the rest of the night off." He grumbled, but called a cab on his cell.

Ten minutes later, this California girl had resolved she needed another shopping trip to Saks for a wrap to match her new dress.

My already healthy disrespect for Welton was at a new high. The cheapskate was stealing millions from unsuspecting investors, yet he wanted to hitch a ride with a hooker to avoid paying a few bucks in overtime?

The cabbie made great time. Within 15 minutes, we were sitting at a red light one block from Welton's swank apartment building. Twenty-two floors. A tower of gleaming light in downtown L.A. Somehow, it fit Welton's persona. The company owned the apartment, which gave him complete access according to Anita. The apartment cost was buried somewhere in the real estate holdings of the company's financial statements.

According to Anita, using the condo to seduce women was Jack's M.O. She was one of the latest "girls" who had been to the condo, one more who wanted to join the "I Hate Jack" fan club. Their plight should piss me off. It was why I should be here. I should be doing this because this guy preyed on his female employees. I wasn't.

I gave Welton a sweet smile as he worked his hand up my thigh. I turned the tables by moving his hand back in his lap with mine resting on top of his. "Honey, you've got to pay to play."

The brash conglomeration of tambourines, drums and whiny voices spewing from the radio set my nerves on edge. The cabbie put on a good show by singing along, but the mirror was a little cockeyed. I knew this one, like most cabbies, wasn't missing a thing.

Our cab surged forward the moment the light turned green. I removed my hand. Even in the dimness, I saw Welton's eyes flash. He was pissed. Excited. The vein in his neck pounded furiously. A wave of self-satisfaction washed over me. I was the one Welton would go looking for afterwards when this was over. That risk got me a 50-50 split with Anita. A half million dollars.

The more complex the con, the harder it is to keep all the moving parts in sync. My ideal option was to have Welton voluntarily access his bank account from his laptop. His one mistake would save me from having to bring in an expert hacker, to avoid the hassles of dealing with yet another partner, but raised the pressure on me to perform.

The lines on Welton's face, the way he breathed, everything indicated a mark on the edge. It wouldn't take much to have him tapping the keys for money at a frantic pace to get laid. He forced a smile. "You're one tough bitch."

"You do know how to flatter a girl." I pursed my lips.

"Upstairs."

"Can't wait." I laced my left arm through his right with my free hand on his elbow. "This will be a night you'll never forget. I promise."

The doorman, a young innocent with shoulders broad enough to stretch the fabric of his uniform, did an admirable job of attempting to remain impassive. His buzz cut gave him a conservative appearance, but that didn't stop him from stealing a glance at me. I winked; he blushed six shades of red before he averted his eyes. Welton, who caught the whole interaction, puffed up his chest like a proud schoolboy as he jabbed the elevator up button.

Even though the ride to the 22nd floor took less than half a minute, his breathing became more shallow and rapid with each passing moment. The doors were barely open when he slipped sideways between them to wait impatiently in the hall. The way he fidgeted worried me. Had I lost him to some weird elevator phobia? It felt like I'd been transported to con-game hell, a place I might never escape. Was I destined to repeat the same moves until I died?

Keys in hand, Welton reached for the doorknob. I stopped him with a firm grip of my hand on his.

He glanced at me. "Slowly," I whispered. Together, we inched the key toward the lock until it slipped in. The ridges and grooves sent a vibration into his hand as each slipped past a pin. "Very . . . very . . . slowly."

He exhaled—his breath raspy, catching in spurts. According to Anita, he'd always controlled their interactions. He'd probably acted the same with every woman he'd ever known, but maybe Jack had a secret wish to be dominated. The key settled in. Welton started to turn it, but stopped when I applied a slight counter pressure while massaging the back of his hand. With my shoulder resting against his, his tension felt like an electrical charge jumping through the material of his jacket.

"Enjoy the moment." I released the counter pressure.

CHAPTER 4

S K I P

A beautiful woman with flowing blonde hair, a white diaphanous gown clinging to her every curve, beckoned. Skip felt her almost irresistible call, her power, pulling him closer to the precipice he'd already confronted once in his life.

"Not again." He spoke, but his words seemed lost in her beauty.

He felt her touch deep within. Her perfect skin, her smile, the way she floated before him, she tugged at his heart. He knew this woman. Knew her all too well. He'd invented her warm touch, her cold heart to help him fight her real-life counterpart. Known by many names—morphine, Oxycodone, Fentanyl—she was loving, yet selfish. Soothing, yet callous. She would forever be a part of him, ready to exert her grip on his soul.

"I will not give in to you."

The beauty before him licked her lips. "I'll be waiting."

His creation disappeared. In her place was an IV drip chamber, half-filled with clear solution. He watched each drop grow larger, heavier, then fall. 1 . . . 2 . . . 3 . . . 4. What time was it? He had no idea. He drifted back to sleep, this time counting drops, the equivalent of tiny liquid sheep, through the IV.

The sounds of a crash cart rattled down the hallway. Hospital personnel ran past his room at a speed they reserved for crises; their voices sounded almost like echoes.

"Clear!"

A sickening whine. The jolt of an AED.

"Clear!"

He whispered to the darkness. "Poor bastard. He won't even know how to fight back."

Again, it repeated. He pushed harder to block out the chaos. He wondered how much blood they had given him. What else might they have pumped into his veins? And the dream—the seductress. She'd been so real. No less real than the room or the dim hallway outside the door.

CHAPTER 5

R O X Y

During my reconnaissance earlier in the day, Welton's condo had been spotless. Nothing had changed. The carpet still showed no signs of wear, not even a footprint. Marble flooring, which ran from the entryway to a second master suite down the hall, gleamed as though it had been polished by hand. A dining set with a glass table top, black lacquered base and four leather captain's chairs positioned precisely for maximum visual appeal commanded the dining area. A daily maid service kept the place looking pristine.

On one wall in the living room hung the obligatory big screen TV; a collection of oil paintings dominated the others. Jack liked to frequent the local galleries, where he picked up works by the "up and comers." I had little doubt these were all originals. I admired a particularly bold oil on the wall. Broad brush strokes in shades of red, black and gray along with touches of blue. It smacked of a cross between the aurora borealis and sunset off the California coast. It was peaceful, yet surreal at the same time.

"Like it?" Welton said.

"It's very bold."

"Anton's gonna be big someday."

"You know him?"

"I've commissioned a few pieces."

"Nice place you have here." I kept my hands at my sides while strolling to the window to admire the spectacle of lights—L.A. dressed up for the evening. A string of yellowish dots snaked from the valley floor into the hills where a quarter moon rose over the horizon.

I could make any number of mistakes tonight, but one of the big ones would be to leave behind a fingerprint. I'd worn gloves to plant my "toolkit" in the powder room on my previous trip. This time, I'd have to wipe down everything I touched.

Jack's charm, power, and money—partially gained through marriage, partially though his stock scam—had lured Anita here. For some reason I couldn't fathom, Anita was surprised when her sugar daddy tired of his mistress as he had with the women before her. Welton slipped his arms around my waist. I thought, show me the money, Jack, not what you think you can do with those paws. I turned to face him.

His eyes were cold. "Since I'm paying for this, let's get to it, shall we?"

I gently pushed him away, wagging a finger in front of his face. "That's just it, you haven't paid yet. So, we need to settle the business end before we get to the—other end." I winked.

For the briefest of moments an angry fire flared in his eyes. From what Anita had told me, Welton was strong, but not trained to fight. If he decided to force himself on me, my red belt in karate gave me the edge. I could handle him unless he went totally gonzo or landed a lucky punch.

"A thousand an hour, right?"

I stroked his neck with my index finger. "If that's all you can handle, sure."

He swallowed hard. "Fine. Wait here."

Twenty-two floors up in downtown L.A. What a view. Off in the distance, a set of red taillights crawled along the horizon. Welton's image reflected in the glass when he returned to the room. He held out a piece of paper; I suppressed a laugh. "Is this a joke? You want me to take a check?"

"It's good. I didn't know I was going to have expenses tonight."

"So tomorrow morning you call your bank to stop payment? Sorry Jack, I don't work on credit. I need guaranteed funds. Cash usually works well."

Welton's cheek twitched. "What do you want me to do, for chrissake, go to the corner ATM?"

"There is another way." I wrote a bank account number on the back of one of the escort cards. That particular con had netted me a cool twenty grand. It was nice to know my business expense was giving me a good return on investment. "Transfer the money into my account. Don't worry, it's secure."

"My wife will see the transfer."

I laid a hand on his chest, a move he interpreted as a green light to feel me up. I backed away a few inches, feigning incredulity. "You think she won't see the check? You must have another bank account. Isn't this, like, a business expense or something? I thought you had a very profitable business. Did you fib to me, Jack?"

"Damn right I run a big business. I deal with millions of dollars every day."

"I have some clients who like to call our time . . . a retreat."

"I don't know."

What? Now he was afraid of an audit? This guy—the one who was stealing people blind—didn't want to misclassify a personal expense? Give me a break. I lowered my hand from his chest to his stomach. His eyes grew large when I traced a heart with my fingertip.

He nodded, slowly at first, then more vigorously until I thought he might explode with self-satisfaction. "Shit, yeah. A business retreat."

"While you're handling your end, I'll freshen up. Where's your ladies room?"

He pointed toward the hallway, the same place I'd been earlier.

"Be right back."

"Perfect. I need to use the computer anyway." Welton crossed the room to a desk with a lamp, a telephone and a laptop that looked like it, too, had been staged. From the hallway, I saw his reflection in the window straightening out his pants before pressing the laptop's power button.

Inside the bathroom, I pulled on a pair of latex gloves. This room also had a professionally decorated appearance with high-end accents done up in a tasteful combination of brushed nickel, grays and blues. The luxury amenities were perfectly maintained without a speck of dirt, dust or clutter to spoil the image. Another of the amenities, one Jack didn't know about, was the black leather case containing a Taser C-2 in the bottom drawer of the bathroom vanity.

I'd planted the Taser during my reconnaissance trip. Now, I weighed it in my hand. Seven ounces of pure agony for Jack Welton. Seven ounces. I placed the Taser next to a brushed-nickel bowl containing a delightfully scented potpourri, then texted Anita to meet me at the door.

I leaned into the hallway. "How's it going?"

"Almost done. Give me a few more seconds."

Armed with a four-hundred-dollar cocktail clutch from Saks in one hand, an equally expensive Taser C-2 in the other, it was time to do battle. Twenty feet of open space broken only by a glass dining table separated me from Welton. I stepped around the dining set, my arm held straight out in front of me. Engrossed in the job of transferring money, Welton never saw me coming.

His back made the perfect target, wide and still. I'd convinced myself this was no different than aiming at a paper target on the gun range. So, why was I walking stiff legged? I pulled the trigger. The crackle of the unleashed electrical charge froze me in my tracks. Two darts shot across the room at fifty-five meters per second. The darts buried themselves into the skin beneath his custom-tailored shirt. The paper target was suddenly all too alive.

I stood, frozen in place with my stilettos feeling like a pair of snowshoes buried deep in a drift as Welton writhed in agony. It felt like an eternity before he slumped back in his chair and fell to the floor.

"Son-of-a-bitch. Never again." I swallowed hard, precious seconds ticking by as I fought to shake off what I'd just witnessed.

I walked to the front door, rapped twice and waited. The person on the outside knocked twice in return. My two amateur partners donned ski masks the moment they entered the apartment. Dom rushed to Welton's side, where he checked for a pulse while Anita watched from one side.

Dom wasn't an MD, but a veterinarian with access to some great drugs. "This asshole almost cost me everything I have. It's my right to put him down."

Anita shook her head. "It's only money, Dom!"

"You didn't deserve what he did to you."

Anita knelt next to her ex-lover. She started to reach for his face, but the caution in my voice stopped her. "The money's got to be enough."

"After what he did, Sis? Really? Get his feet." Dom muttered to himself as he grabbed Welton's arms.

"You're right." Anita wiped at her cheeks. "He's the one who screwed up, not me. We only have a few seconds left."

Noises from the black leather couch almost sounded like moans when they positioned Welton. Dom opened his little vet's bag. While he administered a sedative and Anita worried, I went to work on the computer. For someone who was running a multimillion-dollar scam, Welton was incredibly stupid. Not only did he leave a key in the office where anyone could grab it, but his legitimate bank account was linked to his illegal account. I nearly choked when I read the balance in that account.

"Christ, he's got two and half million in cash."

Anita gawked at me. "Say again?"

I spoke slowly, the number still sinking in. "$2,498,999.12."

"Piece of shit," Dom rolled up Welton's sleeve.

"Easy. Don't let your emotions get in the way." I said.

Dom seemed fixated on the hypodermic needle he held inches from Welton's arm. "I could give him a little extra. He'd never wake up."

"No!" Anita said.

I shook my head. "Would you really want to live with his death on your hands? I couldn't." Nor could I have lived with the possibility of having the cops trace the Taser back to me. It had cost another small fortune to get a C-2 cartridge without the built-in anti-felon confetti, but the entrepreneurial spirit was alive and well in the black market.

When Welton stirred, Dom jabbed a syringe into his arm. "This will hold you—at least for now."

Shit. Amateurs. Right about now I totally regretted becoming involved in Anita's retribution scheme, but it was way too late to back out so I did what my instincts told me to do next—check out all three of the open computer programs. The first was for email—nothing of any importance there. The second was for his internet browser, where I had access to his bank account. The third was called "Notifications."

When I clicked on the Notifications icon, a list of email addresses filled the screen. I gave my two amateur partners a stern warning while I scanned the list. "This is business. Keep your emotions under control. Believe me, you do not want to add murder to your rap sheet. If you get caught, this one's bad enough."

"We ain't getting caught," said Dom.

Spoken like a true amateur. How many incarcerated felons had made the same assumption? "Pull the darts and give me back my Taser. Just remember, Dom, the only way we're not getting caught is to keep this quiet. That means no one—I do mean no one—outside this room, can ever hear about this. It's all about containment. Got it?"

Dom scowled at me, but nodded his agreement.

Anita approached to within a couple of feet, where she stood watching over my shoulder. "What've you got there?"

"Goddamn. This is his spam list." I hadn't even realized she was leaning over me. I pointed to a link at the top of the page. "Dumb shit left it open. See? The link will allow me to send a new message. Talk about a stroke of luck, we can grab the million you wanted. We can even use his business tool against him. Break him instead of these poor people."

Anita's brow furrowed, the confusion on her face apparent. "I don't get it."

"It's called pump-and-dump," I said. "Using this bogus ID, he buys devalued stock. Step 2 is to send an email with bogus good news about the company he invested in to his email list. The greedy ones buy; the stock goes up. He sells before the real news hits the market. Once he's out with his profit, he notifies everyone to sell. When the dust settles, the game starts all over. It's a ridiculous cycle, but some people are making tons of money so there's always a supply of references and new investors. We could alert all these clients to dump their stocks in the morning."

Dom left his patient so he, too, could see the screen. "It would serve the son of a bitch right."

"You are a genius, Roxy. He'll be ruined." Anita hugged me.

Not being a hugger, I patted her hand before slipping out of her embrace. "Hell hath no fury . . ."

My purse vibrated. Probably Skip again. I checked the display. It was Skip's friend Baldorf. Why was the resident computer genius calling me? I put the phone to my ear while I continued typing with the other. The email would expose Welton for what he was, bringing with it a massive selling binge he would never see coming until way too late. This time, he's the one who would be caught off guard and taken down in the undertow. "What do you want, Baldorf? I'm busy right now."

"Skip's at the trauma center at San Diego Regional. I guess I'm his emergency contact, but they couldn't tell me anything. The lady who called said it was too soon to know anything."

My blood ran cold. "The trauma center? What the hell happened?"

"He got picked up in an Oceanside alley. Somebody tried to kill him."

Shit. The ringer on my phone—I'd shut it off. "Is he alive?"

"All they said was he's lost a lot of blood. They don't know who attacked him."

I looked across the room. Dom was again standing over Welton; Anita had joined him. She looked like she was ready to crack, her gaze flitting around the room, never resting in one place for more than a moment.

"Roxy, I'd go, but I'm in San Francisco."

"I'm in L.A."

"What if he doesn't make it?"

Rage coursed through me. "No! He'll be fine." My God, the phone call earlier had been Skip. "I'll go," I said and disconnected from Baldorf.

"What's wrong?" The voice I heard was from Anita, but it sounded disembodied.

"He's out," said Dom. "He won't remember much of anything tomorrow."

"Skip's been attacked." It sickened me that he'd called for help and I'd hung up on him. "What?" Anita's jaw fell.

"I need to go."

"You said you broke up with him. Is he okay?"

I pushed away a tear. "Damn him! How dare he ruin this!"

"Roxy, is he okay?" She peered over my shoulder at the screen. "Did you finish the transfer?"

"The transfer? No." I turned back to the computer.

Anita gently rubbed my shoulders. "You're not over him at all. Go on, Roxy, we can finish up. We'll send the email. You've already done more than enough."

Yes, I had. I'd driven Skip away. I'd become the most larcenous, lying, cheating bitch I'd ever known. Had I ever done enough already. I tasted salt on my lips. "I have to leave."

"We'll finish up here. It's okay." She hugged me, but I didn't feel better.

"No, it's not." To hell with Jack Welton's money. To hell with Anita. To hell with Dom. Screw this job. I stuffed the Taser into my $400 clutch. My life was a mess. The only way to salvage it was to leave. Now.

CHAPTER 6

S K I P

Skip slept fitfully until a male nurse dressed in hospital scrubs and a surgical mask entered his room. The man's motions were deliberate, yet hurried.

"What time is it?" Skip asked.

The nurse didn't answer; he only shrugged.

"Sounded bad, earlier," said Skip.

The nurse let out a heavy breath behind the mask. "Got something to help you sleep."

Skip rubbed his face with his free hand. Clarity. Where had he heard that voice before? "Where's Oliver?"

"His shift ended. I'm in for the night."

A chill ran the length of Skip's spine. How could Joey Santino have found him? How had he known Skip was here? He fumbled for the call button, found it and pressed hard. "You work nights?"

"Nice try, Cosgrove. But you ain't at the top of your game."

"You owe me an explanation, Joey."

"Go to hell. I don't owe you shit. You owe me my life back. My girlfriend. A kid I ain't never seen."

"That's what this is all about? You're a dad and you're going to kill a few people for the opportunity to see your kid? She was right to leave you. You're no good for her."

"Screw you. This'll only take a moment. You ain't gonna feel a thing."

Where the hell was the nurse? Skip pressed the button again, this time, harder. He had only his wits. "What's with the mask?"

"I been sick recently, don't want to expose no one."

"Turn on the light, Joey. You screwed up in the alley, so now you want to poison me? Man up."

"I never want to see your face again." Santino reached for the IV. "Not alive, anyways."

Skip grabbed the line in his right hand, desperate to pull out the IV, but Santino had him pinned. A wave of nausea flooded through Skip—he had no doubt Joey could outlast him. "You do this, you'll never see your kid. Back off."

The needle shook in Santino's hand. "I should've finished you off in the alley."

The lights in the room flickered on, casting Joey Santino in a fluorescent glow. Joey glanced at the doorway for a second, then back to Skip. "Why can't you just goddamn die, Cosgrove?"

Nurse Oliver's voice came from the doorway. "Who the hell are you?"

"Lucky son-of-a-bitch." Santino jerked the needle away from the IV line.

The nurse yelled down the hallway. "Get Security!"

CHAPTER 7

R O X Y

The doorman, who apparently remembered me from my earlier grand entrance, called for a cab while I went outside and stood, shivering in the night. He came out moments later, but stopped when I backed away. "Miss? Are you okay? It shouldn't be too long. You can wait inside if you'd like."

"I'm fine." My stomach churned with the realization that, above all, I needed to get to the hospital. I pasted on a weak smile even though it was apparent from the doorman's face he didn't believe my claim any more than I did.

The cab driver barely paid attention to me. Instead, he listened to mariachi music and a radio announcer who spoke without ever pausing for a breath of air. At the parking garage, I handed him a twenty, then left without thinking to ask for change.

It's amazing a cop didn't ticket me for reckless or aggressive driving during the first part of my trip. Common sense should have stopped me from getting behind the wheel under these circumstances, but I'd left my reasoning skills back in the condo along with two million bucks. I drove like bridezilla late for her wedding.

Where US 101 merged into I-5, it became five lanes of equally maniacal drivers. Between the ones pumped up on caffeine, those dulled by too much alcohol or lack of sleep, and those who wanted to get someplace fast, this was not a safe place to be for a woman whose concentration was 90 miles south.

It wasn't until I reached Anaheim that I began to wonder what had happened in the condo after I left. "Shit!" My voice was the only sound other than road noise in the car.

When I dialed Anita's number, it rang only twice before forwarding to voicemail. "Damn it!" I hung up and tried again. Same result. I left Anita a message. Less than thirty minutes later, I was passing through San Clemente, caught up in the middle of a one-woman debate.

—You never should have left without finishing your job.

—Anita's fine. She's honest. She submitted the transaction.

I switched lanes to avoid a slow-moving car. Headlights from the vehicle fell further behind while the debate continued.

—She's probably asleep now.

—Don't be a fool, you know people. There was too much money for the taking.

—You should go back.

To my right, the San Onofre Power Plant lit up the landscape.

—No! You need to get to Skip. What if he dies?

—He can't die. You should call.

—What? After you threw him away? You did this. This is your fault.

—Shut up! You're driving me fricking insane!

I turned on the radio, but the late-night DJ pissed me off even more. About an hour after the beginning of my drive, I settled into a morose silence. Road noise became the only sound in the car while tears dribbled down my cheeks.

Blurry white lane marker lines whizzed by, the only sign of distance passing. A few miles outside of Oceanside, my thoughts shifted from fear to anger. One thing was certain, whoever did this to Skip, my one—my only—what? What should I call him? Screw titles. Someone was going to pay for this.

CHAPTER 8

S K I P

When Nurse Oliver called for Security, Joey Santino ran out of the room. Seconds later, the nurse was at his side. "Who the hell was that?"

"Someone I didn't think I'd see again."

"Do you need something for pain?"

"I'm okay," he lied. Isn't that what people did in these situations? Lie. Make the other person feel better. "My head's almost clear. He must have seen them pick me up in the alley."

"He's the one who tried to crack your head open?"

Involuntarily, Skip raised a hand toward his head. "How bad is it?"

"I said tried. He only broke the skin. The blow caused profuse bleeding, which could have been deadly, but you were lucky. It could have been much worse."

"That's Joey. He likes poison and shooting people in the back. I remembered that too late."

Nurse Oliver left the room to stand in the hallway, where she flagged down a passing young man in dark blue scrubs. He had shoulder-length hair pulled back in a ponytail and a neatly trimmed goatee.

Skip thought he remembered the guy from before. He attempted to eavesdrop, but their conversation was quiet with the nurse distinctly in charge. Moments later, the young man left and the nurse returned.

"I'm moving you to a different room," she said.

Be the tough guy, thought Skip. Don't make her jeopardize her job. The truth was that the night had taken too much out of him. He didn't have the will to resist or complain. The best he could muster was, "What if someone else is trying to find me?"

"The girl you keep talking about in your sleep?"

He felt heat rise in his cheeks. Had he talked about the seductress? He hoped not. "Her name's Roxy. We had a fight. She's not happy with me, but I am one step closer to understanding her."

"How so?"

"She's built different than most people."

The nurse unfolded the blood pressure cuff she'd pulled from the wall. "What? She's an alien?"

"Let's say she's a work in progress."

"Aren't we all?" Nurse Oliver fitted the cuff around Skip's arm. "Be quiet for a second." She positioned the stethoscope earpieces before placing the chest piece against his skin.

"Why are those things always so cold?" He smiled when he said it, knowing what would come next.

"Shut up!" She made a zipping motion across her lips.

Skip closed his eyes while he listened to the soft whir of the mechanical pump. When the cuff deflated, he said, "Am I normal?"

She ignored him. "So you two had a fight. Big deal. What are you going to do about it? That's the question."

"She's pretty strong willed."

"You think you're not?" Nurse Oliver draped the stethoscope earpieces around her neck before hanging the blood pressure cuff on the wall. "No, you're not normal, your body's under stress. It's no surprise your blood pressure is elevated."

"Can you get me off the morphine? The pain, I can manage. No problem."

Nurse Oliver raised an eyebrow at him. "You're not on morphine. Why would you think that?"

"Weird dreams. I almost became addicted after an auto accident a few years ago."

"Do you carry a card in your wallet? What drugs to avoid?"

"I guess so. I didn't think anyone checked."

She leaned closer, her voice a whisper. "It's our little secret. We try not to let the patients know."

He still felt too dazed to determine whether Nurse Oliver's comment had been a joke, but his chance to ask was interrupted when two orderlies, one male, one female, entered the room. He recognized the guy with the goatee; the second was a young girl with deep-set eyes above hollow cheeks reminiscent of those seen in haunting "help stamp out hunger" photos.

Nurse Oliver tilted her head in their direction. "This is Jake and Gracie."

Jake fingered his single earring after raising his hand in greeting. "Hey, how're you Mr., uh . . ."

"Cosgrove," said Skip.

"Marcus," said Nurse Oliver.

Jake inspected the chart over Gracie's shoulder. "That's what the chart says, Wendell Marcus."

Over a pair of wire-rimmed glasses straight out of an old western movie, Gracie locked her gaze onto Nurse Oliver's. Skip almost smiled at the classic power move.

"What gives, Nance? Mr. Marcus was discharged. I took him out myself." Fire in the girl's blue eyes invited confrontation.

Now the center of attention, Nurse Oliver shifted uncomfortably.

Skip said, "I'm stealing identities?"

The nurse pointed at Skip. "You, hush." She turned to the female orderly. "Gracie, someone tried to kill this man. Forget Mr. Marcus. The other one. It's my judgement call. I'm hiding him until the police arrest the guy who snuck into my hospital."

Gracie stiffened. "I can't do that."

"You'll do what I tell you to do, Gracie. I'm the one who will deal with the consequences."

Skip nodded in Nurse Oliver's direction. "She's pretty tough."

"Someone in Billing is gonna have a cow when they hear about this," Jake said. "Glad it ain't my problem."

"Jake, just move Mr. Marcus."

"Right-e-o. Let's go Gracie, I'm getting paged for ER."

Gracie mumbled something about rules under her breath, but helped Jake roll the bed into the hallway. They angled it to the right, slipping through the narrow opening between another bed and a beige wall. The other bed had been made up with crisp white sheets pulled tight all around. Even the blanket across the bottom half was stretched smooth with its ends tucked under the mattress. He pointed at it. "Someone does nice work."

Gracie leaned forward from behind so Skip could see her face when he looked straight up. "Made it myself. Note the regulation corners." She gave Skip a snappy salute accompanied by a wink. A moment later, she huffed at Nurse Oliver.

Skip couldn't have felt more conspicuous if he were standing on a parade float giving the crowd a fake smile and a princess wave. But, he wasn't waving—or smiling. He was trying to ignore the skinny old man who had sparse clumps of gray hair and toothpick arms. His blank eyes bulged out of a face tattooed with age spots. Another staff member, this one behind the station counter, pretended to ignore the one-bed procession, but peeked a couple of times. Unlike the old man with the blank stare, the staff member averted her eyes when she saw Skip watching her.

Being in the spotlight was not something Skip enjoyed; hospitals, he enjoyed even less. This parade through the hallway would make even Roxy uncomfortable, of that, he was sure. But, the little parade brought him one step closer to understanding the woman he loved. She liked the spotlight—when it was on her terms.

The move was blessedly short—down only a couple of doors before crossing the hall. Nurse Oliver dismissed Gracie and Jake after they had positioned Skip's bed. Alone again, she said, "Gracie's right to be upset, there's going to be hell to pay for this."

"Will you get fired? What about them?"

"I'll be fine, so will Jake. Gracie's new. She's coming up on the end of her probationary period. She shouldn't get in trouble on my account—I'll make sure she's okay."

"So you're Wonder Woman, too? Where's your red corset?"

She bit her lower lip, then gave him a fake smile. "I was married to the hospital administrator's brother and my ex will kick his brother's ass on the basketball court the next time they play if he tries to pull any crap."

"So I'm Mr. Marcus now?"

"Shut up, Mr. Marcus-Cosgrove. I'm documenting everything. You will get billed."

"I never thought I wouldn't. Your ex? He'd take on his brother to help you out of a bind?"

"We have a complicated relationship."

"Friends with benefits?"

"None of your business." Nurse Oliver's lips curled ever so slightly. "Be right back. By the way, is there anyone who we should tell about the move—other than the police?"

"You're calling them?"

"Someone sneaks in here and tries to kill one of my patients? What do you think?"

"You're in charge. Roxy Tanner. I want to see her."

"Right."

"Also, Barry Finkledorf. To be clear, he's a friend, not a girlfriend."

Nurse Oliver raised her eyebrow again; Skip felt his face begin to color.

"I mean he's not, uh, we're not—"

The nurse winked. "Got it. I'm just messing with you." She left after writing the names on a slip of paper. In the hallway, she did an about face. Her smile looked genuine. "Work it out with her. Friends are overrated. It's the benefits that count."

CHAPTER 9

ROXY

I'm not a crier. Even the worst tear-jerker movies seldom phase me. But, there comes a point when even the toughest of us snap. Unbeknownst to me, my breaking point must have come and gone somewhere between L.A. and San Clemente and I'd been on autopilot since San Onofre, oblivious to anything other than headlights, taillights, and white lines on the road. So, when I pressed the little button on the remote to lock my car door, I heard two sounds. One was the obvious thunk of my doors doing their thing, the other was someone hurling open the vault where I sealed away my emotions.

My sobs filled the night air in a parking lot where not a soul would care about me or what I was going through. I was alone. For the first time in my life I realized what the word meant. Alone.

It meant no Skip.

It meant no love.

No us.

Solemn voices—those of a man and a woman—broke the silence. My legs felt numb; it was time to move, but I found myself eavesdropping.

"Do you think he'll survive?" The woman's voice was weak, filled with desperation.

"Your dad's tough, but the surgery is dangerous."

"I'm praying for him."

"Me, too." The man's voice cracked, car doors opened, and the voices were gone. I was alone again without even a stranger's pain to comfort me. My first step came slow and forced. Each step brought me closer to the entrance, but also made the weight on my heart heavier. My path, like that of a moth, weaved toward the light. My destiny lay before me in this hospital—I had no more cards to play in the game. The glass doors slid open, but I didn't have the courage to enter.

A woman's voice said, "Miss? May I help you?"

The words I spoke weren't mine, but those of a stranger. "Do you have a chapel?"

The woman took my name before asking who I wanted to see. She must have taken pity on me because before I knew it, she'd placed a little badge on a string around my neck. She took hold of my arm, then guided me down a hallway. I was again operating on autopilot. She opened the door to a small room filled with wooden pews.

"This is the chapel," she said. "Are you sure you don't want to go upstairs first?"

It had been nearly twenty years since Mom had stopped forcing me to attend church. I stood, still unable to see clearly. "I think maybe this is what I need to do."

"Come back to the front desk if you need anything. Anything at all."

Genuine kindness seldom came my way. Overwhelmed, I said, "Thank you."

The door whispered shut. I was alone. There was that word again. Why was I here?

I moved slowly to the second row. The pew's wood felt cool to the touch; the polished firmness where it met my back somehow gave me encouragement by suffusing my body with its strength. The soft seat cushion, even the soft blues and earth tones of the fabric welcomed me.

My throat felt constricted; my eyes were still hot with tears. I closed my eyes and rubbed my fingers over the wood. It was the way

I'd been once—strong. Now—what was I? A hoarse whisper escaped my lips. "God?"

A wave of embarrassment surrounded me over how I was dressed. Would—he—care? I set the stilettos off to one side and kneeled, folding my hands like Mom had taught me. "It's me, Roxy Tanner. I . . . I've made a mess of my life."

Tears streamed down my cheeks; I probably looked like a raccoon. Or worse. "I don't know if you can hear me . . . or if you even care. Why should you? After everything I've done. You don't have to forgive me, you probably shouldn't. I get that. If you can hear me, I have a request. And it's not for me."

I snickered. "For once—sorry, I don't think you're supposed to laugh in church. Are you?"

My hands felt cold, so I worked them slowly, massaging the back of one, then the other. The action was futile. I swiped at my cheeks with blackened fingers. Maybe God wouldn't care. I laced them together. Somehow, the simple movement gave me courage. "What I need is for a good man. He doesn't deserve me . . . he deserves better. But, he might be dying or dead . . ." My head fell forward onto my hands. Between sobs, I said, "I'm too afraid to ask."

My forehead was still on my hands on the pew in front of me. "Please, he almost threw away his entire life for me. If anyone deserves to die tonight, it's me. So if you have to take someone, take me, not him."

The silence in the room was almost more than I could bear, but my legs wouldn't move. My energy reserves were exhausted; my tank, empty. I curled up into a tight ball on the pew's cushioned surface. One minute. I needed to rest for just one minute.

Would there ever be hope for me? Probably not. Tears dribbled down my forearm before soaking into the seat cushion. Finally, exhaustion overtook me.

CHAPTER 10

S K I P

Skip hated hospitals. Yet, here he was, trapped in a bed with two cops on one side and a nurse at the foot, all arguing over what should happen next. Finally, Nurse Oliver gave in. "A few minutes, that's all you get. I have to check his vitals first."

She elbowed past the two men, positioning herself with a deliberateness he might have found painful if he were feeling better—or if her delay didn't displease the cops enough to make them shift from foot-to-foot. Nurse Oliver gave Skip a knowing wink before removing the blood pressure cuff.

Before he could speak, he realized his mouth tasted foul. He longed for the strength to brush his teeth, but settled instead for a sip of water the nurse gave him. "It's okay," he said.

"A few minutes, that's all," said Nurse Oliver.

The introductions had barely been completed when the criminologist in Skip recognized the roles of good cop and bad cop. It didn't matter if he was the victim this time. Thanks to Roxy, his fall from grace had been fast and hard. He now wore the label of "questionable character" in the eyes of the law. The "good cop" was Tom Holmes, a thin man who had topped off his faded green T-shirt and blue jeans with a tan windbreaker. He wore a Bears cap that made him look the same as any other fan at a game except for the telltale bulge on his left side where he carried his gun.

The other man, Cam Franken, wore a suit distressed by signs of wear from a long day—a wrinkle here, a small spot of soup or coffee left over from lunch there. He blinked excessively, was significantly wider in the middle than the Bears fan, and had plenty of scalp showing through his short-cropped hair.

Skip remembered Holmes from Joey Santino's trial. For some odd reason, Holmes had never been called to testify, yet had attended the trial every day. Franken stayed in the background, firmly anchored in the role of recorder. He watched—a human video camera with the ability to take in everything. What concerned Skip most was the difference between him and a video camera. This recorder would judge what happened here without mercy. He'd judge Skip's every word, gesture and inflection. He'd wait until Holmes ran into a roadblock or missed something. If his partner did get stuck, he'd be the one to drill down incessantly for information. He'd be on the watch for details Skip might have distorted or an opportunity to leverage his partner's questions.

They went through the events in the alley. After that, Holmes backtracked while Franken continued watching. Holmes said, "So tell me again why you followed Joey Santino to that alley, Mr. Cosgrove."

The blood pounded in Skip's temples. The anesthesia was wearing off fast now. How many painkillers had they given him? He desperately wanted to ask Holmes why he'd been at the Santino trial, but never testified. "Santino swore he was going to kill me when he got out of prison. They released him last week. That's when he started stalking me."

"How come you didn't call us?"

"I did. But he was cautious. At first, anyway. He kept his distance on day one, but got more bold the next day. He made a threat to kill Roxy Tanner tonight. You have to get in touch with her."

"You think? We can talk about that in a minute."

"You need to warn her."

"You called this in you said?"

"Come on, Detective. I already answered your question. Twice."

"So why didn't you have us handle it?"

"You guys couldn't do anything until he did something illegal."

"So you took matters into your own hands."

"I didn't feel like waiting for him to find me in a dark alley."

"Which he did."

Skip locked eyes with Holmes. "Yeah. Which he did." Out of the corner of his eye, Skip saw the movement of Nurse Oliver's blue uniform. He caught her determined expression, the sudden crossing of her arms—everything about her demeanor said the cavalry was preparing to charge in.

Franken watched. His eyes darted right to observe the nurse for a moment, then returned to Skip. He said not a word.

Nurse Oliver made a move to interrupt the interrogation, but Skip shook his head. She regarded both men with obvious impatience before taking a step backward, her jaw set in an unhappy frown. While she waited, she read a message on her pager.

Holmes either didn't notice her—an unlikely possibility in Skip's mind—or was ignoring her. "So your, um, proactive approach seems to have accelerated the process."

"You're an asshole—sorry."

"You didn't answer my question."

"Yes, what I did seems to have pushed Santino into action. So are you going to arrest him? Are you going to warn Roxy?"

"He might claim you were harassing him. You did follow him to Oceanside," Holmes said.

"I did. He went into a bar to meet some guy at a back table. Short guy, big attitude."

Franken said, "So you did harass him." The words were the first he'd said since the introduction.

"Great. I tell you what Santino did so you can make me the bad guy? Let's not forget whose head got bashed in."

"About that," said Holmes. "Did you see him hit you? In my experience it's tough to see a guy when he comes at you from behind."

"No, I didn't see him. He went in the alley. I never saw him after that."

"I saw him," said Nurse Oliver. "He tried to kill my patient."

"That's why we're here, lady."

"What time is it, anyway?" asked Skip.

"Four-thirty. A.M." Holmes nodded to Franken. "Maybe he needs a morphine chaser."

"Coffee would be better," said Skip.

"We could maybe get you some."

Franken left the room without a word.

"Tell me about this visitor you had. You two think it was Santino."

"He had a needle with something he said would help me sleep."

"I'll bet it would. Didn't bother leaving the evidence, did he?"

An image of the standoff played out in Skip's mind. Where had the needle gone? "No, he took it with him. I should have asked him to be more cooperative."

"Nice." Holmes chuckled. His friendliness seemed almost genuine. "I like that. Guy's behind the eight ball and he keeps his sense of humor. Too bad for you, nobody's seen the little slime. He's in some rathole waiting for an invite to coffee."

Franken returned with a styrofoam cup; he placed it on the wheeled bedside tray out of Skip's reach. Holmes smiled at his partner while eyeing the cup. "Black for our friend?" Franken nodded, but said nothing.

Skip scowled at the two detectives. They'd shifted back to their roles—interrogator and observer. "What do you want from me? What did I do anyway?"

"About that," said Holmes. "I mean, since you asked. I got one question a good friend of mine would really like answered. If I believe your answer, you get that nice little cup of Joe. If we don't like your answer, we might need a second cup and a couple of doughnuts."

"Fine. What? I can't believe this."

"My friend's name is Grimes," said Holmes. His gray eyes turned cold. "You probably know him—Sergeant Grimes. He got passed over for a promotion 'cause of you and your girlfriend. So the only thing he really wants to know is this. Did she do it?"

"She who? Do what?" Skip was instantly on alert. Grimes had said the investigation was closed. Had he lied?

Holmes eyebrows went up at the outburst. "Tanner. Did she embezzle the five million?"

"No! No! Dammit!" Skip grabbed at his head. Damn, that hurt, but he had to play this through. "How many times have I got to tell you guys I used my inheritance to pay the ransom for Roxy's father." It was the skeleton in the closet, the lie that could bring them both down. It was the question that, answered incorrectly, would lead to a minefield full of more detailed questions. If that happened, one would be posed to a jury—guilty or not.

"You could make this all go away by showing us the check."

"I thought Grimes was satisfied." Skip's voice held the sarcastic edge of an offended man. If he wasn't angry about this line of questioning, if he was indecisive, if he wavered, these two would see it.

"He got passed over."

"If Grimes wants to get his promotion, he should be telling his superiors what he did, not what he didn't do."

"Such as?"

Skip began counting off on his fingers for emphasis. "He got the guy behind the kidnapping. He got the hired gun. He wrapped up the whole case. He got it all in a neat little package. "

"Maybe too neat."

"What? You think I perjured myself at the Panaman trial? The guy kidnapped Roxy's father. I loaned her the ransom. What the hell else could you possibly want?"

"I'm new. I'm curious. Mostly, I wasn't there to see you tell the story, so it's real easy for me to be extra suspicious. Especially when there are questionable facts."

"What questionable facts?"

"The money," said Holmes.

"So that's what this is about? Grimes thinks I lied about where the money for the ransom came from? I can't believe it."

"Your testimony was pretty clear. Hers, too. But, Panaman claimed she was running a con."

"So you believe a convicted felon over us?"

"He wasn't convicted at the time, but everybody from the judge on down believed you. Even Grimes."

"What? You said Grimes didn't. He got passed over."

Holmes shrugged. "You were almost a cop once, you might even understand why I . . ." He smiled. "Stretched his reaction a bit."

Unfortunately, Skip did understand. All too well. Roxy's life was one game of chance. The stakes could destroy lives. Which way should he turn? He remembered something she'd said once—keep the lie simple. Stick close to the truth. He had to be indignant, but sincere. "Okay, Detective Nosey. Here's the deal. My uncle's estate was huge. Terms of the will were to be kept confidential. The only reason I disclosed what I did was to prevent a woman I'd fallen in love with from going to jail for something she didn't do. Are we clear? I mean, really clear?"

When Skip was done, he let his arms fall onto the sheets, hoping it looked like the move of an exhausted man. If he showed tension, these two would see it.

Franken frowned while he rubbed the back of his neck. "You know, Tommy, I think I believe him."

"Cam, I might just agree with you." Holmes held eye contact with Skip.

Everything depended on the next few moments. Skip knew he had to believe the lie. Maintain the indignant attitude. Anything less than the perfect response and these bloodhounds would sniff it out. "I understand being new. I'd rather we pay attention to the guy who wants to kill me."

"Like I said earlier, he dropped off the grid. We're looking, but we don't have the resources to be searching all over for him. You know we don't have enough to get a warrant for every dump he ever visited. So if he's holed up, lying in wait, so to speak, we can't help."

"Til he comes after me again."

"Something like that." Holmes shrugged. "If you got any suggestions, I'm open. I don't like people trying to kill each other, especially when one of them is someone I like."

"So now you like me?"

"Maybe. I'm thinking you might have just had a bad run here—my jury's still out."

Waiting for Holmes to make a decision was better than being on the outs. "I can live with that," Skip said.

"You better, I don't want nobody getting rid of you before my jury decides."

"On whether you can trust me or not?"

"I think you're basically an honest guy. Your girlfriend? Not so much."

"Never trust a beautiful woman?"

"Especially a beautiful woman."

"Sounds like a guy who got burned pretty bad. You have an ex, Holmes?" Skip guessed three, but didn't want to be a smart ass. He needed to be a little dense for his new buddy—if he was a buddy.

"Two."

"Wow. Got burned twice."

Franken leaned back on his heels, his laugh coming from deep within. "Don't believe him, Cosgrove, number three already filed."

"Thanks, partner." Holmes glared at Franken, then pushed the tray in Skip's direction. "Enjoy the coffee, Cosgrove. And don't do anything to make me regret my decision."

"Have you checked with Santino's parole officer?" asked Skip.

"What? You think we're stupid? That was our first call. He's involved, so don't you worry about us doing our jobs."

"Santino's up to something big. I wish I knew what it was."

Holmes said, "Just because your boy gave a bum address doesn't make him a killer. Maybe you ID'd the wrong guy. You said it was dark, that you didn't see the guy who did this."

"You can't win 'em all, Cosgrove." Franken's tone was flippant. "If you don't mind my saying so, it looks like you're on a bad streak 'cause unless something concrete turns up, there's not much more we can do. We cover violent crime, not scuffles."

"Man, my head is killing me." Skip winced.

Nurse Oliver stepped forward to occupy the space between Skip and the two cops. She shook her head at them. "Enough. He needs rest. The doctor's on his way up. You two will have to wait until tomorrow for your questions."

"Attempted murder trumps pain, lady." Franken let his gaze bore into Nurse Oliver's. "And we are the police."

The nurse pulled herself up to her full 5'2" height to square off against Franken, who easily stood six feet. "I don't give a damn who you are. This man is my patient. He's alive. It's my job to see he gets well. Now you, Detective, can step away from the bed. Understand?"

Franken's eyes darted from side to side. It was obvious he hadn't counted on a fireball like Oliver. Skip could almost picture the man as a boy, a stern grandmother grabbing him by the ear for punishment when he sassed her.

Nurse Oliver stepped forward, tapping her watch. "Visiting hours are over."

"Yes, ma'am," said Franken as he backed away.

CHAPTER 11

R O X Y

The sensation of falling through darkness completely freaked me out. I justified my momentary panic by telling myself the cushioned pew was comfortable for sitting, but only birds were made to sleep on something this narrow.

Something had wrapped itself around my neck; my heart pounded with the vague impression of being strangled. Is that what Jack Welton felt at the end? I sat, realizing it was only the little plastic badge holder string, not a killer seeking vengeance. Talk about feeling stupid. It was five-freaking-thirty in the morning. I'd been asleep for two hours. Why hadn't I gone to see Skip right away? Because I was tired? Deep down, I knew that was a lie. It hadn't been exhaustion, but fear.

At the door, I peered back into the chapel, uncertain why I'd allowed my fears to rule me. Did my actions last night mean I'd needed this? My line of work required me to understand human behavior—to use it to my advantage. So be it. A talk with the big guy. The only one who might listen. I said, "Thanks," before slipping out the door.

A young woman wearing blue scrubs approached from down the hall. According to her name badge, she worked in Radiology. I was about to ask for directions when I realized I'd forgotten Skip's room number. The woman's eyes widened; she let out a low whistle. "I want one."

"Excuse me?"

"Your dress is gorgeous. Where did you get it?"

My thousand-dollar Lela Rose cocktail dress resembled something straight out of a laundry basket. Were the wrinkles permanent? Screw it, I needed to find Skip. "Saks. I think it's ruined."

"I can't afford that. You do look like you had a rough night. Must be someone important."

"My boyfriend. He's here—somewhere." I glanced both directions. "I'm lost."

"Let's see." She flipped my visitor's pass over to examine it. "You want 316. Go down the hall, take the elevator on your right and up to the third floor. The nurse's station will be straight ahead of you."

"Great. Thanks. What about a restroom? I must be a sight."

"If I looked half as good as you do now—even when I'm at my best—I'd call myself a lucky lady. Right by the elevators."

Heat rushed into my cheeks. Compliments from men? Sure. I'm used to them. But most other women make catty remarks or scowl. In the restroom, I caught a glimpse of myself in the mirror. Damage control was in order. Making myself presentable for Skip would be a job akin to sending a firefighter into a three-alarm blaze armed with nothing more than a small bucket.

Seven minutes later I was exiting the elevator doors. Directly ahead was an unmanned nurse's station. Fine by me. I knew the room number. The direction I needed to go was obvious, so why ask for help? I arrived at Skip's room, took a deep breath, and entered with a smile on my face. The blood that had rushed to my head earlier drained. I was staring at a vacant bed.

White sheets. Nice neat little corners. No Skip. I swallowed hard. Maybe he'd been discharged. Maybe they'd . . . what? Had a room emergency and needed to shuffle him off to . . . where?

"May I help you?"

"Jesus!" I jumped at the sound of a woman's voice.

"Sorry. I didn't mean to surprise you."

"There was man in here last night. His name is Skip Cosgrove. I'm here to see him." A perverse thought burst into my mind. What if Skip had requested to be moved? I'd hung up on him when he needed me most. Had our relationship cratered?

"What's your name?"

I glanced down, once again my name tag was showing its rear to the world. I cocked my head to one side, fingering the badge holder as though I was about to flip it over. "Lucy Kravitz." The alias I'd used for the first time a couple of months ago rolled off my tongue with the practiced ease of a lifelong liar who'd played dozens of roles. "Skip's girlfriend asked me to check on him."

The nurse nodded, excused herself with a peremptory "be right back" and disappeared down the hall. It seemed odd she didn't know immediately where they'd put Skip. What if she'd just come on duty? Maybe she needed to look him up in the computer system. By now, my suspicious genes were waging all-out war against their molecular brethren. My nervous system was on full alert.

Panic set in when I heard the nurse say something about needing security. My instincts told me to run like hell, so I slipped off the stilettos and headed deep into the ward. Halfway down the hall, I whispered to myself, "Just because you're paranoid, doesn't mean they're not out to get you."

Figuring out what happened to Skip would have to come later. Right now self-preservation had become my priority. Logic dictated I had nothing to fear; living on the wrong side of the law for twenty years made that statement pure bullshit. A bearded, burly man dressed in blue scrubs entered a room, a chart held before him— he didn't even notice me. Despite the man's bulk, the scrubs hung loosely on his frame. They looked like grocery bags he'd stitched together to make a full suit. Ten seconds later, I turned the corner and found myself in an empty hallway.

My little helper's nervous prattle again broke the silent veil hanging over the ward. "She's in here. Nurse Oliver said to call if anyone came to see him. Last night, someone tried to—oh damn! Sorry! I didn't mean to swear. Where is she? She was here a minute ago."

"Nurse, we better go check on your patient."

"Right! Maybe she's looking for him. He's across the hall. Oh my God, if she finds him first! My Lord, Nurse Oliver will have my head!"

Their voices easily carried through the vacant corridor to my location. I was about to peek around the corner when movement in a convex corner mirror mounted high on the wall caught my attention. The mirror gave me a perfect view. I slipped back a few feet to watch the reflection of miniature, unnaturally shaped people scurry up and down the hall, into and out of the nurse's station.

Another of those nifty mirrors also hung immediately below the ceiling in the corner to my left. In the mirror, I saw miniature people scurry across the hall into another room. Unfortunately, I didn't think to count doorways, but I had a general idea of where Skip was. I waited about ten feet from the corner, watching until the nurse and the two security guards stepped out of the room.

The nurse still yammered like a hen laying eggs. "Sorry! Sorry! I didn't mean to disturb you, Mr. Marcus!" The little nurse in the mirror faced the guards. "I guess she must have left when I went to the elevators. Oh, I'm so sorry. I'm . . ."

"We'll find her. What's she look like?" The guard's curt tone indicated how tired he and I were of the woman's apologies. He and his partner split up. The bigger one was headed in my direction, the other had gone the opposite way. No doubt, he'd circle around the floor. I was trapped between two rent-a-cops coming at me from opposite directions.

I heard the nurse call out, "Nice dress! She's wearing a fancy cocktail dress!"

The guard raised his hand dismissively, poked his head into another doorway and continued in my direction. He would be here in seconds. Where the hell was I to go? I spotted an exit at the other end of the hall and double-timed it halfway down the vacant corridor to a door marked "Linens." The door had been left ajar. In the mirror, the guard approached the corner.

It was an all-or-nothing gamble that was so cliché it would probably work. I ducked into the closet to slip on a disguise. It was easy to find the light switch on the wall, not so much for the scrubs I wanted. Towels, bedding, and those awful hospital nightgowns that leave your ass hanging out lined the shelves. But dammit, no scrubs.

The plan was flawed anyway. What good would a disguise do me when the guard caught me coming out of a damn closet? Even a pekinese would know immediately what I'd done. I had one last option. Gently, I pushed in the button for the lock and flipped off the light. If nothing else, the delay would give me time to formulate a plan. The darkness closed in around me. The hospital-grade linoleum cooled my feet. Unlike in the movies, I hadn't seen a man-sized air conditioning vent to use in a miraculous disappearing act.

The guard's footsteps became louder. Seconds passed. I could almost hear my mother's voice through the silence, "Roxy, stop lying. Tell the truth for once!" Damn. How many times had she said those words? Better question—how many times had I?

I held my breath when the doorknob jiggled.

"Well, ain't that the shits. They actually followed the rules for a change." I heard a grunt before his footsteps faded away.

I slumped against the wall, breathing slowly while I counted the seconds. How long would it take for them to clear the floor? A few minutes? I'd never mastered the waiting game unless I was the one calling the shots.

The corridor remained quiet. The room, with the exception of my pounding heart, was the same. I turned on the light switch. Beige. I hate beige. My eyes felt like they'd been dusted with sand.

My escape had been way too close. What about lying to the nurse? Pure reflex, I thought. The act of a desperate, exhausted woman. I'd compounded the problem by running, automatically placing myself into the guilty classification. For once, I wasn't. Or, was I?

At least I knew where they had Skip. I opened the door, stilettos in hand as I walked toward Mr. Marcus's room. I couldn't hide from the truth any longer.

CHAPTER 12

S K I P

Skip kept his eyes closed as he conjured an image of a pulsating, fiery orb, almost a miniature sun, rotating before him, then connected the heat from the ball with the pain in his head. He told it to move closer; its glow and the consequent throbbing, intensified. He formed words in his mind, momentarily enjoying his success in isolating the source. "Good. I found you."

Now, it was all about manipulation. He pictured the imagined orb inching away, its size decreasing, the pulsing diminishing, the rotation slowing. "Cooler. You should be cooler." He changed the color from white to blue.

"You're getting smaller. Smaller. Move away." When he reached the point where he was in control, he opened his eyes. He had work to do; he needed to sort through why Santino was after him. Simple revenge made no sense. He couldn't investigate this himself, not without arousing the suspicions of Detective Holmes. Under the radar. That's where he'd keep both the pain and the investigation.

The chatterbox nurse who had jarred him from the trance earlier appeared at his doorway. "You're still awake."

"Where's Oliver?"

"Nurse Oliver left hours ago. She pulled a double last night. That's the trouble with trauma, it can get crazy." She stopped and giggled nervously. "That's our little joke, the trouble with trauma."

When Skip didn't laugh, her mouth turned down in an embarrassed frown. Her voice reminded him of a recording running at double speed.

"I'm sorry about earlier. I'm—rambling—again. My husband tells me all the time—sorry, there I go again—you have a phone call. Are you up to talking?"

"Unless it's a guy named Joey Santino, yes."

Chatterbox raised an eyebrow. "Who's he?"

Skip craned his neck to see who had come into the room behind the nurse.

"Hey," said Roxy.

His initial elation at seeing her fell flat. She was dressed to kill. It could only mean one thing. Roxy had been working last night. A job. Nurse Chatterbox whirled to see who'd followed her in. Her back stiffened. "You! How—how did you—?"

Roxy held up her phone. "Follow the trail." She smiled, "I called the switchboard. They transferred me to you. I gave you my real name when I asked for Mr. Marcus. You were kind enough to check on him before transferring the call." Roxy gestured at Skip. "I need to talk to Mr. Marcus now. Who came up with that, anyway?"

Chatterbox was heavier than Roxy. She had both hands raised, fingers splayed. "Get out! You can't be here!"

Roxy shook her head. "Not happening, Missy. I'm a red belt in Karate. Don't push me."

Skip recovered his composure. "It's okay! I want her here."

"But Nurse Oliver gave explicit instructions."

"It's okay," Skip said firmly.

The nurse threw her hands in the air and marched out the door, muttering something Skip couldn't understand. He smiled at Roxy, who rushed to the bed, but Skip motioned for her to stop. "You need to be careful." He needed to warn her about Santino; his questions about where she'd been last night would have to wait.

She stood with her hand on the side rail, worry painted on her face. "Are you okay? How's your head? It looks painful."

"I meant you're in danger."

She frowned while she lowered the railing. "Is it okay if I sit here?"

He took her hand in his to pull her closer.

"I was so worried about you." Roxy eased herself onto the bed next to him. "What happened? Why'd they move you?"

"That dress is—wow—you look incredible. But, no makeup?"

"I washed it off. Answer me. What happened?"

"You remember Joey Santino?"

She frowned for a moment, then seemed to remember the name. "You testified at his trial and he threatened to kill you, right? Is he the one who—"

"He could be coming after you next. I know he'll be back for me."

"Is that why they moved you? This whole secrecy thing didn't work out very well."

"You didn't give them your name? I cleared you through Nurse Oliver. All you had to do was—" He stopped in mid sentence. "You lied to the nurse."

Roxy bit at her lip and avoided his gaze. "I thought you didn't want to see me. Maybe you'd given orders to shoot me on sight or something."

Skip's breath caught when her eyes grew moist. He wanted nothing more than to kiss her lips, feel her touch, but he had to know what she'd done. It was the wedge. The one thing that came between them. He squeezed her hand. "Never. I wanted you here. But you were—busy."

Roxy grimaced. "Yeah."

The almost invisible crinkles around the corners of her eyes tightened; her cheeks flushed slightly. He knew if he pushed much further, they'd be right back into another argument. Her work was driving them apart. He needed to learn more, but he'd have to lead into it. "Did you sleep at all?"

"There you go, trying to make me feel good again."

"Bloodshot eyes with carry-on luggage. You've been crying."

"You know me, I don't do the whole crying thing."

"You were, I can tell."

"Damn you, a girl needs some secrets." Her jaw tightened.

"If you want to talk, I won't say a word."

"I never learned how to—"

"Trust?"

She feigned interest in the drapes. He waited. Maybe, just maybe she'd—

"Got a nice view?" She sounded almost chipper, but the sniffle at the end gave her away.

"I never regretted lying to the cops."

She stiffened at his matter-of-fact statement; the gap between them filled with tension. They were the words he'd never said before. It was the subject they'd avoided for months—until the argument.

Skip felt her fingers quiver before she removed her hand from his. "You lied to the world! You never had five million dollars."

"I got something worth much, much more."

"Yeah, a penniless con artist." A tear traced a lonely path down her cheek.

He knew the woman he loved was in foreign territory. A master at the art of the con, in love, Roxy Tanner was a lost traveler unable, maybe unwilling, to ask for directions. What was bothering her? He guessed something even more dangerous than Joey Santino.

"Can we talk about something else?" she said.

In the hallway, a couple stood hugging each other. It took only an instant for him to recognize their grief. Who had they lost? Would he lose, too? Tightness in his throat almost prevented him from speaking. "Gorgeous dress. Where'd you get it?"

She sniffled, "I couldn't resist it. My credit card limit might need some adjustment. The bank hasn't called yet. Maybe they'll fix it automatically."

"Not what I was looking for. Why'd you buy it?"

"I was in L.A. visiting Anita. I thought we were going someplace special for dinner. But, we ended up in a little Mom and Pop place near where she lives. We had fun. Until Baldorf called."

"You wore that dress to a Mom and Pop shop. Right."

"I thought it would be fancy. Besides, Anita was broke—she wanted to split the bill. It looks like you're in a lot of pain."

Skip winced at a hot poker stabbing at the back of his head. Roxy was, as usual, taking every bit of energy he had. He lightly fingered the bandages. "They said I got really lucky. No concussion. The blow only broke the skin, but I bled like crazy. I've got a few stitches and a bruise." She stroked his brow; Skip closed his eyes to savor the moment. "I'm so tired and can't take a chance on the meds. The doc will probably be kicking me out today."

"I know. Will you need a ride?"

"Baldorf's coming. He can take me home. I'll be fine once I get this under control." He pointed at the back of his head.

Roxy nodded. "I've got a few things I need to do, anyway. Like get out of this dress."

He opened his eyes to watch her face. "I could help you with that, Hot Rox."

She pressed her lips to his hand. "I was afraid you might never call me that again." She winked. "Lord help me if Sak's ever goes out of business."

"You've got expensive in your blood. It was big, wasn't it?"

There—the way her chest rose. The sudden intake of breath gave her away. The dress had something to do with where she'd been. Anita. The dress. What else?

"We can talk later. I'll go home and change. Call me when Baldorf gets you home?" He felt her lips on his forehead. Soft. Warm. But? Yes, there was a "but." It was like piecing together a giant jigsaw puzzle.

His eyes drifted shut, which made things worse. Not seeing her face strengthened the longing on his skin for her touch. When she pulled her hand away, he opened his eyes—her cheeks were damp. "I think I'll stay for a bit. If that's okay with you?"

Such a stupid question for a lover to ask, but one that revealed how fragile Roxy Tanner really was.

CHAPTER 13

R O X Y

In the moment when I kissed Skip's forehead, my heart nearly fractured. He reached out to caress my cheek. His touch lingered on my skin even after I pulled away. Would I ever feel that again? That thought—and the resulting panic—nearly knocked me off the bed. I'd never felt so—connected. So why was I doing my damnedest to push him away? My complicity in tearing us apart hurt like hell. Fear rushed through my veins. What if he told me to leave?

He smiled, "I'd like that."

I wanted to run to the door, close it and crawl in bed next to him. I wanted to snuggle up and wait for Anita and Dom and Joey Santino to all go to hell and leave us alone. If I could only tell him how much I loved him. My desire to say those three little words nearly smothered me, but if I did—if I even thought them—what we had might end. That ending would leave a scar on my heart I feared might never heal.

I was a big girl, not an innocent seven-year-old who wanted to curl up with her daddy. If I got in bed with this man, I'd want him. More than any other man I'd ever known, and the truth was that I couldn't have him. Not only because he was injured, but more-so because I needed to fix what I'd broken. From Anita and Dom to what I'd done to Welton to—yes, even down to my relationship with Skip. He was the one. The one who had stolen my heart—the one who had made me realize how broken I was—the one who could destroy me.

We sat holding hands for the longest time. In the silence, his fingers danced across my palm. The last time I trusted anyone I was eight years old. Since that day twenty years ago my life had been spent running away. It was time to make a change, but first, like a participant in a twelve-step program, I needed to make amends. Where would I begin? Better yet, how?

I don't know how long we sat like that, but eventually one of the staff showed up with Skip's breakfast. She suggested I grab something from the cafeteria and come back, but Skip needed rest so I excused myself to grab a bagel and coffee before hitting the road. I turned north on I-5; traffic was abysmally slow. By the time I got to the Tamarack Avenue exit in Carlsbad, it was eight-thirty. Drained. The word barely described my state of mind. In addition to everything happening with Skip, I also had to wonder what had happened in L.A. A call to Anita should clear that up. When she didn't answer her phone and Dom didn't answer his, a knot tightened in my stomach. Had I forgotten one detail in my planning? What if the cops had shown up?

I went to see Anita's Aunt Marjorie. She and I had grown close since we'd met a few months ago, so when Anita needed help, I'd volunteered. Something told me Anita would have called her aunt after such a big night even though I'd warned her about the need for containment, especially if things went bad.

I stood before the door with my finger poised over the button, regretting my decision to come here. When I finally pushed the button, she answered right away. "Hi, honey!" She opened her arms and we hugged. Marjorie's embrace was one of those warm, squishy cream-puff holds that reminded me of Thanksgiving or Christmas tables overflowing with comfort food. She had joked that she had my thin, athletic build plus another of her own. While she wouldn't quite make two of me, she came close.

"I hope I'm not interrupting you," I sputtered with my face still buried in her wild mane of grey hair. My hopes were that she was in a hurry so I could make a hasty exit.

"Just on my way to the store, but it can wait. It's nice to see you!" She hugged me again.

Play this out, I told myself. I smiled. "It's been a while since we've been able to talk, so I thought I'd stop by. Got a sec?"

"For you, always. C'mon in. How's that boyfriend of yours?"

"Skip's fine. He's going to take a little time off work."

"Any big plans?" Marjorie grinned ear-to-ear and raised an expectant eyebrow.

"We had a little disagreement, but I think we're working it out."

"I'll put on some coffee. Have a seat."

Other than the glass top, Marjorie's dining set bore little resemblance to that in Welton's apartment. Where his was elegant and had four leather chairs on casters, Marjorie's wore its bad 1980s design like a badge of honor. The chairs had little rubber feet, not casters. I pulled a chair out and slumped down into it, resting my elbow on my knee, my chin on my hand. Exhaustion ran through me. The only thing I knew for sure was that this was the wrong time to be talking to an inquisitive busybody like Marjorie.

"I have so many things to do today. I don't really have time for coffee."

"Sit." She stood before me with her arms crossed over her chest—truly an imposing figure—if you were afraid of cream puffs. "You and me, girlfriend. We need to talk. You might fool your mother, your hot boyfriend, even yourself, but you don't fool me for a second. Something's wrong—I can see it on your face."

Shit. If Marjorie could read my reactions, I was on the verge of a breakdown. Or was she that good? "I'm just tired."

"Bullshit. You didn't panic when you fought off that Wizard maniac."

"Sproutman was just a hired gun for Sonny Panaman."

"That tried to kill you. My point is that you were strong under the worst of circumstances. That's what I liked about you. You're not the same girl; you're nervous and that's not the Roxy I know."

"She doesn't exist." I regretted the words the moment they fell from my mouth.

The coffee maker uttered its final gurgle, but Marjorie watched my face for a moment. "Really?" She crossed the room and filled two mugs with enough caffeine to jolt the dead awake. The aroma of her fresh brew wafted through the air. I watched her hobble back to the table, mugs in hand. "You've still got that limp."

"The doctor says I'm healing, but at my age it takes forever. We'll come back to you in a second, honey, but first I want to ask a question."

"Long as it's not about men, politics or religion." The fire brew went down hard, but it was just what I needed.

"Well, it kind of is and it kind of isn't. What's going on with Anita? You two seemed to be getting kind of close. I thought maybe you'd know. Have you heard from her?"

"She's done with Welton," I said. "If that's what you're asking."

"I knew that. She was done with him when I introduced you two. When's the last time you talked to her?" Marjorie raised her mug and took a sip.

"Yesterday. We were planning on meeting someplace for drinks. What about you? When's the last time you spoke with her?"

"She calls me every Monday morning at eight o'clock on the dot and today she didn't."

"I'm sure there's a good reason. Maybe you should call her now."

"I did, just before you got here." She tried to hide her nervousness by sliding a coaster across the table, but the tightness around the corners of her mouth gave her away. Marjorie avoided engaging me by focusing instead on her Sexy Senior Sinner mug. "I need a cigarette."

"I thought you quit."

"I'm worried about her."

I forced a laugh, then reached out to give her hand a gentle squeeze. "Why? Because she didn't call at eight on the dot?"

"Roxy, did you and Anita ever talk about, um, her past?"

Uh, no. My past contained enough skeletons to fill a small cemetery. If anyone knew how easy it was to make mistakes, it was me. One good rule in my business is to never ask a question you don't want to answer yourself. That meant sharing was a no-no. On the other hand, this might be the information I needed. "What past? What did she do?"

Her wild gray mane hung freely to one side as she tilted her head. "It might be less about what Anita did than what others did to her. Her mother had a drug problem and resorted to selling herself to men to keep herself high. Anita always seemed so levelheaded, but she got beaten up a few times by her mother's 'boyfriends' when she was a child."

The lines on Marjorie's face deepened further; her coloring became splotchy, her eyes brimmed with moisture.

"I fought with her mother to get the kid out of there, but Anita followed Dom's example and ran away on her fourteenth birthday. She was gone for two months. When she turned up at my door, she swore that if she had to go back to her mother's she'd run away again. I had a good job as a corporate trainer at the time—well, at least a good paying job—sometimes it felt more like I was running interventions than training. Anyway, I made a deal. It seemed like a good idea—I still think it was—I paid Anita's mother to let me keep her."

I eyed Marjorie. "What? You paid reverse child support?"

"Anita was stable for about a year, but one day she got busted for shoplifting at the mall. I was mortified and came down on her pretty hard. She disappeared again—until a few years ago. She told me she'd lived on the streets for about a year, met some 'people' who took her in. That's what she called them, anyway. I never asked what she had to do to 'thank' the people. Right after that she joined the Army and got her life back together."

"Everybody's got a past," I said. "Some are just more difficult than others. She acted out when she was a kid. That doesn't make her a bad adult." If only I could believe that—I'd been committing crimes of one sort or another since I was eight. Would I ever stop?

"In four and a half years she's never missed a call. Roxy, I'd really like to know what you two decided to do about that no-good boyfriend of hers. I'll probably be okay with it—just tell me you didn't kill him."

CHAPTER 14

S K I P

When Skip awoke, he fully expected the room to be empty. Instead, Baldorf sat in a nearby chair, hunched over, tapping on his iPad screen.

"How was the conference?"

"Overrated, dude. Besides, I had things I needed to do here. Seen Roxy?"

"Baldorf, she's one of the best liars I've ever met."

"That the boyfriend talking or the forensic hypnotist slash criminologist?"

"It's what she does. You know that."

"She's trying to go straight."

"Only because I forced her to."

Baldorf shook his head. "No way, man. She could've bailed on you, but you showed her how to trust again."

"Again?" Skip snorted. "Don't make me laugh, it hurts."

"It's true, she trusts you. She loves you. You know that, too. Besides, you're right. She's the best liar I've ever seen."

"High praise from someone with a 165 IQ."

Baldorf smiled. "I endeavor to not force my brilliance on mere mortals." He paused, letting his eyes bore into Skip's. "Neither should you."

Talk about being on the losing end of an argument, thought Skip. "I'm trained to watch for the clues and I have trouble knowing the truth from a lie with her."

"Don't feel bad, I'm a genius and I can't see it. I love her, dude, but I always check my wallet before she leaves."

How much, or rather, how little, Skip could trust Roxy hurt more than the bruise on his head. At times, he felt like one of Roxy's marks, never knowing if his eye movements, facial coloring or breathing pattern might give him away. He wondered if she felt the same about him. He winked at Baldorf. "Pity the mere mortals."

"Total control, dude. Girl's in total control every second."

"I knew from the moment we met that she was dangerous. But, I couldn't stop myself from falling in love with her. Now I couldn't betray her any more than I'd commit cold-blooded murder."

"Love is blind, man. I think you would kill for her."

Skip's first reaction was to deny it, but Baldorf's assessment was a universal truth. "Isn't that why it always happens?"

"Why what happens?"

"People kill for love all the time."

Baldorf watched Skip's face, shaking his head slowly. "You. Got. It. Bad."

"This morning, while she sat here on the bedside next to me, she dropped her guard. I've never seen her so vulnerable."

"What'd she do?"

"I asked her about last night and she hesitated."

"She hesitated? For what, like, a few seconds? A minute?"

"Not long."

"A tenth of a second? A thousandth?"

"Long enough."

"Wow. You are one tough—how do you know she wasn't just, you know, having a female problem or something."

Skip chuckled. "A female problem? You've got a 165 IQ and you call it a 'female problem?'"

"I'm basically an introvert." Baldorf blushed. "My verbal communications skills regarding human physiology, especially when discussing attractive women with a strong—uh, sexual appeal—tend to deteriorate."

"We need to get you a girlfriend."

"I'm so over this. Can we discuss something else?"

"You do like girls, right? You've got some hot ones in that video game of yours." Skip smiled, "Barry Finkledorf's—"

"Stuff it!" Skip's friend rolled his eyes. "Why do I put up with you, anyway? It's Baldorf's Revenge and you know it. And, yes, I like girls. But, I'm a geek. I get all tongue-tied around them. Happy now? I said it. I hang out with the likes of you because you two are . . . oh, man, you're like family."

Warmth radiated through Skip. "You'll be the best man at our wedding—if there ever is one." He paused, afraid to take that conversation thread any further. "I thought you just liked us because we're dysfunctional and entertaining."

Baldorf cocked his head to one side. "There's always that. So tell me, Master Human Lie Detector, how you diagnosed this oh-so-insignificant breach of guardedness."

"I told her about Santino. I also asked where she was when she got the call about me. Her eyes darted up to the right. She was constructing a visual memory—a lie. She told me she was at Anita's place. She said they had dinner and spent some time with Anita's brother."

"Where'd they go for dinner?"

"A Mom and Pop place, so she said. Even though she was exhausted, she caught me watching her every move. Her cheeks were puffy; her eyes were red. It looked like she hadn't slept the night before."

Baldorf's brow furrowed. "Dude, it's all so war of the titans. Two communication experts, each vying to outdo the other, each searching for a clue about what the other is really thinking. The sex must be awesome."

Skip held back a laugh. "I thought you were shy."

"You're bringing me out of my shell. Besides, I didn't ask for, like, a description or anything. Let's just call it a clinical analysis. An observation."

"Enough!"

"You started it." Baldorf laughed.

"I need a favor and I'm wondering if you can help her."

"It's part of the reason I came back."

"She told you something?"

"Only that she was in L.A. when I called. But she was upset. Girl wouldn't have cracked unless she was under extreme duress. So, she didn't say anything; it was more like what she didn't say."

Chapter 15

R O X Y

On my way home from Marjorie's, I stopped to pick up a copy of the L.A. Times at Vons market. If I was going to help Anita—or myself—I needed to check the L.A. news. From my first conversation with Anita, I'd suspected that she was into a game she knew nothing about. Now, I was concerned about her emotions. Had Anita made me an accomplice to something far worse than a con?

My former office was on the second floor of a small building near downtown Carlsbad. There had been room for a clueless receptionist and a separate, almost-spacious office for me. My walls had been decorated with beautiful lithographs, my credenza had displayed a cherished photo of me when I was a precocious, bubbly seven-year-old on a trip to the San Diego Zoo with Mom and Dad. Had I realized my receptionist wasn't so clueless after all, I might be on a warm beach working on my tan, not working out of my kitchen. Instead of the oak desk and pictures on the wall, I had a faux-wood dining table and a freebie calendar from some charitable organization I'd never heard of.

Before parking myself at my "desk," I powered up the laptop, determined to take advantage of the amenities so my change in status didn't feel so much like a total comedown. I scanned the L.A.

Times while water heated in the kettle. There was nothing in the front section about Welton, his stock scam, a company crash or anything of the sort. I laid Sports aside and went on to Business. Again, nothing.

The tea kettle whistled, so I put the newspaper down and pulled out a little single filter and plastic holder. I dropped in a scoop of grounds, then poured water through the filter. What happened after I left Welton's apartment last night? While my little drip system did its thing, I went online to check the stock price for the company listed in Jack's email last night. The quote was easy enough to find. It was trading at near zero on massive selling.

I went to the L.A. Times website and typed "Welton" into the search field. The next page popped up with some ads directly below the search box followed by a list of results. The list was separated into four categories: articles, images, video, and blogs. Ten of the articles involved my search term. I suppose they were ordered chronologically, but it didn't really matter. The headline for the first one said it all, "Local businessman found dead in apartment."

Los Angeles businessman William J. (Jack) Welton was found in his downtown apartment this morning by his maid service, Downtown Cleaning. Police are investigating the death and will make no comment, citing an ongoing investigation.

The maid service said that two maids entered the apartment shortly after 8:00 a.m. and found Welton's body in the bedroom. "They called the police immediately," said a Downtown Cleaning representative. The representative refused to comment further.

Anyone with information about the killing should contact the Los Angeles Police Homicide Division.

My pulse pounded so loud it almost drowned out the chirping of birds in the apartment courtyard. The stock crash wasn't a surprise, but Welton's death was. What had Anita—or Dom—done? What had I become involved in? I did another search for current news on Welton. There had to be some word on how he'd died. What about his wife? The cops always went after the spouse first. I typed her name into the search box.

The search engine returned somewhere in the neighborhood of a gazillion entries. What I needed was something to tie her to Jack. It was her money that had given Welton his start, so . . .

Bingo. Just a couple of entries down in the list was one titled "Frederica Gurney-Welton's husband found dead." I clicked the link.

> Jack Welton, husband of Frederica Gurney-Welton, was found dead in the bedroom of a downtown apartment this morning by his maid service. When asked about her husband's death, Ms. Gurney-Welton refused to comment.

The bedroom? He must have woken up. Maybe it hadn't been Anita. I opened another window on my laptop to search for Downtown Cleaning, found their contact information and dialed the number.

A woman's soft voice answered. She sounded professional, but had a heavy Hispanic accent. "Downtown Cleaning."

"This is LAPD homicide calling. One of our officers neglected to ask a question of the maid that found Jack Welton's body this morning. Is she still around?"

"Maria? She not work in the office. She took rest of day off. Felt very bad."

"I understand. I'm sorry she had to go home early. Would it be okay if I called her at home?"

"You the police. Why not?"

That's right, I was. "I'll do that. What's her number?"

The voice turned suspicious. "What was your name did you say?"

"LAPD homicide and you don't want me having to come down there!"

The poor woman caved faster than a horny sorority girl on a date with the school jock. After she gave me a telephone number, I apologized for snapping at her. I also assured her, with absolutely no confidence at all, that we, the LAPD, wouldn't disturb her again. My next call was to the maid's home.

"Hola?"

"Hi, this is LAPD Homicide. Maria, please."

"She's asleep. She's not feeling well." The voice on the other end of the phone sounded like a young second or third generation Hispanic who spoke English with only the hint of an accent.

"When will she be up?"

"One hour. Maybe two. She has a migraine."

"Because of the body she found earlier today?"

"She's never seen a dead man before. She liked Señor Welton; he was very nice to my mother."

I noticed how smoothly the Spanish word flowed off her tongue. "Did your mother say anything about what happened?"

"No. Wait. Yes. She doesn't think he should have to go to hell for what he did."

Hell? What could Welton possibly have done to a maid with no money to invest? "Why would he go to hell?"

"He hanged himself. My mother says only fools hang themselves."

CHAPTER 16

S K I P

Skip found it almost comical that he, the injured one, itched for the smell and taste of a gentle sea breeze, while Baldorf, who could get up and walk out anytime, was immersed in his little online world. He'd swapped out his iPad for a laptop. His fingers moved over the keys with practiced ease. "You should blink more often."

"What?" Baldorf never took his eyes from the computer screen.

"Your blink rate is near zero. If you blink more often, your eyes won't dry out so much."

His friend glanced up, cocked an eyebrow, then went back to typing.

"What's that mean?" asked Skip.

"Nothing," Baldorf said without pausing.

"No way. You always mean something."

"My blink rate's fine." Baldorf huffed at Skip.

"Something else is bugging you. What?"

"Working with you two is no fun, dude. You and Roxy get to have all the secrets. The rest of us have zilch. Don't get me wrong, the cloak-and-dagger part's awesome, but you two are, like, real downers when it comes to letting a guy follow a train of thought. How about if, instead of playing Master Wizard with me, you borrow my iPad so you can play chess with some Buddhist kid in Kalmykia?"

"A what? Where?"

"Kalmykia. It's in the Russian Federation."

"They play chess?"

"Duh. Of course they do. You've never heard of Kalmykia? Wow, talk about a narrow world view."

"I think I just got insulted." Skip felt the call button in his hand. Should he ring for a nurse to distract Baldorf from the inevitable? Too late, his friend had already started.

"Which means, of course, that you might expect their primary religious beliefs to be Russian Orthodox Christianity. Instead, the predominant faith is Tibetan Buddhism."

"So, oh worldly one, I'd play chess with this Buddhist kid there because?"

"It's the world's chess capital. So to speak." Baldorf's fingers tapped on the keys again; his eyes roamed the laptop screen.

"So to speak. In this . . . backwoods . . . Russian Federation . . . town . . ."

"Self-governing member state."

"Of course, a self-governing member state. Keep the iPad."

"Dude. Every Kalmykian elementary school student is required to play. You might even be able to beat one of the younger ones."

Baldorf's attention was fully focused on the screen before him. Skip wondered if Baldorf was even listening when he said, "Screw you."

"I found it!" Baldorf's eyes lit up. "I checked a couple of the online databases and found background on your boy Santino. There's not much intel on his prison time. Not anything I can find, at least. But you know what that means."

"It's secured somewhere?"

Baldorf glared at Skip. "No, man! I haven't had much time to work on this."

"Sorry, momentary lapse on my part."

"You're forgiven. His address before he went to prison? It looks like a rental property. Really shady landlord who does less than zero maintenance. It's a rat hole—in all senses."

"I'm not sure I follow."

"There's some neighborhood activist who's blogging about this place. I've been reading his past entries. Man, if half of what this guy is saying online is true, the place ought to be burned down. Here's the latest blog entry. 'Stanmore Argemi has continued to ignore the pleas of the neighbors, this blogger included, to clean up his properties and rent them to upstanding sitizens.'"

Baldorf shook his head. "Guy needs spelling lessons. He spelled citizens with an s."

"There is one."

"He's got two."

"Don't grade, read."

"Roger. His spelling is atrocious and his grammar sucks so I'll just paraphrase. Dude says Public Health stepped in two weeks ago and served notice on the property to get rid of all the garbage. He also said Argemi reinstated his garbage service after the threat, but rented the property to a group of 'those Asians.'"

"Ouch. Guess he doesn't like Asians."

"Roger that, dude."

"So there's a spy in the neighborhood. Does this blogger have a name?"

"Just calls himself Straight Eddie."

"Have you got any idea what Fast Eddie's agenda is?"

"Straight Eddie, oh name-challenged one. You're the people expert. Human behavior mystifies me. Especially female behavior."

"Like Roxy?"

"She's in a class by herself, dude. She baffles me—and fascinates me—more than any woman I've ever met."

"But you still check your wallet when she leaves the room."

"Perpetually. Constantly."

Skip raised his hand. The clear plastic tubing still taped to his skin reminded him of his need to heal quickly. "Got it. Did she call you yet?"

"Not today, but I'm expecting to hear from her any time now."

"I need to find out what she did in L.A. Can you give her something to do? You know, keep her busy until I can get up there?"

"Why don't you just ask her?"

"I tried. She doesn't want to talk about it. Whatever she's involved in, it's bad."

"You're right, something happened in L.A. I don't know what, but I do know she's going to want your help."

"When she's ready, she'll ask. Right now, though, she's not and I need to get her out of the way. Someplace safe, which means she can't be home since Santino might go looking for her there."

"I've got the perfect solution. I'll send her to this address. The neighborhood is a crappy place to spend a couple of days, but she should be safe with Straight Eddie on watch."

Skip nodded. "It's a former address for Santino and Straight Eddie watches everything. That'd be perfect."

"You ever tell her what I did and my wallet will never be safe."

CHAPTER 17

R O X Y

I hung up the phone, the words of the maid's daughter echoing in my mind. No shit. Only fools hang themselves and Jack Welton was no fool.

There were only two possibilities. Hanging is an either-or proposition—either Welton hanged himself or someone did it for him. I leaned against the counter while a wave of fear washed through me. How had this gone so terribly wrong?

My phone bleeped with the ring tone for Baldorf. "Hey."

"Hey, yourself. What's up?"

"I need a favor. This guy that's after Skip, you know, this Santino character? I know where he lives, but need to do a stakeout for a day or two."

"Baldorf, I don't do stakeouts. They're way too boring." I didn't want to whine, but my own problems were piling up.

"This is for Skip. I'd so do it myself, but you know me . . ."

I had a sudden flashback to how Baldorf had once described himself. "I know, one part genius, one part chicken."

"Chickens are stupid birds, Rox."

"They were your words. I'm just reminding you of what you said."

"Verbatim recitation of earlier conversations is an unbecoming trait when dealing with discussions of personal weakness made during times of stress."

"Are you calling me a bitch?"

There was a long pause, which gave me an immense amount of satisfaction. It took a real shocker to stop Baldorf. Score one for me. I couldn't stop smiling.

"Uh, no. I'm sorry. I didn't mean to upset you."

"Forget it. I'm just messing with you." Maybe a stakeout would be a good thing. Helping Skip might help get my mind off my problems. That would give my subconscious an opportunity to sort out my next move. I fingered the faux-wood table top. Another benefit would be having Baldorf owe me a favor. Help from the boy genius when I needed it would be a definite plus. "Skip really needs this done?"

"It's critical."

"Fine. What's the address? I'll do this for the rest of the day. After that, we have to negotiate compensation."

"Cool. Today. After today, we negotiate. Are we, like, talking about money?"

"No. A favor."

"Maybe we should just deal with that now?"

"Not a chance. Gimme the address." I wasn't about to reveal my cards. The stakeout would give me time to think about how Baldorf would pay me back.

CHAPTER 18

SKIP

Skip flashed Baldorf a thumbs up at his friend's sincerity. He'd so do it himself. Not a perfect lie, but with a hint of beginner's luck, Baldorf just might have fooled Roxy. "Nice," said Skip. "It went okay?"

"I assure you, she's in no danger at all. Santino's not going looking for her at his old place. He's been gone for years."

"You did good, my friend. I owe you."

"Really?" Baldorf's eyes lit up. "It was sly, huh? She'll be sitting there the rest of today. I'm sure I can figure out something for tomorrow, too. Very cool if I do say so myself."

Skip winked. "You said it, sly."

With a wide grin extending from ear-to-ear, Baldorf boasted, "Exquisitely sly. Would you say?"

"You had the element of surprise on your side. Enjoy the rush. How long does it take you to figure out scenarios for Baldorf's Revenge?"

"The longest was a day and a half. The problem was that I needed a way for a player to escape a Vesuvian-style eruption. There were fourteen different variables to account for."

"Stop!"

"The algorithm was extremely complex. Depending upon the IQ, it's entirely possible and within the realm of statistical probability that—oh, sorry."

Skip held his hand up in a sign of surrender. "I get it. I'm sorry I asked. Okay, okay. It was exquisitely sly, but you're making my head hurt."

"Sorry, dude. What can I do to help?"

"You can help me get all my questions lined up before I go to L.A."

"I'm a genius, but don't read minds. You want to give me a hint?"

"Whatever Roxy's into has something to do with her friend Anita. Roxy bought a very expensive cocktail dress for the trip."

"She wanted to impress someone?"

"Exactly." Skip said nothing while he watched an orderly roll a patient on a gurney past his door. The IV, the masks, hospital gowns—he hated these places. He continued, "That probably means a very swanky party."

"I'll check the hyperlocal news sources for intel on the mucky-mucks."

"Now local news isn't good enough? We're into hyperlocal?"

"Sign of the times, man. It's like, written by locals about locals for locals. It's the tabloid for the little people."

"All I need to know is if this is going to tell me where she went Sunday night. Can you do that?"

"There are times when you so disappoint me. You might consider daily meditation as a methodology to help you resolve your attachment to negative assessments of others' capabilities."

"What the hell are you blathering about?"

Baldorf winked and turned his attention to his laptop. "Chill, dude, I've so got it covered."

CHAPTER 19

R O X Y

Face it, girls, the problem with being a woman on a stakeout is not being able to use a water bottle when nature calls. At least the stakeout gave me time to think. Hours, in fact. I'd been sitting half a block down from a total dump, a place that reminded me of something between a rat's nest and a garbage pit. Once-blue exterior paint had long ago begun to peel. The place had a tired, beat-up appearance. There were gutters, but no downspouts. Windows? Sure, but they were either boarded over on the outside or covered on the inside by blinds hanging crooked. The landscaping on the block was indicative of slum neighborhoods, but Santino's front yard made the others look like they'd been manicured. It was the classic TV drug haven and the only thing breaking the monotony of bare dirt and parched weeds was a lonely tree stump.

Twice during the last three hours I'd gotten hateful stares from the neighbors. Periodically the neighborhood dog pack would bark in unison—probably the dog equivalent of a detailed complaint session about their living conditions. There was also the dumb ass in the red T-shirt with a crew cut. His shirt had "Neighborhood Watch" in giant white letters. He'd made a big show of taking down my license plate number, which only reinforced the fact that this place gave me the creeps. The sooner I could get out of here, the better.

The good news was I knew what payment I'd extract from Baldorf. Some of the identifying information for Welton's illegal bank account was still fresh in my mind and given the task I was performing here, it wasn't enough that I'd want Skip's little computer genius to hack Welton's account. Oh, no. Let him bitch about the amount of time it would take, but he'd do my bidding. If anyone could, he'd find out where the money had gone. He was the only person I knew who was remotely capable of accomplishing such a feat—if it could even be done.

I needed a restroom, but wasn't about to go anywhere near one of these houses to use the facilities. I was thinking a trip to the nearest safe-zone gas station was imminent when a kid snuck around the back of Santino's place. He wore typical kid garb—a black hoodie with ragged jeans—and carried a bulging backpack.

The kid scanned the area while he approached one of the few windows that hadn't been boarded over. I wondered if I was about to witness a break in. To a drug house? Was this kid insane? Gunshots would bring the cops. A raid would seriously screw with my surveillance. The kid dropped the backpack at his feet. He pressed his hands against the glass. The window jerked open a couple of inches.

There was no way I could let this happen. Everything would go to hell and Baldorf would probably refuse to help me. I was out of the car, walking quickly toward the house while the kid was engrossed in breaking and entering. He put his hands under the sill, then pushed up again. With each attempt, the window inched open a fraction more. I sprang forward just as the kid got the window open enough to slip through. He saw me and ran in the opposite direction, but tripped over his backpack. He went sprawling, scrambled to get up, but wasn't fast enough. I grabbed his sweatshirt hood to pull him toward me.

A small fist slammed into my shoulder. A high-pitched voice yelped, "Lemme go!"

Holy shit, he was a she. I grabbed her arms, pinned her against the side of the house and clamped my hand over her mouth. She took another swing, but I stilled her by digging my thumb into the tender spot on her neck just beneath her jaw. Her eyes got wide and she stopped resisting. To my surprise, she didn't cry.

I glared at her until she nodded. I reached up and lowered the window, hoping the kid didn't run the minute I released her. With everything back to normal—whatever that was—I grabbed the kid by the arm and scooped up her backpack. "Come with me."

She hissed, "You won't, like, get away with this. People will, like, be looking for me."

"Who? That neighborhood watch guy? Real impressive, kid."

"Lily. It's Lily, pervert."

"Roxy. Nice to meet you, Lily." From a distance, I hadn't seen Lily's features, but now that I did, her natural beauty—and the bruise around her left eye—struck me. "Who gave you the shiner?"

"Some moron who won't, like, mess with me again."

We reached the car where Mr. Neighborhood Watch awaited. Momentary panic engulfed me. How many things could go wrong in the next ten seconds? Too many, starting with the kid. I gave him my most sincere smile while tightening my grip on Lily's arm. "Thanks for helping to keep the neighborhood safe. The City appreciates your hard work. I've got this one. Thanks again."

Mr. Neighborhood Watch stammered, "You're—you're welcome."

Lily didn't say a word during the whole conversation. I'd fully expected her to rat me out, so when she didn't, I concluded she was smart enough to know when to stay your hand. My respect for this kid was growing by the second. She reminded me of myself at her age. When Mr. Neighborhood Watch scampered away, probably in search of someone easier to intimidate, I opened the back door, tossed in Lily's backpack, and shoved her into the passenger's seat. "I only want to talk. When we're done, you can have your stuff back. Deal?"

Lily nodded. I closed the door, unsure if she'd bolt the moment I was on the driver's side of the car. To her credit, the kid kept her word. I liked that. Once I was behind the wheel, I turned sideways to assess her—dirty face, unwashed clothes, stringy hair. She didn't get like this from our little scuffle. The kid hadn't seen a shower in a while. "Are you hungry?"

The longing in her eyes reminded me of others I'd seen living on the streets. "Like, what's it to you?"

"Where are your mom and dad? They don't feed you?"

"My dad's, like, a deadbeat. He split. You know, when he, like, found out. Mom . . ." A tear formed in the corner of her eye as she turned her face toward the side window. "Mom likes drugs more than me."

The crack in her voice sent a lump into my throat. Shit. Talk about baggage. I took a deep breath. "When's the last time you ate anything?"

"What do you care? You, like, want something. What is it?" She faced me, all fire and defiance again.

"Chill out, kid. There's a fast food joint not very far away. Would it be okay if we went and got something? I need a restroom something fierce and my stomach's starting to growl. How about if I buy you lunch?"

"You're, like, a cop. You gonna, like, try to entrap me or something? You ain't gonna get away with it, ya know."

"Believe me, kid, I'm not a cop."

"But you, like, told that guy you were."

"No. I didn't. What I want is information about the house. I've got a hunch you know all about it." I caught her rolling her eyes. "I'm willing to pay for the information."

She stared at me, suddenly interested in more than escape. "Serious? Like, how much?"

I winked at her. "We'll negotiate over lunch. Right now, I need that restroom. Deal?"

She glanced at the backpack in the back seat. I half-expected her to jump out the door, but instead she stuck out her hand. "Deal."

CHAPTER 20

S K I P

In Skip's dream, he walked the beach near his condo, felt the sun warm his skin while small waves cooled his feet. Everything was perfect except for an insistent voice prodding him awake. The familiar voice came again. "Dude. Wake up."

Skip slipped down deeper under the covers. He only wanted sleep.

"C'mon, man. The doc's coming."

Doctor? He remembered beige walls, patterned gowns, masks, surgical caps. Hospital—he was in a hospital. He opened one eye. Baldorf peered back at him over the top of the blanket. "I was having a nice dream," Skip said.

"No time, man. The doc started to walk in, but he got called out by one of the nurses."

The room came into focus; Baldorf rattled on.

"Look, before he gets back, I think I figured out where Roxy went last night. There was a party in L.A. to raise money for a new wing on a museum. Roxy was there with some dude named Jack Welton."

"You sure it's her?" Skip struggled to an upright position, rubbed his forehead and cheeks to wake up. How long had he been out?

Baldorf turned his laptop around. Skip focused on the screen despite his eyes feeling grainy with sleep. Roxy stood, her hand touching a stranger's arm, laughing. Skip's pulse raced at the thought of her with someone else. He had no right to be jealous after their fight, but damn—he studied the photo. Erect posture. Back arched slightly. The killer dress.

"Mr. Cosgrove?"

Skip's mind jerked back to the here and now. The doc was a tall man with a solid five-o'clock shadow who bustled in with the enthusiasm of someone straight out of med school. "Hey, doc."

"I think you're ready to go home. What do you think?"

"I'm past ready."

"That's always a good sign. But you're going to need to take it easy for a couple of days."

"Sure doc. Rest. Maybe some light duty." Like hell. Light duty was the last thing he'd be doing.

Baldorf sat like an antsy six-year-old, but Skip wasn't willing to screw this up just because his friend was bored. The moment they were alone, Baldorf said, "Sorry I couldn't finish earlier, but you need to know something else. Welton is dead."

CHAPTER 21

R O X Y

I sat across a red laminated table from Lily, checking out the others in this depressingly predictable fast food restaurant. The pimply faced kid behind the counter wore a lame uniform with weird stripes that reminded me of an escaped convict in a black-and-white movie. He'd recognized Lily, a fact they'd tried to conceal by exchanging only a nod. I chalked up their exchange to the equivalent of an encrypted teenage code of questions asked—hi, how are you, need any help?—and answered—hey, it's cool, not around the adult.

A man wearing a ragged US Army jacket, dirty jeans, and wool cap sat about fifteen feet away at another window table. He divided his time between arguing with his soft drink and staring at the shopping cart filled with plastic bags, clothing and other miscellaneous personal crap he'd parked outside. I nodded in his direction. "He here all the time, too?"

"Maniac? Yeah, he, like, hits the streets. If he gets enough cash, he shows up here. He don't spend much on food." Lily pointed out the window at a liquor store across the street. "His money, like, goes there."

"He's an alcoholic?"

She didn't answer. Instead, she stuck a ketchup-doused French fry in her mouth and chewed. "What, I gotta, like, break it down for you?" She began counting on her fingers. "Here, you're so, like, a drunk, an addict, or fighting to stay alive."

I swallowed hard. Where did Lily fit in? Behind those salty, ketchup-coated fingers was a streetwise kid. I suspected she knew far more than most people. She licked salt and ketchup from her fingers while daring me to challenge her with a dispassionate game face. I avoided the wordless taunt by taking a deliberate sip of my drink; she countered by bathing another handful of fries in ketchup.

"So is your mom in rehab?"

Her face clouded over. She lowered the fries, placing them on the paper next to the remnants of her burger. Her eyes teared up, then she swallowed the lump in her throat. "Mom got busted. She, like, hit up a cop by mistake last time the City Morons decided to crack down."

"City Morons? You mean the City Council?"

"Same thing."

"Was it for prostitution?"

"She didn't do nothin' ain't, like, been done before."

I couldn't bring myself to even ask the next question. I shoved the thought of what this little girl, this child, might have had to do herself. "How long is she in for?"

"Like, three more months."

"Where do you live?"

"Foster home." She shoved the fries into her mouth. Between chews, she said, "I'm cool. You, like, so owe me for butting in at that house. There wasn't nobody there. They were, like, off making one of their drug runs. So what do you wanna know? I, like, got stuff to do."

I felt a pang in my heart. Personal experience told me how anger and defiance wore on your soul. No matter how strong she might be, how long could Lily last? "I need to know who lives inside that house."

"Morons." She shrugged. "They been around a month, maybe. When they leave out the back, like they did when you butted in, they ain't gonna be there for fifteen, maybe longer. I had time. Plenty."

"Wait a minute! There's a back entrance?"

Lily jabbed a fry into the ketchup, a smirk on her lips. "Duh! You're, like, so right, you ain't no cop. What do you care about that place, anyways?"

"It's a long story, so don't push it, kid. I'm the one paying for information. Not you. What's in the house?"

"So, like, how much you gonna pay me?"

"We'll settle when I see how much you know. What else is inside?"

"They ain't got much. Like, maybe a coupla mattresses. They got a TV in the living room. They even decorated—they, like, kinda got a couch for some of their drug deals."

"How do you know that?"

"These guys ain't smart. Like, I was in the house when one went down. Morons were so messed up they, like, didn't know nothin'."

I couldn't believe what I was hearing. "You were inside when they were there? Have you got a death wish?"

"It ain't no big deal, if their customers weren't, like, stupider than them, they'd so be out of business. Ya' know, they never even, like, knew I was there."

"Promise me you won't go back in the house!"

"You ain't my mom."

I sat up straight, embarrassed at how quickly I'd stepped over a line I thought I'd never cross. "You're right. I shouldn't tell you what to do. I'm sorry. But, I like you. I got in a lot of trouble as a kid. I know how it can screw up your life. Be careful, okay?"

She answered through a mouthful of burger. "I'm always careful."

Her bravado felt forced, even uncertain. By the time we'd finished our food, Maniac was pushing his cart across the street. Never, even on my darkest days, had I slipped to Maniac's level. Or to where fate might force Lily. I reminded myself of why I was here. "Is there a guy in the house? Hispanic. Maybe five-four. Medium build. Bad attempt at a mustache. His name is Joey Santino."

She shook her head. "Ain't no Mexicans in that dump. But, ya know, they got somethin' out for some loser. They're all, like, we're so gonna kill this dude once we find him. So what do you do makes you, like, go looking for this guy? He, like, a friend of yours?"

"Hardly. What I do for a living isn't your business. They want to kill him? Did they ever say a name?" What she said made no sense; Lily had to be wrong. Baldorf didn't make mistakes like this.

Lily leaned to one side, letting her eyes roam my figure in a frank assessment that was innocent and honest and made me incredibly self-conscious. She said, "You're, like, really hot. You a dealer?" Her voice grew excited. "Are you, like, gonna boot these Asian morons out?"

It was my turn to do the eye roll. "Not happening, kid."

"FBI? CIA?"

"I already told you, I'm not a cop."

"That can only mean one thing."

I snickered. "What?"

"You're, like, a CI working for the cops. Is there going to be, like, a crackdown on the drugs? You're so gonna close down all their crack houses and put them away. Man, that's sick!"

I held up my hand. "Enough! These guys have more than one place? Wait a minute. You said they're Asian?"

"Well, duh. Everybody knows that. Like, what kind of CI are you?"

"Where's their other place?" Maybe that's where Joey hung out?

Lily shook her head. "I dunno. But, I could, like, take you there."

"If you don't know where this place is, how are you going to find it?"

"Follow 'em. Big & Ugly's, like, at the drive through."

CHAPTER 22

SKIP

Waves broke a few hundred feet away from the patio of Skip's condo. White surf punctuated the gray sea; salty air filled his lungs with welcome moisture. He listened, eyes closed, to the ocean's rhythmic spell, then took a deep breath. "It's good to be back."

He returned inside to be a couch potato while he tracked down old acquaintances, knowing he'd feel less guilty if he made nice before pumping them for connections. Within an hour, he'd found a former classmate from the police academy who was working in LAPD Homicide. Buddy Winestock had never been a close friend. While their relationship had always been more professional than personal, Skip made sure to spend time catching up on their days from the academy and talking about Buddy's kids. When the time was right, he launched into the reason for his call.

"A friend of mine was doing some research on an investment firm in L.A.—he's thinking of putting some money into their recommendations. Anyway, he discovered that the owner, Jack Welton, died recently. Is your department investigating?"

"You're wasting your time. I can't comment."

"So there is an investigation into Welton's death."

Suspicion edged into Buddy's voice. "You're pretty persistent on this. What did you say your connection was?"

"I hate to say the name because you guys probably hate him. But, he's a defense attorney. Wally Price."

"Yeah, I heard of him. He doesn't practice much up here. Lucky you."

"Why's that?"

"Because if he did practice up here, I probably wouldn't talk to you at all. You want to know if we're investigating Welton's death?"

"Right."

"No comment."

"What would you tell me if Wally did practice in L.A.?"

Buddy chuckled. "Same thing. What else?"

"I read that his maid service found him in the bedroom— that he hanged himself. Doesn't the M.E. consider that 'unusual circumstances?'"

"That would be procedure."

Two for two, thought Skip. "By luck or happenstance my path seems to be crossing with that of Jack Welton. Would you like me to pass along what I find? Assuming, of course, I come across something of interest to an investigator."

"What do you think? Of course. We'd want all leads funneled this way."

"Got it, Buddy. I'll be in touch." Skip disconnected the call before his friend could press him for a promise. Had Buddy asked for one, Skip's answer would have been, "No comment."

CHAPTER 23

ROXY

I slammed the driver's door, shoved the key into the ignition, and barked at Lily. "Why didn't you say something?"

"Hey, it ain't my fault you, like, eat so slow!"

By the time I was backing out of the parking space Big & Ugly's Explorer was making a left on the Coast Highway heading north. We pulled up to the exit, my lunch heavy in my stomach. "That burger was awful."

Lily yelled, "Clear!"

Without thinking, I gunned the engine after a quick glance to my left. A horn blared to my right. "Crap!" I yelled. "I almost sideswiped that car!" Lily leaned forward in her seat, a wide grin plastered on her face. I barked, "Seatbelt!"

"That was awesome!" She was turned sideways in her seat, watching the car behind us. "Totally cool driving!"

"Don't you ever pull that on me again!" We were a block and a half behind a white Ford Explorer with enough identifying dents to make it an easy tail in a world filled with less accident-prone vehicles.

"Chill. He was, like, so in the other lane."

"She. It was a woman and she was in the other lane after I almost hit her!"

"Stop, like, being so picky. It was so my side of the car that would'a got hit."

"Spoken like a twelve-year-old with no idea of how to drive," I snapped.

Lily's smile fell away. She stared out the side window. Immediately, I wanted to take the words back. I knew so little about this poor girl's background. How fragile was she? I kept one hand on the wheel, simultaneously reaching over to pat her knee. "It's okay. Don't worry about it."

The SUV turned right onto Surf Rider Way. How was I supposed to handle this? No clue. "Did I—upset you?"

"You're so not like the others." She had a huge grin on her face. "Hands on the wheel. Pervert." She winked.

I bit my lip, embarrassed. The kid had played me?

When we made our turn at Surf Rider Way, Lily whooped, "Awesome! There! Like, two blocks. Hang a left."

At Ditmar, the street where the SUV had turned, I kept going straight. The Explorer parked midway down the block. "We'll come around from the other direction."

I could almost feel Lily's enthusiasm. Did she have any idea how dangerous this was? These were the people even I dreaded dealing with. The realization that Baldorf had made a mistake was more than I could handle. I pulled to the side of the road, tears in my eyes, unable to stop laughing.

Lily watched me, her mouth agape. "You're not, like, messed up, are you? Are you, like, using?"

I wiped my cheek, indulging myself in one last chuckle over how Baldorf would react to this turn of events. "I finally get why I was at that house. It was a wild goose chase. I was on stake out because someone thought it was totally safe. He'll sh—have a cow, when he realizes what's happened."

Lily rolled her eyes. "That sucks." It was her turn to put her hand on my thigh. She leaned toward me while staring me in the eye. "You think I don't know shit? It's, like, got four letters. S-H—."

"Got it! You know the lingo. So, what do you think? Is this their other place?"

"Duh! Let's, like, check it out."

She unlatched her seatbelt, but I grabbed her arm before she could get out the door. "I have to make a call first." While I filled Baldorf in on this new development, Lily's impatience grew. Baldorf yammered on, trying to convince me to leave, but I was sticking to my guns. The debate was heating up when Lily opened her door. She was halfway across the street by the time I was out of the car. I almost dropped my phone in my rush to catch her. "Whoa! We can't just waltz in there. Have they seen you? Even if they haven't, who knows what will happen."

"Chill. Those morons? They, like, so never saw me."

"All right. We'll check it out, but we're keeping our distance." Securing Lily in the car while I took a short walk around the block seemed like the appropriate adult action to take. But, from what little I knew about Lily, I could picture her picking the lock or convincing some stranger to call the cops on her abusive mom, the one who'd chained her to the car. Felony charges? No thanks.

"Stay with me, " I said. We walked slowly in the direction of the house where Big & Ugly had parked.

We reached the corner at Ditmar when I spotted our guy. Lily sucked in a breath. The kid might have bravado, but she also seemed to sense how much danger we could be in. "Keep going straight."

To my surprise, I felt Lily's hand slip tentatively into mine. My heart nearly stopped. I caught a glimpse of Lily's face. This time, there was fear in her eyes.

"They're, like, in the third house. Blue. You saw him?"

I squeezed her hand; she returned the gentle pressure. "You named him well, kid."

Her green eyes lit up when she smiled. Her olive skin was flushed with the excitement of the chase, but there was no way I could put her in jeopardy. If these guys knew what we were up to, they'd kill us both. We had to get out of here. Coming even this far had been a mistake. One I never should have made.

CHAPTER **24**

S K I P

Once Skip had the information he needed, he took a nap. After that, he called Baldorf and dressed for his next role. When the doorbell rang, he straightened his blue blazer, smiling in anticipation of the reaction he was about to see. Sure enough, Baldorf's jaw went down; his eyebrows did the opposite. He didn't blink once during the time it took him to examine Skip from combed hair to polished shoes.

"You like the look?" In addition to the blue blazer, Skip wore a white shirt paired with a navy tie accented by subdued silver stripes. Instead of his normal tennis shoes, he wore black wingtips.

"What are you doing wearing a suit, man? You're not going to court, are you?"

Skip ignored his friend's questions. "Welton is a dead end until I can get to L.A. Nobody's going to talk on the phone."

"Dude, you're not in any condition to be making that drive. Besides, why would you get dressed up for a trip to L.A.?"

"When you called, you said Roxy thinks there's a connection to Santino at the old house, right? You finding anything on him?"

Baldorf scanned Skip's attire again. "The head bandage thing is a bit disconcerting, but other than that, you cleaned up well. What are you into, man? You're not making any sense. Nothing about that house makes much sense, either. According to the records, your boy Joey hasn't been there for years. So why would Roxy think the guys who are there now want to kill him?"

"He's not my boy," growled Skip. "Santino may not be involved with those guys, but there's got to be a connection."

"Maybe the dude was feeding a habit. You know, stiffed his supplier."

"Joey's not a junkie. I always suspected he had ties even though there were no drug charges. It all tracks with what one of the detectives told me in confidence. He always thought Santino was linked to some big drug gang, but they had no proof."

"You got a job interview?" Baldorf eyed Skip again.

"When Joey confessed, he said the robbery was a way to get some quick cash."

"Dude, you're driving me nuts. What's the deal?"

Skip crossed the room to the kitchen counter. He showed Baldorf the "Jesus Saves" flyer someone had stuffed into his doorjamb. His first impulse had been to throw it away, but the flyer had given him an inspired cover story. "I wonder if there's anything in the house that will link back to Santino."

Baldorf buried his face in his hands. "Oh, man, we're not breaking the law again, are we?"

The tightening in Skip's stomach reminded him of how far from grace he'd fallen since meeting Roxy. He forced a smile. "I haven't used my lock picks in months. I wouldn't want to get out of practice."

CHAPTER 25

ROXY

All the way back to the car, I told myself getting Lily home was the right thing to do. Her foster parents would be missing her. By now, they had to be worried sick—even if Lily didn't think they were. I packed her into the car, my internal pep talk in full swing while I told myself worrying was ridiculous. She was a kid, I was the adult, I had the stronger will, the intellect. If all else failed, I had the drivers license.

"I need to get you home," I said.

Her smile dimmed, sending pangs of guilt into my gut. A second later, her smile was back. "Nuh-uh. We, like, so need to watch those guys. If we go a coupl'a blocks back, we can, like, see the house."

"As you so eloquently put it—nuh-uh."

"Hello! What's your handler gonna say when you show up with nothing? We gotta, like, stake out that house. The moron you're after might, like, be in there."

I was dangerously close to having what was, for me, an almost surreal experience—a parental moment. A vision of Lily being forced to walk the streets because she couldn't get a decent job played in my mind. Dammit, she wasn't my problem. But, these guys were and what would I tell Baldorf? I could have found out more, but got tired of sitting in my car? A twelve-year-old knew what to do and I didn't?

I texted Baldorf to have him check out the property records for the house.

"So, like, how long's that gonna take?"

"He's usually pretty fast. Not long. But, we stay two blocks away and you do what I say. When I decide it's time to go, we go. Agreed?"

"Deal."

A perk of being a professional liar is that you can almost always tell when someone is lying to you. There was no doubt in my mind I'd been suckered by a twelve-year-old.

Chapter 26

S K I P

Baldorf drove Skip to Oceanside on the Old Coast Highway. As they passed Buena Vista lagoon, Skip studied the view outside the passenger's window of the blue Prius. Condos and single-family homes lined the shore—all were characterized by an abundance of windows. The classic California-scenery homes, presumably sold primarily for their spectacular views, soon gave way to Oceanside's older commercial section with its conglomeration of auto repair shops, used car dealers, burger joints, and mini malls. To Skip, this section of the highway typified the growing pains experienced by California coastal communities.

"Baldorf?"

"What, dude?"

"Thanks."

"For what? Giving you a ride? No problemo. You got me away from some research I had to do."

"For the game?"

The young man hesitated. "Yeah."

Skip suspected that there was something else going on, but didn't want to press too hard. "I know you classify yourself as a big chicken, but where we're going—that takes some guts."

Baldorf's cheeks flushed. "Look, dude, we know several things. Fact, Roxy was at this party. Fact number two, the guy she was with is dead. Fact three, she's now sitting over on Ditmar watching a drug house."

"You said she's in no danger, right?"

"Roger that. What's the deal with Welton?."

"The guy was found dead. Whether it was a homicide remains to be seen. In this case, no comment from LAPD probably means yes, we're looking at this case. There is, however, a logical conclusion. Roxy was running a con on this guy."

"How do you know that? Now you're the one confusing facts and conjecture."

"Maybe, but I know her, Baldorf. She wouldn't have been up in L.A. at that party if there wasn't money—big money—involved. So, what we can be pretty sure of is that Roxy got involved in a job that went bad. I have to go to L.A."

"Dude, you're in no condition for that."

"The doc said light duty, not bed rest."

The car drifted to the right as Baldorf turned to look at Skip.

"Watch the road!" The outburst sent shooting pains into the back of Skip's head. "That hurt."

"Sorry! Driving's not necessarily my strong suit. How's your head?"

"How do you handle video games?"

"Different world, man. Too many outside stimuli to process in a car."

"What?"

"I'm a point and go kind of driver. I go where my eyes are pointing."

Skip hadn't realized it before, but Baldorf's driving scared the crap out of him, so he switched subjects. "I won't be leaving for L.A. until tonight. I'll get some rest, but I need to do this first."

Ten minutes later, they were parked in front of the house Baldorf had sent Roxy to earlier. Baldorf fidgeted behind the wheel, his discomfort obvious. "This is a bad idea. What if there's someone inside?"

"While these guys are over on Ditmar, they can't be here. Besides, I always have the Sig." He patted his blazer and straightened his tie with both hands. "See? Good as new. How do I look?"

"Don't bullshit me, dude. Your head's killing you. What in the hell do you expect to find in there, anyway?"

"Joey Santino. Maybe his girlfriend."

"He's gone, man! I doubt if she ever stayed in this place. No self-respecting woman would. Look at that dump. She's probably the reason he moved. Besides, how could you sleep with all these dogs barking?"

"It's a hunch, Baldorf. I'm not really expecting to find Joey, but maybe there's something to connect him with these guys."

"There's not a shred of evidence for that kind of leap."

Skip grabbed the dozen fake flyers they'd printed at a copy store on the way. "Online. There's no proof online. There might be inside that house." He was about to close the door when he leaned back inside. "Jesus saves. Just call me if anyone shows up. Make sure you call Roxy, too. Have her keep watching that place on Ditmar. Tell her to get license plate numbers or something. Also, make sure she calls you if they leave. I don't want them showing up here while I'm inside the house."

Baldorf smiled. "Sure, I'll call her." He flashed a thumbs up. "You'll do fine."

Being up and moving felt good, but it was tiring. Skip's lack of energy made it easy to appear worn out as he climbed the steps trying to fulfill his role of someone who'd had a hard day traipsing door-to-door discussing how religion could help practicing heathens improve their lives.

He knocked. No answer. Even out here on the front porch the odor of cigarettes and marijuana hung in the air heavy enough to make Skip's head spin. He rang the bell. Again, nothing. He knocked one last time, waited a few seconds, then placed the flyers at his feet. He pulled his pick set from his inside breast pocket, inserted the tension wrench into the keyhole and twisted the wrench slightly left, then right. Once he knew which way the lock turned, he inserted the pick above the tension wrench. In under a minute, the door drifted open. Skip grabbed his flyers on the way in. "Hello?"

When he got no reply, he pulled the Sig from its holster, slipped inside and locked the door after doing a quick sweep of the room. The flyers went on the floor. "This place stinks."

Should there be trouble, he'd never miss at this distance. He moved from room to room, clearing each as he'd been trained. The house was quiet. No sign of anyone. In the kitchen, the stench of rotting food assaulted him. He muttered, "You guys need a housekeeper. Or a match."

A tattered cotton curtain that should have been ripped down years ago barely covered the back door window. He slipped across the room to peek out back. There was nothing outside other than a few dead plants interspersed with pockets of dried-out crabgrass. Behind that, an alleyway.

He checked the lock on the door as he surveyed the room. Mountains of dirty dishes and trash filled the sink and the countertop. A trail of ants scavenging, then returning to their nest, traced a crooked path down across the dirty linoleum countertop. The trail snaked down through a small opening between the faucet and the food-stained formica surface. Across the room, an old green rotary phone hung on the wall, its coiled cord a twisted jumble of knots anchoring the receiver to the cradle. Next to the phone was what he'd hoped to find. Tacked onto the wall was an old picture of a smiling Joey Santino.

It was the same picture he'd seen during Joey's trial, the one in which Joey stood next to his girlfriend in a tropical setting. They were just another happy couple posing for a lifetime memory, except that someone had circled Joey's face in blue ink.

Skip dialed his cell phone to call Baldorf. "The house is clear. Anybody outside?"

"Wait. Got a car that just turned the corner. Oh, it's just a lady with a couple of kids. They went into a different driveway. You're clear."

CHAPTER 27

R O X Y

My phone began to bleep with Baldorf's ring. "Finally!" Normally, when you ask Baldorf for information, he has an answer almost before you can finish your question. At least, that's the way it seems. The fact that it had taken more than two minutes to get an answer had me wondering if he hadn't just blown me off.

"Is that, like, your source?"

I nodded. "Speak to me, Baldorf."

"Sorry this took so long, but it turned out to be a convoluted path. The house is owned by a Sybilla Killen. Ms. Killen is an unemployed dancer. She's been unemployed for a year and a half and, get this, she just paid cash for the house three weeks ago."

"So she's got what, a sugar daddy?"

"Ms. Killen supposedly received a cash settlement from her previous employer in the amount of $500,000 for emotional distress caused by his overt advances, which, she claims, she dutifully cautioned him to stop. When he didn't, she supposedly sued and won. Here's where it gets interesting. She bought the house from a company owned by a guy named Stanmore Argemi."

"Should that name mean something to me?"

"His property management company owns the place you were at earlier. There's nothing about this in the public records either. I found zip about Ms. Killen receiving any kind of settlement."

I'm not a public records expert, but I have learned that if Baldorf says something doesn't exist, it doesn't. "So where did the money come from?"

"She recently married one Michael Ingle. Two weeks after that, she was flush. Michael Ingle is an unemployed stockbroker. It's an alias. His real name is Fu Zhang—a guy who has a rather impressive record with the courts."

"Meaning?"

"He's been arrested, but never convicted."

Out of the corner of my eye, I caught Lily doing a little happy dance in her seat. Good call, kid. "Anything else I should know?"

"Yeah, this is, like, serious shit. Keep your distance, but I need you to let me know if the guys you followed leave. It would also help if you can get me the license plate numbers of all the cars around that house. I can check them out."

"You want me to stay away, but write down plate numbers. Seriously?"

"Uh, yeah, it would be a nice favor—I mean, if you could."

I smiled at Lily. Oh, this was too sweet. The boy wonder would owe me two favors. "Okay, I'll do it. Just for you."

"But, keep your distance, okay?"

"Yeah, yeah, is that warning from you or Skip?"

"Both. Believe me."

Even better. Maybe I could parlay this into something really big. "Let me guess. People die around this guy. Thanks, Baldorf." I watched Lily's face as I disconnected. "So, you were right."

"Awesome!"

"You, my little spy-girlfriend, have pretty good instincts. Looks like we're just going to be sitting her for awhile, so get comfortable. Can you read the plate number on the SUV from here?"

"Duh, of course. Can't you?"

"And here I was starting to like you. Just read me the damn plate number."

When the SUV driver got ready to leave, I called Baldorf. I thought he'd want me to tail Big & Ugly, but instead my instructions were to sit tight. To my surprise, the SUV returned with a new passenger. The driver and passenger carried grocery bags into the house, then left a few minutes later. Lily and I watched the house on Ditmar for another hour.

"This is the weirdest drug house I've ever seen," I said.

"How many times have you done this?" Lily eyes were wide with anticipation.

"This is my first one."

Her disappointment was almost heartbreaking. Obviously, she was still under the impression that I was a high-powered confidential informant or agent with some super-secret law enforcement organization chartered with bringing down the world's bad guys. Sorry, kid.

"So tell me, why were you at that house when we met?"

She shrugged.

"C'mon. Why weren't you in school?"

"We, like, had a stupid math test."

"Math's good for a lot of stuff."

"Whatever."

Our conversation was almost a test of wills. On balance, we were about equal on wins and losses, but all the while I kept thinking there was something she wasn't telling me—something that bothered her deeply.

We got distracted again when a guy with neatly trimmed black hair came out of the house to weed the flower patch. When he finished, he sat on the front porch. At five o'clock, a woman came out of the house to join him. She wore her blonde hair tied back, carried herself well and had smooth, fluid movements. She was the total package—sensual even at this distance. I figured she knew how to get what she wanted from a man. She carried two glasses; they sat, sipping their drinks while enjoying the unusually warm summer afternoon.

"Roxy?"

"What, kid?"

"Like, maybe I was wrong."

"About what?"

"Maybe I, like, messed up. Maybe this ain't a drug house."

"It doesn't seem odd to you that the SUV came here twice—both times with a different passenger."

"Maybe. I dunno."

I faced Lily—no easy task now that we'd been sitting for hours in my little car. "You have good instincts. You need to learn to trust them."

"Like, how do you know? We just met."

"Because I have good instincts." I winked. "There's a lot of things I've screwed up in my life, but the one thing I'm really good at is judging people." Good grief, I was starting to sound like my mother. "Look at the guy on the porch."

"So?"

"Look closely. What do you see?"

She shrugged. "I dunno. Like, a moron drinking a beer?"

"Maybe you're right about the beer, we're too far away to tell. That shirt is a Tommy Bahama print. Not cheap. His shorts? They're khakis. He didn't wear a T-shirt and jeans to work in the yard, he wore resort wear."

"What if they're, like, knockoffs? Maybe he, like, just went to the outlet mall."

"I was in a men's store recently where that print was hanging on the rack. Believe me, it's the real thing. What else did you see?"

"He so wore gloves when he was, like, working in the yard."

"He also never once put his knee on the ground. What's that tell you?"

Lily's face screwed up in confusion. "He's, like, a priss?"

I smiled, but the arm candy sitting next to our guy told me he was the kind of man who got what he wanted. That meant these two were perfectly matched—at least, for now. "Are you hungry? I'm starved."

"We ain't gonna keep watching?"

"Nope. You ever take a class in logic?"

Lily made an ugly face. "Hello! I'm twelve."

"Right. Sorry. Here's what I think. Baldorf sent me on a wild-goose chase. What's so funny is that it turned out to be not so wild. This Fu Zhang guy and Joey Santino are somehow connected. Given their business, it has to have something to do with a drug deal. Based on what you told me earlier about these goons wanting to kill some guy, that can only mean Fu Zhang will be making Joey—"

"I know! I know!" Lily tucked in her chin. "An offer he can't refuse."

It was the worst Brando imitation I'd ever heard, but it was cute in a weird sort of way. "You've got the idea."

"So what's, like, gonna make your dude crack?"

"He's got an ex-girlfriend and a kid."

"That's messed up. They'll, like, be looking for her."

"Right again, kid."

CHAPTER 28

S K I P

Skip climbed into the seat next to Baldorf. "Wow! That felt great!" He burst out laughing, adrenaline pumping up his every thought and action.

Baldorf shook his head. "Dude, you are, like, out of your freaking mind. You haven't even had a full day out of the hospital and already you're looking for danger?"

"Don't worry," Skip leaned back against the headrest. "When the adrenaline wears off, I'll remember why I'm not a danger junkie. Let's go back to your place so you can work while I rest."

Half an hour later, Skip found himself in a precarious state. On one hand, he was anxious for more activity; on the other, he felt drained of all energy. Still, he couldn't shake the desire to know what was really going on with Joey Santino. His eyes flitted around the room, eventually settling on a crack in the ceiling across the room. Baldorf was still scouring the Internet for information about the man who'd tried—and failed—to commit murder twice. This was so unproductive. Skip was bored. He needed something—anything— to occupy his thoughts. He stood, tested his balance, then slowly crossed the room to stand under the crack.

Without taking his eyes from his monitor, Baldorf said, "Dude, you're doing that thing again."

"What thing is that?"

"That mystic-voodoo thing where you look at a Rorschach inkblot test and pick out the numbers."

"Inkblot tests don't have numbers."

"Exactly."

"Baldorf, you scare me sometimes." Skip pointed at the ceiling. "Have you ever wondered why these popcorn ceilings always have cracks?"

Baldorf pointed at the spot. "It's an acoustic ceiling material that was used for about thirty years because it was inexpensive, had good sound insulation properties, and masked building defects buyers weren't supposed to know about."

"Poor workmanship? That's it? I think there's more to the story."

"See? There you go again. The fact that some wannabe carpenter back in the 60s didn't know how to wield a hammer isn't what you're after. I can't wrap my head around how you think up this shit. Put me out of my misery, dude, just tell me what you're after."

"Why there? Why did that one spot crack?"

Baldorf watched the corner of the ceiling where Skip pointed. After a few seconds, he turned his attention back to his computer. "You want my landlord to, what, bring in a structural engineering firm to analyze why my ceiling is cracking after fifty years?"

"No. We know the reason. The pressure got to be too much. So, it's cracking. Right?"

"If you insist on oversimplifying a complex structural issue, yes."

Skip quieted Baldorf with a wave of his hand. "You're missing the point." He motioned with his head in the direction of the ceiling. "That crack is Joey Santino. Someone squeezed him hard enough to break. The look in his eyes in that hospital room—there was hatred, but something else. He could have jabbed that needle into my arm or even my neck. I don't think he wants to kill me."

"C'mon, man. That crack is not Joey Santino. That crack was caused by a complex process of aging, ground settlement, material shrinkage, and other structural variables. Would you like me to list them?"

"Baldorf, focus."

Baldorf's eyebrows went up. "Oh, I get it. We're talking in metaphorical terms. Could you maybe hold up a little wand or something the next time you're shifting into the dark arts? I missed the transition."

"You suffer from the forest and trees syndrome."

"Dude, I write video games for a living. Where you see a forest, I see photosynthesis—a chemical process—never mind, you probably failed biology. Let's assume for a moment that you're right—say Santino doesn't want to kill you. Guy's got a funny way of showing his indifference."

"He's not doing it because he hates me, it's because he needs me out of the way. The only time we had any dealings at all was during his trial."

"Shazam!" Baldorf smiled. "See? I can speak that magic mumbo jumbo language, too. Okay, I get it. You think there's something from the trial that didn't come out. That I can work with."

"Not something, someone."

Baldorf's smile fell; his brow furrowed. "That would be bad. Especially if you're talking about this Fu Zhang dude."

Skip nodded. "Joey lived in that house. We think he moved out to live with Shaina. Then, she disappears. Next thing you know, the gang Joey's in splits and Joey commits armed robbery. For what? Maybe he didn't want money, but protection. I need to go home so I can check my files. There's got to be something I'm missing." He paused, letting Baldorf's comment sink in. "You might be right. Fu Zhang and Joey are linked. I testified at the trial that Joey had a motive for the robbery that went beyond money. Maybe that's it."

"Was this Fu Zhang dude always in the shadows?"

"I don't know—yet. I need to confirm my hunch."

"I don't think I like the sound of that hunch thing. But, spill."

"I suspect Fu Zhang's got at least one dirty cop on his payroll."

Baldorf's eyes defocused and his brow furrowed. After a moment, he said, "Dude, I'd give that scenario a 42% probability."

Skip blinked back his surprise. "That's pretty specific. What do you have, some sort of life-probability calculator in your head?"

"No, man. I made that up. I just wanted to see if you'd buy it. It could, however, explain why he got the urge to wave a gun around when he walked into a fast food joint. Please, don't tell me you're gonna want to spy on the house where Roxy is to prove your point."

"Wouldn't think of it. Not before I get some sleep anyway."

CHAPTER 29

R O X Y

The aroma of baking dough, simmering sauces, and melting cheeses filled the air along with the clamor from a sports team decked out in blue-and-yellow uniforms. While the team celebrated their latest victory, three TVs blared from the corners of the room. Candles in standard red glass holders on each table cast flickering circles of light onto the faces of those who packed this bustling pizza joint. Lily and I were caught in a showdown. We each had elbows planted on the wooden table. Just like gunfighters in an old western movie, we each eyed the last slice on the platter.

"I want it," said Lily.

"You didn't eat the crust on your last two pieces."

"Here." She grabbed her crust leftovers and tossed them onto my plate. "You can have 'em."

It was like someone pulled my happy pin. I nearly went into hysterics. At one point, I laughed so hard I had to rest my head on my forearms. When I looked up, Lily was stuffing the last piece into her mouth. Her cheeks reminded me of a cartoon chipmunk. "You're evil. That's so unfair."

"I an . . . st . . . d."

Another laughing fit overcame me. All I could do was watch her struggle to swallow. When I'd recovered enough to speak, I said, "If you're going to talk with your mouth full, at least wait until you can pronounce a few of the letters."

Lily's eyes grew wide and teary. She looked like she might gag on the pizza, but finally swallowed and began gulping down her soft drink. When she was done gasping for air, she said, "I ain't, like, stupid. I, like, knew you'd try to outsmart me. It's what grownups do."

A cheer went up at the sports-team table. All around the room, TVs played while people did their own thing. For a split second, I wondered if I should do what I always did with others, ignore her feelings. No. Not this time. Not with her. "Have I treated you like that?"

She shook her head. "You're, like, different. You're cool."

I swallowed hard, relieved that one person in the world thought better of me. "We need to get you home." I didn't add the rest of my thought—before you learn who I really am.

Lily rolled her eyes. "That's messed up. I'm, like, having fun hanging out with you."

"You have school tomorrow, right? Don't you have homework?"

"Seriously? You're, like, kidding, right?"

"What grade are you in?"

She hesitated before answering. "Sixth."

Even I knew the school year had started more than a month ago, so Lily shouldn't have to think about what grade she was in. "What's you're favorite subject?"

In the dim light, I watched her take a last bite of pizza. She shrugged while she chewed, apparently contemplating her answer. Finally, she tossed the uneaten crust onto her plate. "Recess," she said.

"Here's to recess." We raised our glasses in a toast, but I couldn't stop wondering what was going on with this kid.

When we stood to leave, Lily wrapped her arms around my waist. She hugged me and buried the side of her face into my shirt. "Thanks, Roxy. Today was, like, awesome."

I hugged her back and kissed the top of her head. "You're welcome, sweetheart." The room felt suddenly warm—everything got kind of blurry. My jaw felt tight when I held Lily close. I was way too young for hot flashes—it must be the air conditioning. After a few moments, I cleared my throat. "So, um, where do you live?"

She took a deep breath. "I can, like, walk."

"No way. I'm delivering you to your front door."

"Whatever. Let's go." She pulled away, her smile replaced by a sullen cloud.

Ten minutes later, we were two blocks from the house where I'd met Lily. In this old neighborhood, the streetlights left long stretches of sidewalk in near darkness. She guided me to the only house with a light still on. The dim bulb left the front yard in darkness. I parked in front of the house, but left the engine running. My throat felt tight. "I'll wait until you get inside."

"It's, like, okay. My foster mom takes, like, for-ever to answer the door. They don't, like, give me a key." Lily shrugged; her eyes glistened in the dashboard glow.

I felt a tug on my heart, but forced myself to think about practical issues. Twelve and no key? "What do you do when she leaves for groceries?"

Instead of answering me, Lily shoved her door open. She stood in the street, gripping the backpack close to her chest. Her voice trembled. "I gotta go." She slammed the door before I could ask her for a phone number.

Who was I kidding? Relationship challenged—that was me, to put it nicely. The kid was better off as far away from me as possible. She approached the front porch and trudged up the steps. Talk about for-ever, I smiled, recalling the way Lily had almost split the word into two. Instead of happiness at being rid of my obligation, my cheeks burned with worry. At the top of the stairs, she turned and waved. I wiped at my wet cheek.

It was time for me to do what Roxy Tanner always did, disappear. "Get out of here," I said to myself. Hollow words. The words of a true loner. I pulled away from the curb, periodically glancing in the rear view mirror. But, the porch was no longer visible. At the next cross street, rather than making a right, I hung a U-turn for one last pass by Lily's house.

I could barely breathe from the ache in my heart. How had this kid gotten under my skin so easily? So fast? It was time to move on. Again, the words. "Get out of here." Again, hollow. I spoke to the emptiness in the car. "She'll only bring you down."

Lily wasn't on the front porch. A lump filled my throat. Her foster mother must have come to the door quickly. I rubbernecked it down the street, trying desperately to see what happened at the front door while inching the car further away. A half block later, I almost sideswiped another car. At the next corner, a silhouette moved beyond the edge of the streetlight circle into the darkness. Though it was little more than a shadow, I recognized the outline immediately. I jammed the accelerator to the floor.

Chapter 30

S K I P

At just after 8:00 p.m., Skip returned home for a quick change of clothes. He needed something dark. He threw on a navy T-shirt and jeans and a black sweatshirt. He stepped out onto the condo's deck, soaking in the moist evening air that flooded his lungs with its freshness. After a few more breaths, he whispered to the ocean. "Wish me luck."

He returned to Baldorf's, where he found his friend hunched over something about the size of a golf pencil. "What're you working on?"

"It's a video camera. It'll send a signal back here."

"You've got to be kidding."

"No, serious. Actually, it can send a signal over the Internet or store video on its internal drive."

Skip pointed at the device. "That's got a hard drive?"

"In layman's terms, it's a flash drive on steroids. It will store up to an hour's worth of video at this resolution. Not the greatest quality, but on a limited budget, it'll do the job."

"How the hell do you fit all that in this—pencil?"

"Dude, chill. All you need to know is that once it gets a connection, it'll upload the stored data. Without a connection, you could turn it on and it will run until it reaches the drive's capacity. It's also got a self-contained battery. We cool?"

The twinkle in Baldorf's eyes reminded him of an eager child. His spiky hair and lack of discernible facial hair gave him an immature, almost impish, appearance. "How are you going to get an Internet connection without asking someone for permission? We can't just call the cable company and ask them to hook it up for a couple of days."

Baldorf admired the contraption he held between his thumb and index finger. "Dude, we're just borrowing. Call it a little friendly sharing, that's all."

"Bullshit," said Skip. "You're going to hack someone's wireless connection, aren't you?"

"The term hacking has such a negative connotation, don't you think?"

Skip licked his lips, not sure what to say next. "I'm the people-voodoo guy, remember? I'm not really proficient at this hacking stuff. So you're going with me?"

"Unnecessary. Never fear, my technologically challenged friend, I have you covered." He pointed at the messenger bag on the floor next to Skip. "Boot up that laptop, start one program, it'll do the rest."

Skip shook his head. "What's in there?"

"Call it my voodoo magic. It will find and secure a connection—encrypted or not."

"Wait a minute. You're telling me it doesn't matter what I do to protect myself. You can use anybody's cable?"

"Dude, security is purely a function of time and money. If you've got the money, it's going to take me more time. At some point, the economics don't work out. That's when I give up because there are other lower hanging fruit to pick." Baldorf placed the camera into the messenger bag before handing the bag to Skip. "Ready?"

"What? Me? No. I'm not ready. This is—this is wrong."

"Dude, this is such commonplace shit in my world. You either join in or get frozen out. The technology on both sides gets more sophisticated every day. What do you want to do?"

Skip closed his eyes and rubbed his temples. Even when he lay bleeding on the ground in the alley, he never thought he'd go this far down the rabbit hole. He grabbed the bag at his feet and stuck out his hand. "Fine. Give me the damn pencil. Let's just hope I don't get caught."

CHAPTER 31

ROXY

I made a sharp left around the corner where I'd seen Lily running into the darkness. My poor little Toyota's tires squealed. The back end fishtailed through the turn. The suspension groaned. Shit. Parked car dead ahead. I swerved. To my left, I saw Lily on the other side of the parked car.

My car screeched to a stop—half in the street, half in the driveway in front of Lily, but she'd already doubled back to the corner. I pulled the handle, threw my weight against the door, and broke into a dead run.

Wisps of fog drifted through the light. Already a thin film of moisture clung to everything. If I lost her in this neighborhood, I'd never find her. I yelled, "Lily, stop!"

She faltered when the backpack shifted to one side, then stumbled when she overcompensated. I caught her. We went down on the sidewalk in a heap.

"Lily! What the hell are you doing?"

Even the damp blanket slowly settling around us couldn't silence her sobs. "I don't live there," she wailed. "I, like, made that up. Leave me alone."

I kneeled next to her and stroked her hair.

"You don't want me! Nobody wants me! Just—go!" She continued to blubber.

I pulled her close. "Oh, sweetheart." It felt like someone had kicked me in the stomach. What a complete idiot I'd been. I, Roxy Tanner—Queen of the Con—had been taken in by a twelve-year-old. Again. "You don't have a home, do you?"

She shook her head. I felt the movement against my shoulder. "I, like, have to find a place to sleep. Just, like . . . let . . ."

"You're coming with me. At least tonight, you'll have a bed."

Her tears soaked into my T-shirt. It didn't matter. Nothing did. "It's okay," I stroked her hair while whispering to her. "It's okay. It's okay."

"I don't need nothin'. Just—just, I won't cause no trouble."

"Shhh." I squeezed her tighter. The damp chill of the pavement penetrated my jeans; we were both shaking. "Let's go, huh? It's freezing out here."

She looked into my eyes; tears stained her face.

"Okay?" I asked.

She gave me a weak smile, but her body shuddered against mine.

CHAPTER 32

S K I P

Skip parked a half block away from Fu Zhang's house on the opposite side of the street. A sheen of moisture cloaked everything. The fog had arrived with a vengeance. Cool, moist air flowed through the open window. Already, the streetlights cast halos—in a sense, circles of influence that projected the illusion of safety onto the surrounding houses, streets, and sidewalks inside the circle. But, outside—in the surrounding darkness—you could do almost anything. In about an hour, the moon would rise. But tonight? Fog or moon, stars or pitch black, nothing mattered. He would be long gone by then.

Lights in the living room were off, the flickering glow of a TV the only illumination behind the drawn drapes. At 9:30 p.m., the glow from the TV changed color and intensity several times in rapid succession. Skip smiled. Someone channel surfing. What did a drug dealer watch? A cop show? Sitcoms? Old war movies? Another thought sent a chill down Skip's spine. If Fu Zhang caught him planting surveillance equipment, he'd be interrogated. His death would be slow and painful. No rescue force would come to find him.

Skip grabbed the messenger bag Baldorf had given him before stepping into the street. He turned off his phone. No distractions. No noise. Even the hum of a vibrating cell phone could give him away. He scanned the neighborhood in all directions as he approached the house. At the brick-lined walkway, he gave the street one last quick visual inspection before turning up the walk. He was halfway to the house when headlights appeared at the corner.

CHAPTER 33

R O X Y

Where Lily lived remained the biggest mystery of the night. Perhaps that house where I dropped her really was her foster home—maybe not. I wasn't about to force her to go back, nor was I going to start banging on doors in that neighborhood at night. The bottom line was that the kid was desperate—perhaps I was, too.

What I did know was that Lily hadn't had a shower in a couple of days, so when we got to my place, I insisted she get cleaned up. The poor kid didn't even have a nightgown, so I loaned her a T-shirt and put her in my bed. By the time I turned out the light and closed the door, she was already out. The couch would be fine for one night, but the adrenaline running through my system would keep me awake for hours. The problem was that I had two mutually exclusive goals. First, I wanted to find Santino's girlfriend. Second, I needed to know the truth about Lily. Was her mother really in jail? Was Lily in foster care or not? When I had answers, or my adrenaline rush ended, I'd either sleep until noon or be begging for a mug or two of that witch's brew Marjorie called coffee.

I booted up my laptop and started checking public records. Lily had said her last name was Jameson, so that's where I began my search. A "Judith Jameson" had indeed been convicted of prostitution last month—she had three months left on her sentence. I pulled out the phone book and looked up the name Tucker. There was one listed at the address where I'd dropped Lily off. The same place she'd run away from how many times? At least once that I knew of.

It was time to ask Baldorf for a favor, so I sent him a text message. "can u find info on foster parents? Call if ur up."

Just in case Baldorf was still working, I set my phone to vibrate mode. No sooner had I placed it on the table than it began a little dance across the faux-wood surface. I answered, my voice barely more than a whisper. "Hey, I caught you."

"Skip's got me working on a project. What's up with foster care? You're not, like, thinking of taking in ruggers I hope."

"Are you kidding? I can barely keep my own life together. But I did wind up with a house guest. She's a foster kid—tells me the place where she's living is a money farm. Can you dig into what these people are up to?"

"It would be pretty difficult. The records are protected. You know, encryption, passwords—blah, blah."

"Oh, so you can't."

Baldorf snorted. "That's not what I said. It would be a challenge. A serious hacker could find a way in if he really wanted to. I'm also working on tracking down Joey Santino's girlfriend. So, where'd you meet the kid?"

Was Baldorf saying yes or no? I couldn't tell. I thought I heard a noise in the bedroom. Had Lily woken up?

"Roxy?"

"What? Oh, Lily? She's great. We met on the stakeout. She's really bright."

"Hey! Focus. What's gotten into you, anyway? Tell me about the stakeout."

"You got lucky."

"The kid again? Don't get attached, Rox, she's not a puppy."

"I know. She's just—she's skipping school. What kind of parent—any parent—lets a kid get away with that?"

"The kind who'll lose their contract with the state if it happens too much."

I winced. Baldorf was probably right. "She lied about living there, too."

"I think you've got a juvenile delinquent on your hands. That type of relationship can only go one direction."

"Pretty cynical view. Forget it. Sorry I asked. So the place you sent me was a dead end, but you knew that already. You wanted to keep me out of the way while Skip works on finding Santino. Am I close?"

There was a momentary silence. "Shit," he muttered. "I—I told him it wouldn't work."

"He had you lie to me?"

"Call it a community effort. I'm sorry I deceived you."

"Well, I'm not. It's like I told you earlier, Lily said the guys in that house are after someone who fits Santino's description."

"So you said."

"Baldorf, come on, the good news is—well, this assumes these guys are smart—anyway, he's probably safe until they find the girlfriend. She's the key. If it were me, I'd grab her so I could use her and the kid to force him into revealing himself. That means we need to find her before they do."

There was an unusually long pause on the line, so while I waited I tiptoed across the room and slipped the door open. Lily was still asleep, breathing softly. Baldorf said, "I know where Santino's girlfriend is."

I inched the door shut just like my mom had done when I was Lily's age.

"Roxy? You still there?"

How did I explain what I'd just done? I didn't understand it myself. Through the tightness in my throat, I whispered, "You know where—how?"

"Skip and I were using the same logic. Not to do anything so bold as to kidnap her, of course, but to see if she knew where Santino might be holding up. Good old-fashioned deduction with a pinch of high-tech brilliance."

"Don't get too smug; you don't have her yet."

Another pause, probably Baldorf's ego rebooting. "So you think these guys are after Santino? What do you know about them? Can they use an online database?"

"Look, I didn't get invited to tea. Those guys don't exactly look like computer geeks. How long did it take you to find Joey's girlfriend, anyway?"

"Hours. In fact, it was just a little while ago. She tried to bury her tracks, but she screwed up."

Had she made the same mistake all runners made their first time out? "Didn't cut her ties?"

"You and Skip—you're no fun at all. Man, now I'm depressed."

"Go on, tell me. I want details."

Baldorf seemed to perk up. "The only reason I found her was because we started checking on her relatives. She moved in with a cousin a couple of weeks ago. That's where she is now."

"They'll find her sooner or later," I said.

I checked the time—almost eleven. Next thing I knew, I was inspecting the refrigerator. What would I fix Lily for breakfast? I continued rummaging. "Joey might not care what happens to his ex, but he's not going to want to see his daughter suffer. If they find the kid, he'll turn up." All I could offer the poor kid was coffee and a croissant. Was there a grocery store open at this hour?

"I can tell you one thing, Santino dying wouldn't make Skip very happy."

That news derailed my breakfast musings. I would have expected Skip to be the last person who'd be upset by a world without Joey Santino. "I'll bite, why?"

"Skip thinks Santino has ties to Fu Zhang."

"The guy whose house Lily and I were watching this afternoon?"

"Exactamundo. We're just brainstorming at this point, but it's bizarro that our dude Fu rose to power right after the top dog got himself killed. It was like a huge food-chain fiasco. Everything went the wrong way."

"A food-chain fiasco? Never heard it called that before. Fu Zhang's not going to hesitate to throw Joey's ex into the chain—or his kid." Another reason to get Lily home, too much danger. But how?

Baldorf's voice held a dark edge. "From what I hear about this guy, he'll take out anyone who gets in his way."

I glanced nervously at the bedroom door. "I met Lily while she was breaking into that place where you sent me on the stakeout. If I take her home tomorrow, she'll probably go right back there. You know how kids are, they're fearless. She's too young to understand how dangerous these guys might be. Can we get the cops involved?"

"Not likely. The detectives who were looking for Santino told Skip that they didn't have the resources. Who knows? Maybe the Feds are involved. They could be watching, too, but we have no intel on that. We have to compile data."

That was Baldorf-speak for something, but what? "You want to wait?" I hissed. "Why?"

The bedroom door opened. Lily stood, staring at me. My insides melted—long legs, tangly hair, sleepy eyes—dammit, I should have waited until morning to call Baldorf. I motioned at the seat next to mine.

The firm, yet insistent, tone of someone making a point interrupted my thoughts. "I didn't say wait. I said, compile data."

"Sorry," I mouthed to Lily. I still didn't get Baldorf's meaning.

She whispered, "It's okay."

Baldorf said, "Skip is, um, installing some surveillance equipment."

Suddenly, all my mental detours ceased. Someone had opened an emotional trap door beneath me. I plummeted down a dark hole with no bottom in sight. A hand touched mine. Lily. Could she read the fear on my face? My voice cracked as I forced out the question I didn't want to ask. "Where, Baldorf? Where is he installing this equipment?"

"Fu Zhang's house."

Shit. Of all the places for him to go. I clicked the disconnect button and dropped the phone on the table. Glancing around the room, life's cruelty overwhelmed me. Though we'd only been together for a few months, Skip was everywhere. He'd put his mark on every single thing—including me. It had been complicated enough before Lily.

Somehow I had to help her and Skip. How the hell was I going to choose between them?

Chapter 34

S K I P

Skip ducked behind a giant hibiscus just as headlight beams lit up the street in front of the house. He slipped the Sig out of its holster at the small of his back with barely a sound as he watched—just the simple action of getting ready felt like pure insanity. Nine rounds. If things spiraled down that far, everyone would lose. Nine rounds. Could he even get that many shots off before they killed him?

The car rolled to a stop. Headlights dimmed. Front doors opened. Two men got out. The driver, a hulk who lumbered up the sidewalk like an overweight sumo wrestler, came first. The porch light illuminated his features, another reminder of the world these men came from. Shaved head. Sprig of dark hair sprouting from underneath his lip. Small scar, right cheek. Skip wondered who could have gotten close enough to even strike that blow.

The driver barked at the second man in a staccato language Skip couldn't hope to understand. Mandarin? Tagalog? Maybe one of a hundred others. The smaller man stared at the bush where Skip hid. Had they heard him? Seen him? Skip's hand tightened around the butt of the gun. A male voice commanded both visitors to silence from the front porch.

Skip suspected the man from the house was Fu Zhang. When the passenger said something, Fu Zhang silenced them with an abrupt, unintelligible order. The passenger watched the ground while the conversation between the large man and Fu Zhang continued. The discussion became more animated, punctuated occasionally with one word he did recognize—Santino. Fu Zhang's tone grew more insistent. No matter the language, Skip knew the indicators of a hot temper.

The messenger bag lay at Skip's feet. He eased the camera out, pointed the device in the general direction of the porch, and flipped the miniature switch. The longer the men talked, the more he picked up words that seemed forced into the conversation. Already, he'd mentally logged a name other than Santino—it was Shaina.

The back of his head ached, but he had no time right now. Fight back. Be strong. Despite his training, his energy was flagging. Lowering the camera wasn't an option. He needed to know what these guys were saying, so he waited. When the conversation ended, the visitors left abruptly. Fu Zhang wasted no time in turning off the porch light, then the TV. Apparently, the day was over. Skip waited for the throbbing at the back of his head to subside. He envisioned the pain growing cooler, softer. When he stood, his surroundings turned white; a wave of nausea rushed through him. He leaned against the house, letting the chill of night seep into his bones.

With the visitors gone, the neighborhood turned silent. Skip waited in his hiding spot, his senses becoming attuned to the quiet. He recognized the sounds of a city—the drone of a vehicle's exhaust, a dog's bark, the almost steady hum of traffic that never stopped in Southern California. With the blanket of fog came clarity. He'd only recognized four words in the conversation on the porch. All names. All tied to Santino. He hid the camera where it would capture video from the front walk, then returned to his car, turned on his phone, and waited for Baldorf's message.

A couple of minutes later, his phone bleeped with the good news. "Got video."

He was exhausted, both physically and mentally. Going home to sleep for a full day was the sane thing to do, but he couldn't do that if he was going to help Roxy. He turned the ignition key. "Goddamn, I'm tired."

CHAPTER 35

R O X Y

I was engulfed by the sickening sense of falling into an abyss where there was no bottom, no end, and no light.

"You look like you're gonna puke."

"What?" I buried my face in my hands. "I wish I could. Maybe I'd feel better."

"What's the matter?"

How could I explain what I was feeling to Lily when I didn't understand it myself?

"Duh. You ain't got the market on being afraid. When they, like, busted my mom, I couldn't hardly even eat. I was totally messed up."

Lily came into my arms, her thin body conveying a sense of comfort. "I think you understand all this better than I do. That place we were at today on the stakeout? The second one? Skip's gone there to install a spy cam."

She reassured me, "He'll be okay."

"How can you be so sure?"

"Duh! Cuz he's like you. Ya know? Smarter than all those morons put together."

"Sweetheart, I hope you're right." I kissed her on the forehead. "If he gets caught—well, bad people can get mean no matter how resourceful you are."

"I, like, know all about mean. Old Man Tucker sucks. He, like, makes these random threats all the time."

I held her at arm's length to eye the bruise on her cheek. "Has he ever hit you?"

"Seriously? Are you, like, kidding? He ain't nothing but a blowhard."

I almost burst out laughing. "Where did you learn that one?"

"Zane, he's a friend that's, like, on the streets. Whenever he's, like, trying to get money and these random people start, like, yelling mean things at him, he calls them that." She smiled. "Maybe worse."

My phone buzzed; I pulled away from Lily to answer. "Baldorf, any word?"

"Mission accomplished. He's safely on his way."

My breath caught. "Here? He's on his way here?" My pulse quickened. I must look awful, my hair—

"Uh, no. He's on his way out of town. He's got important business to handle elsewhere."

"I'll call him." It was okay that he wasn't coming over—I had Lily. I needed a shower. The place was a mess—

"He says he won't answer until morning. You have to trust him."

Someone opened the damn trap door again. If bracing myself with a hand on the table would have helped, I'd gladly have done it. But, help was out of reach. I gripped the phone tighter. How badly had I screwed up this relationship?

"Roxy! Listen. He told me to tell you that this isn't about the fight."

Anger replaced my fear. "So what's it about? Give me something, dammit!"

Lily jumped. Her reaction made me feel terrible about showing her this side of me—the bitch capable of destroying the lives of others. I felt worse when she backed away, gripping her sides tight with those stick-figure arms.

"Trust, Roxy. It's about trusting him."

"I have to go." I reached for Lily. "I'm sorry. I didn't mean to scare you."

"Whatever." She stepped closer, relaxing just a fraction. "I ain't scared. I just, like, thought you might need some space."

"You're one smart kid." But I did see fear—the same kind I'd felt at her age. We were so much alike, two kindred souls separated only by time. Could I prevent her from making the same mistakes I had?

She searched my face, then said, "Roxy?"

"Yes, sweetheart?"

"Would you, like, hold me? I dunno if I can, like, get back to sleep."

"Do you have bad dreams?"

"Sometimes."

"About Old Man Tucker?"

She shrugged.

I guided her back to the bedroom. We laid on the bed with Lily nestled in my arms. The next thing I knew, the sun was streaming through the window while some damn bird chirped out a frigging concerto.

I slipped away from the bed, being careful to not wake Lily, then eased the door to the bathroom shut behind me. My first order of business after my shower would be to get Lily home, but when I came out of the shower, she was already gone.

"Lily?"

Sobs from the other room caught my attention. I wrapped the towel around myself and padded toward the kitchen. There, sitting at the dining room table was Lily. She had tears streaming down her cheeks.

What the hell? "What's wrong?"

"Nothing! This sucks!" Lily grabbed her backpack from its resting place on the floor at her feet, then stood, clutching the pack close to her chest.

"Where do you think you're going?" My stern tone shocked me. It even seemed to take Lily aback.

She stood as though frozen in place. "I need to, like, borrow some money."

"Why?"

"Cause you're just gonna send me back!" She stuck out a hand—a seasoned panhandler looking for a free ride.

So this was how it worked? You gave someone your heart and all they really wanted was—shit, how many times? How many people had I done that to? Though I willed myself to be strong, the pressure of the tears grew. My jaw felt tight. I croaked, "So is that what you want? Money? Straight up, kid. Look me in the eye and tell me the truth."

Her lower lip quivered; she kept her attention glued to the floor. When she raised her eyes to meet mine, she dropped her pack and rushed into my arms. "I can't go back there. But you're gonna throw me out. You don't want me—nobody does."

What had happened to this poor kid? "You don't have to leave yet."

"That sucks. One night? Like, what good's that do me? I'd have, like, been better off on the streets."

I put my fingers against her lips. In my heart, I knew she didn't mean what she was saying, but no matter what either of us wanted, she couldn't stay with me. She pushed away and my towel began to slip. Years of practice kicked into gear—I instinctively grabbed it.

Lily giggled through her tears. "That was close. But I ain't goin' back to them. I, like, can't."

"Can't? Or, won't?"

"Old Man Tucker, he don't beat me or nothing. But, me and him don't get along."

"So you've been living on the streets. For how long?"

"A few weeks. I got three months to go before they, like, let my mom out."

"Did the Tucker's report you missing?"

She nodded. "Maybe." With a smile, she added, "I been keeping a low profile."

"Pretty high concept for a kid. Zane, again?"

She wiped at her nose with her hand before glancing away. "He's, like, been good to me."

I felt like I was standing two feet away from a railroad crossing with a train rushing by at high speed, warning bells clanging and red lights flashing. I'd bet he had. "How old is Zane?"

"Old. Maybe forty."

"Has he ever touched you or come on to you in any way?"

Lily's face lit up in recognition. She chuckled. "No way! He's gay."

"Are you sure? Really sure?"

"I'm really, really sure. I, like, caught him with another guy one night. It was, like, really gross."

The time had come for me to put my foot down. Whether she wanted to go home or not, this wasn't Take Your Homeless Kid to Work Day. "I need to take you back."

Lily stood with her back ramrod straight. "Whatever. I'm outta here."

"It can't be that bad."

"How would you know?" The bitter edge in her voice cut through my defenses. "I'll run away." The resolve on her face was clear. Even if I somehow forced her into the car and drove her back to the Tucker's home, within a day, she'd be back on the streets.

The thought of this little girl having to beg for food and do who knows what just to eat—I couldn't live with myself if I caused that. "What about school? You have to be going to school."

"Duh. You don't, like, go to school when you live alone on the streets. I'll go when my mom, like, gets out of jail."

How long would that last? A week? A month? How long would it take for her to get busted again? What had I done to deserve all of this? Anita and Dom had most likely screwed me out of my share of the Welton score. The man was dead, probably thanks to me. Skip had almost been killed—that was probably my fault, too. The image of Lily standing before me with her hand out flashed into my mind again. How long before she followed in her mother's footsteps?

For once in my life, despite my best defenses, my feelings were rising to the surface. No matter what it cost me, I couldn't send Lily back. I swallowed hard. "All right. Look. If I allow you stay to here for a couple of days, will you promise me you won't run away?"

"Really? I could, like, stay here?"

"A couple of days. That's it. We need to sort out how to get you someplace more permanent."

"You won't, like, send me back to them?"

"I'll do my best not to. But, you have to promise me one thing. No running away. No matter what I tell you to do."

"You're cool, I wouldn't run from you. We can, like, talk. I can't talk to . . ."

Her voice trailed off. "I get it, sweetheart. Believe me, I so get it." How was I going to keep a twelve-year-old occupied? "Okay. First thing is I have to get dressed." Her eyes misted up and I remembered what had been in her backpack last night—a blanket, a toothbrush, a wool hat and a jacket. I put my hands on her shoulders. "If you're going to be hanging out with me, you'll need something else to wear. We need to do some shopping." I felt a little surge of enthusiasm. I'd never taken a girlfriend shopping. I'd never even had a girlfriend to go shopping with. Where should we go? "How about—"

"Forever 21?"

Her wide-eyed enthusiasm got me. How could I refuse that offer? "I like your style, girlfriend."

CHAPTER 36

S K I P

The ringing of Skip's cell phone jarred him awake just after 8:00 a.m. He fumbled around the nightstand, found the phone, then held it to his ear. "Hello?"

"Skip?"

"Hey, Hot Rox, I miss you."

"You sound terrible."

"Just had a late night. How's it going?"

Her voice became more insistent. "Where are you?"

How did he tell her he was in a cheap L.A. hotel room, wishing instead that he was with her? "Can't say. I'm out of town working on a case. I'll be back soon."

"Did I do something? Are you mad at me?"

"We're fine."

"You don't sound fine. What's up?"

"I have to find someone. You know, just normal stuff." Skip listened to the faint hiss of cell-phone communications filling the void between words.

A moment later, she said, "Skip, I want this to work."

"This? Us?"

"Yeah, I want us to work."

"I just have a couple of things to deal with here. I'll be back soon. Promise. Until then, please, do what Baldorf asks. Okay?"

"You trust him more than me?"

"That's not it. Not at all. Baldorf and I worked out a game plan yesterday. I'll explain everything when I get back. Until then, I need you to do what he asks. Please don't beat him up for not telling you the plan. He's only the messenger. It's his skill set driving this whole thing right now. You know Baldorf, master of the Internet universe." He chuckled, but there was no response on the other end of the line.

"Roxy?"

"Tomorrow? You'll tell me everything then?"

Could he? Maybe. Maybe not. "Yeah, tomorrow." Was he lying to her or himself?

"Skip, I . . ." her voice trailed off.

He knew the three words she was afraid to say. "Me, too." They ended the call. He focused on his stitches, visualizing the skin soften and become less tender. In his mind, he encased the tender spot in cotton until it was nothing more than a memory. He gave himself ten minutes before logging into the hotel's Wi-Fi system. His chest felt heavy while he waited for his laptop to boot up.

The worn paths in the carpet reminded him of trails through a grassy meadow. One led to the front door, another to the bed, a third to the bath. Unfortunately, the room smelled like anything but a meadow. "Why can't she and I just be honest with each other?"

They were like travelers passing through the meadow. Each used the paths, each covered the same ground time after time. Only the strong paved new paths. Were they both so weak?

Skip tossed his phone onto the bed. Rather than feeling refreshed, he was still tired. Not a good way to start the day. Maybe later, after checking his email, he'd call Roxy back just to hear her voice. "Can't believe a place this cheap actually has Wi-Fi." While his email trickled in, he spoke to the empty room. "I guess you're not so bad. I'll give you five half stars."

A second later, he spotted an email from Baldorf. "Call me ASAP."

CHAPTER 37

R O X Y

By the time I finished my little dealmaking session with Lily and my call with Skip, my hair had dried flat and my damp towel felt like it had just come out of the freezer. That, however, didn't stop me from sitting around staring at my phone, no better off than a morose drunk at a bar. Lily's presence jarred me from my woe-is-me cycle.

"Boyfriend trouble?"

"Stay away from boys. They're nothing but trouble."

"Don't worry, I ain't gonna, like, have anything to do with them ever."

"I said that once, too." We both laughed as I gathered my towel around me and went to the bedroom to change. I dressed in a pair of jeans, a black camisole, and a dark blue, sleeveless shirt. Lily was already in the kitchen sitting next to the window.

Her eyes widened when she saw me. "You're, like, hot."

My cheeks grew warm. "We're going to make a stop—coffee for me and hot chocolate for you."

"I, like, drink the hard stuff."

"Hard stuff?" I snickered. "That's going to stunt your growth."

"Whatever. I only drink it when I'm, like, really tired."

I nodded knowingly. "Gotcha. Well, you got a good night's sleep, so hot chocolate should be all you need, right?"

"That's cool."

On the drive to the mall, I noted Lily's growing eagerness. I suspected she had a lot of pent up shopping angst. My suspicions were confirmed when we arrived at Forever 21. While I watched Lily select three pairs of jeans and four tops, I started a mental review of my recent credit card spending. It had taken her less than 15 minutes to do some serious damage to my credit line and we hadn't even gotten to underwear. My credit limit would need some serious adjustment in the near future.

Lily disappeared into the dressing room only to reappear moments later, a pre-teen model showing off a navy blue T with a scooped neckline and a pair of jeans that fit like a second skin. I was about to suggest a larger size when she rushed over and wrapped her arms around me. "Can I? I ain't never had nothing this nice before."

I rested my hands on her shoulders, momentarily enjoying the softness of the shirt's material, yet fully prepared to deliver the bad news.

She must have sensed my concern, because she backed away, nodding, her jaw set. "I get it. Not . . . sensible."

My suggestion about a size change caught on the lump in my throat. This girl was going to be so much trouble—just like I had been. I brushed at my cheek and mumbled. "They're perfect. Let's see what the others look like."

She bounced away, doing the twelve-year-old version of a runway walk. I put my hand to my throat, wondering if this was what Mom felt when I was growing up. My phone vibrated the moment Lily returned for a second showing. Great. Baldorf. What bad news was he bringing me now? I answered, "I'm busy."

"How soon can you get to Oceanside?"

"What? Why?"

"I think we can get Joey's girlfriend to safety if you pick her up."

"Why me? Why not you?"

"I have some other things I'm working on for Skip." I remembered Skip's request. Help Baldorf.

"I'm done with your wild goose chases, Baldorf." Lily wore another pair of tight jeans, this time with a black tank top. She didn't yet have the curves to make the outfit look provocative, thank goodness. I flashed her a smile and a thumbs up.

I flicked a couple of hangers on the rack in front of me to one side. "I told you, I'm seriously busy right now."

"This is important. Skip needs you to do this."

"I talked to him. He said you'd fill me in." I eyed a lacy top that would give Lily a nice "dressed up" look.

"That's not what he told me. Can you go pick her up?"

I jammed the hanger back onto the rack. "First you try to keep me out of the way. Then, he doesn't say a damn thing to me but he asks you to ask me. Are we back in grade school or something? What gives?"

"There are lots of guys assembling at Fu Zhang's house this morning. Looks like they could be mobilizing for something. They're all yammering away in Chinese, but she could be in danger."

I backed away from the rack, my irritation growing. "Who's they?"

"The guys you followed. Plus others. This has to be done fast. The pow wow's in progress now."

"I don't like being left out of the loop."

"Roxy? This isn't for Skip. It's for me. He doesn't know I called you. He wants me to go there, but I'm—" Baldorf's voice cracked.

I didn't make him say it. We both knew what was going on. Baldorf was afraid. Congratulations, Roxy, the bitch strikes again. I was forcing a nice guy to admit his fear. "I understand. Text me the address."

Lily stepped out in the third outfit. I nodded enthusiastically. "Sweetheart, you should have been a model." I waved at the clerk, a thirty-something woman who was dressed conservatively. "Hi, can you take off the tags? She's going to wear that one." To Lily, I said, "Sorry, but we have to go."

"Another caper?"

I nodded. "You might say that."

Her eyes lit up. "Awesome!"

The sales girl winked at me as she removed a tag. "You have such a lovely daughter."

A surge of longing ran through me. "If you only knew."

CHAPTER 38

S K I P

Skip sat on the edge of the motel mattress, tapping his foot on the cheap carpet while he waited for Baldorf to answer the phone. With each ring, he grew more impatient and apprehensive. He was about to hang up when Baldorf answered. "Hello?"

"What's up, Baldorf?"

"Nothing, dude. Just some logistical issues to deal with."

A siren signaled the beginning of another typical day in Los Angeles. Skip hated big cities because there was always another crime or fire or grave emergency that put someone's life in danger. The siren's wail faded, but was quickly replaced by a symphony of other noises: the steady whoosh of an adjacent room's shower, someone clumping along the outside walkway with a rolling bag in tow, the blare of a car alarm.

"Did something happen with the camera?"

Baldorf chuckled. "You might say that."

"Spill it."

"Dude, this is going to rock your world. You remember how I told you I could use someone's wireless network for the camera?"

"Cut to the chase, will you?"

"Last night I hacked Fu Zhang's network. I'm monitoring all of his communications."

Skip thought for a moment. He didn't want to get overly optimistic, but did this mean what he thought it meant? "This is huge, right?"

"No, dude, it's epic."

"What have you found out?"

"Fu Zhang's working on a huge deal. No details yet, but I'll keep you posted. That urgent message was to put you in a holding pattern in L.A. You need to make another stop."

Skip heard rustling noises on the other end of the line. He said, "Is that paper you're messing with?"

"Dude, even I like to make little scribbly doodles once in a while. It can be super therapeutic sometimes. Especially when my energy reserves are dwindling and my Skipman to-do list is not complete."

"Sorry, I hate using up so much of your time." He cleared his throat, "This will be over soon. What have you got for me?"

"Don't worry about the time. I'm having a blast helping you out. Anyway, there's something suspicious about this whole Jack Welton death thing. There's all sorts of drama at his company. It's like they went into panic mode. Nothing concrete, just . . . weird."

Something weird? Baldorf didn't use vague words like weird unless he was stumped, which was not a Baldorf condition. It just didn't happen to someone with a genius IQ. "You said panic mode, what's that mean?"

"I don't know, dude. It's bizarro. No facts. Just prodigious amounts of chatter around the industry. There's like this huge selloff of investments that all tie back to Welton. Like something—imploded."

"Maybe you're misreading the situation. There's probably a perfectly good reason, you know, a big investment banker dies—shit's gonna happen. It's either that or a scam fell apart—oh, crap, Roxy's trip." How stupid he'd been. Of course, it all made sense now. This woman would be his undoing.

"Dude, what's going on?"

Skip couldn't take his eyes from the blank TV screen. How long? When would the story unfold? What would he have to do this time? "She's done it again, Baldorf."

"Who's done what, man? You're making zero sense."

"Roxy. She pulled another con."

"You think she's behind this? No way. She wouldn't kill a guy."

On that point, he had to agree. Roxy was no killer. "But she might have driven him to suicide by taking him for everything he was worth. How much money does—did—this guy have?"

"I can check it out."

Skip flinched at the wail of another siren. "Get back to me the minute you've got something. This guy Welton was married, right?"

"Roger that. William J., aka Jack Welton, wed Frederica Gurney on September 8, 2007. You want me to look into her too?"

The TV had a security lock and cable chaining it to the dresser. How closely that reminded him of his relationship with Roxy. Their bond could only be broken with tremendous force. The resulting damage would leave them both scarred. "Why not? We're already breaking the law."

"Dude, don't worry about it. They're all public records—well, mostly, anyway."

Skip recalled the TV interviews from the last time—being on the other side of police Q&A's—the endless glares from cops who had once trusted him. He took in a ragged breath. Shit.

"You okay?" asked Baldorf.

"No, but I have a question."

"Fire away, dude."

"What kind of con would get a man killed and cause an investment banking firm to implode?"

Another siren sped past the motel. While the wailing faded into the distance, Skip waited. In all that time, Baldorf didn't answer. Yeah, thought Skip, the question even stumped the boy genius.

CHAPTER 39

ROXY

I explained to Lily what we were doing on the way to the address Baldorf had texted me. The explanation triggered another round of questions about my profession. How do you explain to a kid that you steal money from people for a living without feeling like you're destroying their faith in humanity? Because I danced around the issue, she had even more questions. Thankfully, we arrived just before I had to decide whether to lie or tell the truth.

I turned in my seat to face her. "Remember what you promised. You're going to do exactly what I say."

She rolled her eyes. Ah, yes. Instructions received. Whether they'd be obeyed was a different issue. What Lily didn't realize was that she was dealing with someone who'd been playing this same game almost twice as long as she'd been alive. I leaned in close. This situation could get highly volatile, so I had no qualms about laying down the law. She leaned back against the window to escape the invasion of her space, but her eyes remained fixed on mine in a determined effort to best my concerned-parent imitation. "Stay here!"

Apparently transfixed by my determination, Lily just nodded.

On my way to Shaina's door, I suppressed a smile. Not bad, I thought, this parenting thing wasn't so tough after all. Would time be our friend? We had to get out of here before the goons showed up—that meant I had to work fast. A dark-haired young woman opened the door. Beside her, a skinny white arm clinging loosely to her mother's thigh, stood a little girl, a miniature replica with dark eyes, eyebrows and eyelashes straight out of a fashion magazine. Both had a defined bone structure that made them grudgingly beautiful. I could see why Joey had fallen hard. Whatever feelings he harbored for Shaina, I couldn't imagine Joey being kept away from his daughter—at least, not willingly.

She said, "Yes?"

"Shaina Bowden-Meager?"

She leaned to one side, peering around me as though she suspected I might not be alone. "Yes." The little girl, who had two little spindles with knobby knees for legs, tightened her grip on her mother in response to the unmistakeable stiffening in Shaina's posture.

"My name is Roxy Tanner."

Recognition dawned on Shaina's face. "Joey told me about you." Her voice was cold.

The kid began to fidget. Did she sense her mother's unease or was it just a kid thing?

"This may sound very weird, Shaina, but I'm here to help you. A drug dealer named Fu Zhang is looking for you."

She snorted. "I doubt that. Him and Joey go way back. They got history."

A flowered rolling suitcase, its handle fully extended, sat on the floor behind Shaina. This was taking way too long. I needed to gain her confidence—quickly. I watched her face for clues. "Are you going somewhere?"

Shaina let out a huff as she tightened her grip on her daughter. "Joey's gonna want to see Tina. He told me that when I went to see him in prison."

There had been a slight hesitation in her voice; what had that meant? "I'll bet you don't want him to see her."

"What if I don't?"

"It's not a problem for me. The further away from him you can stay, the better is what I say."

"I thought you was the cab."

"I could drive you."

She eyed me. "Why would you help me? I don't know you."

I nodded toward the car. "Got one of my own out there."

She poked her head out the door and looked at my car, where Lily princess-waved at us as though she'd practiced the move for years.

Shaina gave me the once over. "You're kind of young to have a kid that age."

For once, I didn't need to construct the smile, it was genuine. "Thanks. It's a long story. I'll tell you later—if that's okay?"

"C'mon in. I just have to finish packing the bathroom."

I gave Lily a thumbs-up before entering the house. Shaina closed the door behind me and went to the bathroom, where she stuffed beauty paraphernalia into a bag. She finished her packing in about a minute, despite the distraction of Tina tugging on her skintight jeans.

The next thing I knew, she held up one finger and nodded at her daughter. The bathroom door closed, so I cooled my heels while Tina did her business. While I waited, I looked around. Except for a few sticks of furniture and a still-wet kid's finger painting on the coffee table, the place had been stripped.

I heard Shaina's muffled—and insistent—voice. That was probably a five-year-old kid thing—had to go, but couldn't when under the gun. Either way, I just wanted Tina to get on with her business so we could get out of here. I paced the room until I heard Lily's voice. I rushed to the front door and stuck my eye up to the peephole. My hand went to my heart. The goons were here. My knees nearly buckled—they were on the porch talking to Lily.

Chapter 40

S K I P

Jack and Frederica Guerney-Welton lived in a style that Skip would call California beachfront's most ostentatious. From their front gate, the house looked too tall, too expensive, and way over the top of any sensibility scale. The view from the upper windows probably extended well beyond the Channel Islands on a clear day. Though built on lots not much larger than the house itself, the opulence was larger than life—with the possible exception of the ivory button for the call system. The gate might be bronzed, but the button to ring for someone to open that swanky gate was still white plastic.

Moments after he pressed the button, a woman's voice crackled in the air. "Yes?"

"Skip Cosgrove. I called earlier about seeing Mrs. Gurney-Welton."

A click, followed by a buzz, momentarily drowned out the caw of gulls flying overhead. The gate drifted open when Skip pushed it lightly. He followed a manicured walkway along the short, but soothing path framed by a dramatic canvas accented with orange birds of paradise, queen palms, and hibiscus. A woman wearing a pale blue uniform and sensible shoes greeted him at the front door. Her skirt, which hung just below her knees, reinforced the conservative nature of her uniform. Did that mean that the woman was modest? Or did it indicate a wife's defense against a husband's roving eye?

The puzzle was becoming more complex, thought Skip. He'd come here looking for answers. So far, he'd only found more questions.

Natural light flooding the foyer emphasized the full dramatic effect of the three-story glass wall behind him. He smiled, hoping to establish a rapport with the maid. "Nice little place."

She stared at him blankly, apparently unimpressed by his friendly comment, then motioned for him to follow. Her shoes squeaked on the gleaming hardwood floor as she led the way. The walls had been painted in earth tones accented by shades of chocolate and rose. The colors added a sense of drama to the presentation. Recessed lighting spaced every two feet punctuated the ten-foot-high hallway ceiling. Again, thought Skip, someone wants to show off how much money they've got. Welton? His wife? Or both?

Inside the first room they passed, Skip noted plush area rugs in bright blues and greens with sharp geometric patterns covering sections of the floors. What appeared to be original modern oil paintings hung on the walls. At the end of the hallway, the mini-tour ended in what might loosely be called a family room. The sliding glass door on the back wall, left slightly ajar, looked out over a spectacular pool, fountain, and hot tub setting. Splashing water noise from the fountain drifted though the slider opening.

A man and a woman, both in their early thirties by Skip's guess, hunched toward each other on a red leather couch. The man had draped his arm across the back of the couch so that his fingers rested just inches from her shoulder. The woman wore a black turtleneck sweater with tan pants. She was barefoot, wore no jewelry, not even a wedding ring. The sudden abrupt end to their conversation made it feel somehow more intimate. Did these two have a secret?

The woman stood to approach Skip with her hand extended. "Mr. Cosgrove? I'm Frederica Gurney-Welton." Her tone was purebred Beverly Hills.

Skip shook her hand, noting the firmness of her grip. She seemed a stark contrast to the ostentatious trappings of the house. He turned to the man. "Skip Cosgrove."

The man, whose complexion was almost pasty white, nodded at Mrs. Welton. He rose to return the handshake. "Edward Oz. Jack's business partner."

When Mrs. Welton distanced herself from Oz, Skip instinctively shifted deeper into observation mode. Why had they moved apart? To avoid inappropriate appearances? Or to shed guilt?

"Have a seat, Mr. Cosgrove." Mrs. Welton gestured to the spot where she'd been sitting.

"Frederica," said Oz, "I really should be going. We can finish our discussion later." He turned to Skip. "Nice to have met you."

"Same here."

Oz left without another word to Mrs. Welton. She didn't speak to him, but she looked down to the right when he left. To Skip, it meant she was accessing her feelings—the word that popped into his head was "couple."

Mrs. Welton stood about six inches shorter than Oz. The way she kept glancing at him made Skip wonder if there was something going on between these two. Were they lovers? Or, just close friends? The latter seemed less likely when Mrs. Welton gestured at the couch, but planted herself on the love seat. "Please. Sit. Ynes said you had information about my husband's death."

"Actually, I was looking for information. I don't have anything new to add."

Mrs. Welton's back straightened; her eyes narrowed. "Who did you say you were?"

Skip handed her a card from his wallet. "I'm a criminologist and a forensic hypnotist. I've been asked to look into your husband's death."

The sound of footsteps in the hallway grew louder. Oz returned and stood only a few feet away. Mrs. Welton handed him the card. He gave it a cursory glance, slipped it into his pocket, then took up a combative stance squarely opposite Skip. "Who are you working for?"

Mrs. Welton slipped in close to Oz, subconsciously started to reach for his hand, but stopped when he pulled away.

"Client confidentiality. I can't reveal that."

The other man's face flushed. This display of male bravado only made the investigator in Skip more curious. He baited Oz with a half smile. Oz inhaled sharply, then took a small step in Skip's direction, but stopped when Mrs. Welton grabbed his arm. "Eddie, no."

Skip noted how close they now stood. Eddie? Had Mrs. Welton known about her husband's womanizing? Had she chosen to sleep with his partner? These two were doing a lousy job of concealing any relationship they might have. Were they even trying? He decided to take the offensive by making a move almost guaranteed to irritate Oz—he ignored him. Skip shifted his attention to Mrs. Welton. "All I can tell you is that I've been asked to evaluate the circumstances surrounding your husband's death. And your relationship with Mr. Oz."

Mrs. Welton withdrew into herself, crossing her arms over her chest, while Oz shifted his weight into a defensive posture. It was a textbook reaction, thought Skip. He flexed his knees to bring his balance forward. No sense in being caught off guard.

Instead of throwing a punch, Oz's Adam's apple bobbed from a hard swallow. Skip needed more answers and these two weren't going to do that—for now. It was time to dig deeper. How did Anita play into this? What about Roxy? He'd identified an emotion he could use to drive a wedge between Oz and Frederica. Now, he just needed to figure out where and when to use it.

CHAPTER 41

R O X Y

I stepped back from the peephole of Shaina's door, unable to believe what was happening on the porch. I peered out again and bit my lower lip. "Shit!"

Lily stood between two guys who resembled escaped death-row inmates. One was a six-foot-tall tattooed guy; the other was a little skinny runt who had not aged well. The runt blinked repeatedly, making me wonder if he'd snorted too much coke one too many times. Tattoo Boy had a frequent tick that animated a skull and crossbones tattoo on his left cheek, giving him a fearsome appearance.

Despite the chill running down my spine, I pulled off my sleeveless blouse and yanked one side of the camisole out of my waistband so it hung lopsided. I bent over to do a complete reverse comb of my hair. When I stood, Shaina looked like she might freak out. She kept Tina close with one hand on her shoulder, but there was no need for that—the kid looked petrified as she clung to her mother's leg.

"Call 9-1-1." I hissed, "Now!" I flung the door open, yelling at the top of my lungs, "Hey asshole! What the hell you doin' to my kid?"

Tattoo Boy did a double-take. "Who the hell are you?" He edged in my direction.

"That's my mom, Mister." She began moving her index finger in a small circle next to her ear.

Runt compared me to a photo in his hand. "This crazy bitch ain't her, man."

I got right in Tattoo Boy's face and jabbed him in the chest with my finger. "Leave my kid alone, asshole!" I scowled at Lily. "Get your scrawny ass inside and grab my shotgun! You know how much I hate strangers."

Lily almost fell as she scrambled past the two men. She signaled again that I was crazy. When I lurched in her direction, she jumped, practically stumbling inside. From behind the closed door, she yelled, "Right away, Mama!"

Tattoo Boy glowered at his partner. "You sure?"

I whirled back to face Runt, screaming at him with my face just inches from his. "Who you callin' a crazy bitch, asshole?" He kept backing away until he was off balance on the edge of the porch. I seized the photo, took one glance, then ripped it in half. I threw the pieces in the air, wondering how these two got a photo of Shaina and Joey in a romantic embrace in a setting filled with tropical foliage.

"What the—that was mine!"

I gave Runt a shove, sending him ass backwards off the porch. He landed with a thud that knocked the wind out of him. I turned back to deal with Tattoo Boy. "Little pissant!" The big guy was stunned by what I'd done, so while he digested the situation, which included Runt moaning about his injuries, I calculated my chances of landing a kick to his groin. Runt would run the second the muscle went down, so I prepared for the first strike and screwed up my face. "Hurry up in there, goddamnit! What are you lookin' at!"

Lily's voice came from inside the house. "Sorry, Mama! I'm comin'!"

Tattoo Boy started in my direction, but stopped when the sound of police sirens grew louder. He must have realized he had the cops closing in and still didn't know what to do with a crazed woman who wasn't included in his orders. What would he do? Kill me? Run like hell? He turned suddenly meek and mild. "Sorry to have bothered you, lady." At the foot of the porch, he seized his partner by the collar. He practically ripped Runt's shirt off of him when he dragged the little guy, half-stumbling, to the car. "You piece of shit. The boss warned you what would happen if this didn't work out." He shoved Runt inside, took one look at me, then rushed to the driver's door.

The cops couldn't be more than a few blocks away, but our visitors had enough of a lead that they were gone by the time two Oceanside PD cars converged on the house a half minute later.

Lily rushed out the front door. "You were awesome!"

I pulled her into a tight embrace. "You were pretty good yourself, sweetheart."

We'd survived. My pulse raced. Now I had to deal with one of my worst nightmares, cops in uniforms looking for something bad.

The uniforms took up their assigned positions. We were only halfway home because I still looked like a crazed bitch. With no time for a costume change, everything depended on sincerity. I could only hope the cops didn't realize Lily was a runaway. I hugged her again and whispered in her ear. "Follow my lead. Do not overplay this. These guys will be suspicious."

To my relief, Shaina stayed in the house. Could I finish this before she showed up to blow my act? Lily and I assumed the mom-daughter pose, my arm draped protectively around her shoulders, hers around my waist. I said, "Thank God you're here! The guys we called about couldn't get out of here fast enough when they heard your sirens. They just showed up at our door and started hassling me and my daughter."

The first officer, a tall thin Caucasian whose name tag read "James" eyed me. "Your daughter?"

I rolled my eyes and shook my head. "Seriously? Is that a pickup line?" I brushed at my hair with my free hand, averting my eyes for a moment for extra effect. When I had their full attention, I muttered loud enough for them both to hear, "I must look like a two-bit whore right now. Dear God, this is awful." I crossed my arms over my chest, doing my best to look embarrassed.

James flushed a bright shade of red, his voice got shaky. "Uh, no, ma'am. I mean, sorry . . . Miss. Rudy, maybe you should, uh . . ."

Rudy was a heavily muscled Hispanic with a light complexion. His last name was Jimenez. I took him to be far more seasoned than James because of the way he scanned the area as he spoke. "Ma'am, Officer James is pretty new. I apologize for his faux pas. Did these men drive away?"

I nodded quickly, then kissed Lily on the forehead. "Thank the Lord. I don't know what they'd have done to her if you hadn't shown up so fast!"

Lily tapped my arm with her free hand, but didn't say a thing.

"She's shy," I said.

When I leaned down, Lily whispered in my ear. "Tell 'em I, like, can't talk to strangers."

"It's okay, sweetheart." I smiled at the officers. "She was really scared. Poor kid has a terrible time talking to strangers. If only I could afford therapy for her."

From the corner of my eye, I caught Lily gazing up at Jimenez, nodding solemnly. After a few seconds, he gave her a knowing nod. As if on cue, Lily finished her intimidated-kid act by watching the ground.

The guys were now focused on me, making sure not to further intimidate Lily. I brushed at my hair again, "I must look a sight. Oh, my Lord, her father's going to be showing up soon—visitation, you know? If he hears about this, he'll use it against me." I motioned at Lily. "He doesn't care about my little girl—he'd take her away in a minute if he got the chance just to spite me."

"Do you think he sent those two men?"

Crap. I hadn't thought of that option. It was time to fall back to basics, to keep this simple before the lies got too complex to remember. "You can't be serious. My ex? No way."

Lily slipped away from my side to approach Jimenez. She tugged on his shirt and he leaned forward. What the hell was she doing? I kept the smile on my face, though my knees felt as though they might buckle at any moment.

Jimenez nodded as Lily whispered in his ear. When he straightened up, he gave Lily a nod. "We're done here. Let's go—Romeo." He gave me a sympathetic smile as he led Officer James away.

We waved as both squad cars left. The moment they were out of sight, Lily charged to the house. I yelled after her, "We have to leave! Now!"

Lily waved her hand in the air as she yanked open the door. Shaina and Tina rushed out of the house to my car. As Shaina got Tina situated, she said, "I cancelled the cab. I ain't trusting no one."

We were gone in less than two minutes. Once we'd made it onto Old Coast Highway, I turned to Lily. "What did you whisper to that cop?"

She smiled. "I, like, said that you so overreacted cause you're, like, way overprotective. I told him it was, like, the PMS, that did it."

I laughed. "You're twelve. How do you know about PMS?"

"My mom is, like, always talkin' about that crap. She, like, says if it wasn't for PMS, she'd like, so lose half her johns."

I bit my tongue and did my best to keep my mind on my driving, but couldn't resist checking the rearview mirror, where Shaina stroked Tina's hair absently as she glared directly at both of us.

If I didn't know better, I'd swear Lily and I had the same DNA.

CHAPTER 42

S K I P

The conversation with the widow and her suspected lover revealed far more than Skip imagined might exist. If she was having an affair with the deceased's business partner, what other secrets might she have? How many other secrets were out there? He left, convinced that a visit to Welton's business had the potential to raise more questions about both Mr. and Mrs. Welton and their personal affairs.

He called Baldorf, who answered on the second ring. "Dude, I've got news."

"The spy cam?"

"Fortuitous, man, but that's not why I called."

"Keep watching. There are secrets in that house. I think we need to find out what they are."

"Roger that."

"Also, I need an address for Welton's business."

"Before you go there, check this out. Roxy's friend Anita has gone off the grid. Dude, she's become a ghost."

"You sure she's not just off visiting grandma or something?"

"The brother's gone, too. He's a veterinarian. Runs a small animal hospital called Loving Care for Pets. It's been closed since Welton died."

"You think they're hiding from the cops?"

"That or she's gotten herself killed. Girl's gone, dude. Totally. Her bro, too, which is weird because he treats all kinds of pets. I'd guess that specialization is the more viable business plan, but prescribing pet meds isn't my thing. Seems unprofitable to just close the doors for a few days."

A horn blared behind Skip. "Shit!" he barked. "I've been sitting through a green light. Hang on." On the other side of the intersection, he parked in the lot of a convenience store. "Maybe he can do that. Just close, I mean. Besides, who'd want to kill her? Or her brother?"

"Who'd want to kill Jack Welton?"

"I can think of two suspects I didn't have until a few minutes ago," Skip said. "Mrs. Welton and her lover."

"Serious? Dude, this is awesome! A love triangle is like the pinnacle of motivation. You sure?"

"I'd bet my next paycheck on it."

There was a pause, then Baldorf said, "You—get a paycheck?"

"Figure of speech, my friend. I'll show you my bank statement. So what's Anita's address? Should I go there?"

"Her apartment's in Culver City."

"It's still early, might only take me an hour to make it. Where's Welton's place of business?"

"Where else, man? Downtown L.A."

"Text me the address. If you get me Anita's first, I can go see her before I start stirring up trouble in the world of investments."

"Dude, you might want to hurry, they're in free-fall from what I can tell."

An hour later, Skip was driving along a Culver City street lined with cars on both sides. Two-story apartment complexes built during the cheap commercial real estate heyday of the 70s occupied every available square foot of land. Judging by the conga line of parked cars, off-street parking had been an afterthought in this neighborhood. A half block ahead, an old blue Chevy pulled out and Skip grabbed the empty space.

Beige stucco walls with dark brown wood trim had peeled, giving the building a seedy appearance. Large stately trees added a touch of serenity to the neighborhood's atmosphere. Skip couldn't understand the general lack of maintenance for a complex this size. He went to the trunk to pull out his Sig .357. He also selected two extra clips, a small box of latex gloves, and his lock picks. He slipped the picks into his jacket pocket, the gloves into the back pocket of his jeans and went in search of the manager's apartment.

The flaking paint on the door, along with the tarnished doorknob, reinforced the feeling that this complex was only remembered when it was time for the rent to be paid. He knocked, wondering if this was the best that Anita could afford. He heard a woman's voice and footsteps on the second-floor walkway. The inflection on the last word reminded him of a Chicago Jewish grandmother scolding a child.

"So, what did you say she did again?"

A man answered. "Sorry, ma'am, we can't discuss this. We just needed to ask Ms. Hewson a few questions."

Skip stiffened slightly. Were the cops here already? He wanted to ask questions, not answer them. From not very far away, he heard the rumbling and clacking of a clothes dryer. He followed the noise to the first open doorway. Inside the room, a lone dryer tumbled while two washers and a second dryer sat idle. The units appeared old enough to be original complex equipment. Behind him, footsteps tapped on the concrete staircase. Skip slipped into the unoccupied room.

Irritation tinged the woman's high-pitched whine. "For a few questions you two had to break into her apartment?"

He looked back at the stairwell, which faced away from him. Concrete steps with no back risers let him see straight through—he was in a perfect place to spy.

A different man's voice said, "We had a warrant, Mrs. Jacobs. For the record, we didn't break in, you unlocked the apartment."

Skip slipped back into the laundry room. He found a worn folded newspaper on a plastic chair, grabbed the paper, then returned to the door ready to plop down while pretending to wait for the dryer if anyone came in.

Mrs. Jacobs planted her feet and crossed her arms over her chest as she faced off against the two cops at the base of the stairs. "So is there anything else? Or are you two done ruining my morning?"

The cops quickly excused themselves, but Skip waited. When he was satisfied the manager was alone, he doubled back to her apartment. Inside, a TV talk show blared.

He knocked. When there was no answer, he rapped harder on the door. The TV noises stopped; the woman's voice cut the air again.

"So now what do you need? A body can't get anything done with all these interruptions!" The door swung open, the woman's face screwed up in confusion. "So what is it you do already?"

Skip held out a business card. "I'm looking into the disappearance of Anita Hewson."

"What? Are you working with those two schlemiels that just left?"

Skip whispered conspiratorially, "Do you think anyone could work with those two?"

The woman tittered as she did her own quick check of the hallway. "Martha Jacobs. That schlemiel Montague ought to have his mouth washed out the way he talks to others."

Skip nodded. In a normal tone he said, "I hear you, Mrs. Jacobs." He leaned forward, pretending they were best buddies sharing a juicy secret. "You didn't hear it from me, but I think the department's considering putting him on 'leave.'" He made quotation marks in the air with his hands.

Mrs. Jacobs's eyes lit up. "Would serve him right, the way he is. So what is it you need?"

"I need a decent report on what Montague found in Ms. Hewson's apartment and I won't get it from him. You know what I mean?" He hesitated before continuing. "I'm probably going to get in trouble for being late even though the call to get here didn't come in until the last minute. You think he'd take the blame for that? I doubt it."

"Oi vey. A maven he's not. You want in the apartment, honey? I'll let you in. I already saw the warrant."

"Would it be too much trouble?"

Mrs. Jacobs rolled her eyes. "What that those two should have been so polite! I'll get my keys."

Skip rubbed the bridge of his nose with his fingertips while he waited for Mrs. Jacobs to return. He muttered, "What am I doing, impersonating a cop?"

He rationalized his actions by telling himself that he'd never said he was a cop. He'd only implied it. His life since the moment he met Roxy had been one big complication. A couple of hours ago he'd been criticizing her for conning people. Now, here he was, doing the same thing.

The jingle of keys broke his train of thought as Mrs. Jacobs stepped into the hallway. She motioned toward the outside world with her head as she locked the door. "In this neighborhood, you can never be too sure." With a wave of her hand, she motioned for Skip to follow.

Mrs. Jacobs climbed the stairs without hurry, but Skip's heart pounded nonetheless. Clinically, he recognized the rush of endorphins. Emotionally, his reaction worried him for one simple reason. He was becoming more like Roxy with every action he took. Was he becoming addicted to the rush itself?

Once she'd unlocked the apartment door, Mrs. Jacobs seemed uninterested in hanging around. Skip said, "Mrs. Jacobs, do you mind if we keep this just between the two of us? You know, because of . . ." He motioned with his head to one side a couple of times.

She winked while she made a zipping motion across her lips. "No problem, doll. Close the door on the way out, I'll stop by later to lock the deadbolt."

CHAPTER 43

R O X Y

Distance. It's a concept that can be measured in miles—or feelings. I frequently played on the latter—that's just the nature of my job. In this case, it was physical distance that apparently eased Shaina's mind. Her scowl softened with each passing mile and each time Tina expressed interest in a new sight outside the car. As the excitement of our escape faded, our drive morphed into a normal "family" outing with the girls caught up in the outside world. Although the hard edge of Shaina's mood had softened, I grew more concerned. Where was Skip?

It was time to make a decision about our destination. I called the person at the center of Skip's little information universe, Baldorf, to give him the bad news. "We're on our way to your place."

"We? We, who?"

"All of us. Shaina, Tina, Lily, and me. Let's cut right to it, Baldorf, I want to know where Skip is. Tell me now or I'll feed the kids a ton of caffeine and sugar before we get there."

"You, you can't come here. I don't have room—I don't—"

"Stuff it. We're on our way. You got me into this, so you're in it, too. The only question is how painful I make this for you. If the sugar and caffeine don't work, I can get really creative."

My phone bleeped that a call was waiting. I said, "You got lucky, Skip's on the other line." After disconnecting Baldorf, I took a deep breath while reminding myself to keep cool because whatever Skip was doing was for me. I should not be angry with the man, I should be thanking him. "Hey."

"Hey, yourself."

His voice was soft in my ear, melting my annoyance at having been left out of his plans. "Where are you?"

"Someplace I didn't expect to be. I came to L.A. to get some background on someone for a friend—a very close friend."

Talk about conflicted. I wanted that friend to be me, but I was terrified—what if it wasn't? Could this be our undoing? "Oh? What—did you—find out?"

"This friend of mine got involved in something that went the wrong way. I'm trying to help . . ." He paused for a moment, "Um, solve her problem."

My heart nearly stopped. So far, no names. So far, we had distance. So far, the tightness in my throat wasn't letting me tap into my anger. We could only dodge this issue for a short time. I bit at my lower lip, desperate to not break down and confess. "What problem does—she—have?"

"Several. There's her boyfriend, a guy who loves her deeply, but can't help interfering when he knows she's in trouble."

I cleared my throat—the lump was there, growing. He still cared? "Sounds familiar."

"She's also got a dead body and cops trying to find her friend that got her into the mess in the first place. Her friend's disappeared, by the way."

"Anita's missing?" I blurted. Game over, time to be a big girl. Face this head on. "When did you find that out?"

"Just now. I'm—uh, visiting—her place."

"Visiting? What's that mean?"

"It seems that the manager let me in and, well, she had to leave. Soap opera, TV talk show, whatever. Anyway, I'll be damned if I can figure out where Anita might have gone."

CHAPTER 44

S K I P

Skip listened to the hiss of the open telephone line while he waited for Roxy to absorb the news that he'd lied his way into Anita's apartment.

When she came back on the line, her voice was an angry whisper. "Are you out of your freaking mind?"

"Let's not argue, okay? I have a pretty good idea of what happened. She came vetted."

"Through Marjorie. Anita's her niece."

"She needed help from someone with—special skills. That's how you got roped into some arrangement involving Welton. Am I close?"

Skip could picture Roxy, probably beyond angry at him for getting involved, but even angrier at herself for how much trouble she'd found this time. He was surprised that when she spoke, her voice was calm.

"So what do you need from me?"

"Is there anything here that might connect you to her?"

"I was never in her apartment. There's no physical evidence. Even the Taser confetti was untraceable."

"Black market Taser darts?" Despite his best efforts to not smile, he couldn't help but admire her ingenuity. "You do have connections, don't you?"

"Special circumstances. Please, just tell me you didn't pick the lock."

"No, I told you, the landlady had a key. She opened the door for me."

"Why? Why would she do that?"

"I might have—bent the truth a little."

"Good God, Skip, you can't just run around lying to people!"

Skip laughed out loud. "You're a fine one to talk."

A few seconds later, she said, "Okay, you win. I'll stop if you do."

Was that a smile he detected in her voice? "Maybe we should settle down and have a few kids. You know, like normal people." Skip's breath caught when there was another long pause.

"I've got Joey's girlfriend and daughter with me."

"What? Baldorf called you in on that? He was supposed to— dammit. What about Fu Zhang? He's looking for Shaina so he can flush out Joey—and Joey's after you."

"We didn't leave a forwarding address. We're 'in transit.'"

Skip spotted a small computer desk with a single drawer standing half open. He cradled the phone and checked his gloves before easing the drawer open the rest of the way. Inside, he found only a few pens, a scratch pad, and a tube of lip balm—the same brand Roxy sometimes used. He pocketed the tube as a precaution. He surveyed the room. In some respects, the place looked as though Anita had left in a hurry.

"Hey? You still there?" Her tone had changed to one of concern.

"We'll be lucky to get out of this alive. How did I get you into this?"

"You didn't. When are you coming back?"

"I've got one other stop later today. I should also find Anita while I'm here. Got any ideas?"

"I'll check with Marjorie. Skip, I've gotta go, we're at Baldorf's."

"That's not a good choice. You need someplace secure."

"We won't stay here long. Do you have any other suggestions?"

The problem was, he didn't. "He's going to hate this, you know that, right?"

"Good."

She hung up before he could say say goodbye.

CHAPTER 45

ROXY

Our invasion of Baldorf's little bungalow went well, all things considered. He managed to rustle up some gourmet cookies for the girls. They scarfed down his private stash and some milk like hungry puppies while Baldorf watched—the pain on his face evident.

Baldorf professed to be highly undomesticated, yet he soon had a pot of tea brewing for the adults and was making an honest attempt to engage in meaningless small talk. He broke away only long enough to kneel down in front of the girls to offer them more cookies. Luckily for him, Shaina told Tina "no more." Lily must have decided it would be uncool to laud her independence over her new friend, so she declined also.

As Baldorf stood, Tina burst into tears, her piercing wail shattering the solitude of the man cave. The panic on Baldorf's face would have been delightful had I not been feeling the same. Shaina lifted Tina, clutching her tightly. "Shhh, baby, shhh."

Tina wrapped her skinny white arms around her mother's neck. When Shaina relaxed her grip to put Tina down, the little girl screamed again. "She don't trust men so much." She glared at Baldorf, who put an open hand on his chest and gulped.

His eyes widened and he squeaked, "I can't change that . . ."

"Your gender doesn't always have the advantage." I resisted reminding the poor guy that he could make a change if he were motivated enough.

"We ain't staying here. Tina needs a better environment."

Baldorf nodded his agreement; his eyes darted wistfully at the almost empty plate of gourmet cookies before he gestured at the array of equipment occupying most of the available space. "Man, I'm completely booked. No offense, but my place isn't big enough for guests—with ruggers—I mean, children."

"We don't have anywhere else to go," I said.

Lily watched us with a sly smile. I was beginning to hate the fact that this kid sometimes saw solutions I didn't. "What?"

"You'll, like, figure it out."

I'm glad someone thought I knew what I was doing—I looked to Baldorf for support. "Any suggestions?"

"Get me a cab, we'll go—somewhere," Shaina said.

Baldorf and I shook our heads simultaneously. We both barked, "Not happening." You would have thought we'd rehearsed the reaction. Maybe he was starting to get the hang of this whole dealing with people thing. When I winked at him, he flushed.

Shaina shook her head furiously, the contempt in her eyes obvious. "I'm done with you people. You can't kidnap us."

"No, but where would you go? How would you pay for the cab?" I said.

"I got a credit card. Tina and me, we got people we can stay with."

Baldorf's phone rang; the big chicken scurried away to answer it.

"Are you serious?" I snapped. "How long do you think it will take before Fu Zhang checks with these people? Do you think he won't be watching for credit card activity?"

"So what? He ain't gonna do nothing to me."

"Hey, Tina, let's go over here," said Lily.

Tina nodded, then squirmed down from her mother's grasp and grabbed a doll. They walked hand-in-hand to a corner of the room where Lily plopped down cross-legged and Tina followed suit. Lily's ability to shed her street persona amazed me. I recalled Baldorf's earlier caution to me. *Lily would have to go back.* Would she readjust? Was I destroying her life by pulling her away?

Shaina started to walk toward the girls, but I stopped her with a hand on her arm. "They're doing fine."

She watched Lily use Tina's doll to play Pat-a-cake with her daughter. I'd have expected Shaina to be happy at how well the two girls got along—that didn't seem to be the case.

To one side, I heard, "Yeah, in fact, Shaina's here at my place along with her little girl and Roxy. Gotta go, my other line's ringing."

The girls must have ended their game or grown bored because Tina approached her mom with Lily in tow. "Mommy? Can Lily and me go outside?"

The anger in Shaina's blood rose until the glow on her face reminded me of a hot thermometer. Unsuccessfully, I tried to divide my attention between Baldorf's new conversation and Shaina's. Based on his tone of voice and facial expressions, I could tell that things were not going well for him. Shaina remained focused on Tina, oblivious to everything around her.

I touched Lily's hand to get her attention. She glanced at me and nodded. Already, she knew. My breath caught in my throat as I tried—but failed—to make myself believe she'd be fine when this was over.

"We don't know these people, baby," said Shaina. "I want you to stay with me."

The little girl put on a pouty face that would, someday, drive her boyfriends to do crazy things. But, she didn't complain.

Baldorf wrote something down on a piece of paper. "Are you positive? This is an absolute, dude. No error margin here."

That sounded bad, so I mouthed to Lily, "We have to leave."

She kneeled next to Tina. "Hey, Tina?"

"Mommy says I can't."

"It's cool," said Lily. "There's, like, this game me and my mom play."

"What is it?" In seconds, the pout was gone, her eyes sparkling with the thought of learning something new.

Shaina bristled. I thought, chill, Mom. You can't keep her forever.

Baldorf shook his head as he disconnected from the call. He nodded for me to follow him to his miniature kitchen. "That second call was a buddy of mine who speaks Mandarin. He translated everything about that big meeting at Fu Zhang's."

"Well?"

He licked his lips. "I was wrong. They weren't going after Shaina, there's a shipment coming in tomorrow." He handed me the paper with his notes. "That's the where and when. You'd better talk to Skip about what to do."

"Wait a minute. Does this mean that the guys at Shaina's weren't sent by Fu Zhang?"

He shrugged. "I don't know."

"What's going on? I heard my name?"

Apparently, Shaina had been trying to listen in. I folded the paper while I caught Lily's attention. "You got this? Just stay inside."

She rolled her eyes. "Duh."

Baldorf, bless his heart, jumped in before I had to make something up. "Skip wants to find some level of permanency for you."

"We ain't going no place permanent. This is only temporary."

"He meant more permanent than here," I said. "As in, maybe a day or two while we get this sorted out. Our top priority is security."

Shaina glared at us with cold eyes. Her intimidation routine had Baldorf fidgety as a frightened kitten, but for a change, I felt like the only normal one in the room. How did I get stuck between opposing forces of the universe?

CHAPTER 46

S K I P

Skip closed the door to Anita's apartment with a sense of foreboding closing in around him. His search had turned up nothing. Anita was gone. Temporarily? Permanently? She still had clothes in her closet, but there were no personal items like a toothbrush, hairbrush, or even a razor in the shower. She'd taken her computer, but left food in the refrigerator, dishes and silverware in the drawers. There were no keys, no purse—nothing. Even the two cops had walked away empty-handed.

Skip needed Roxy to help find Anita, but didn't want to call her until after he'd been to Welton's business. He turned to see Mrs. Jacobs, one hand on the railing to support herself, trying to catch her breath.

"She was here." The woman gasped for air. "Her mail. She was getting her mail so I went out to talk to her. When I told her about the police, she turned white as a sheet. Poor girl ran out like a vilda chaya."

"A what?"

"A wild animal. You know nothing? Still, for you my daughter might be interested. Are you looking for a nice girl? I can fix you up, you know."

"Sorry, Mrs. Jacobs. I have a girlfriend. I'm sure your daughter is very nice, however. Did Anita say where she was going?"

"My daughter, she'll become an old maid if I don't find her a man. You got any nice friends?"

Skip started to ask another question, but stopped when he realized Mrs. Jacobs could carry on this conversation all afternoon. He simply replied, "No."

Forty-five minutes later, Skip stood before the impressive glass entrance to Welton's investment firm, seventeen stories up in a downtown office building. Inside, an attractive blonde sat at a receptionist's desk. A young man wearing a white shirt and tie who looked to be no more than a first-year college student burst through a side door. He said something to the receptionist before dropping a sheaf of papers on the corner of her desk.

The young man glanced up as Skip opened the door. Their conversation ended abruptly with the flash of a white shirt disappearing through the side entrance. The roar of keyboard clacking, ringing phones, and jangled nerves rushed through the open doorway, then faded away as the door drifted shut. It must be pandemonium back there, thought Skip. Although he'd never seen a customer-service bullpen before, he recognized the frantic voices of people calling out orders, trying to recover from some catastrophic event. Or was it always that way? He was alone with the receptionist—along with the frustration and fear she tried to hide behind a forced smile. A nameplate on the desk read, "Melinda W."

"Crazy day?" asked Skip.

She pointed at the six-inch stack of papers on her desk. "Insane."

"The boss dying will have that effect."

The receptionist's hazel eyes widened. Her eyes darted back to the top sheet of the papers she'd been handed. She scanned the page, muttering under her breath. A moment later, she again pasted a smile on her face. "What can I do for you?" Her gaze lingered on the top sheet, her eyes darting down the page even as she spoke.

"More bad news, I assume?" Skip pointed at the small mountain she couldn't seem to ignore.

She cleared her throat. "Did you have an appointment to see someone?"

"No. I heard about Mr. Welton and wondered how it might be affecting the business. His death was sudden?"

The receptionist shrugged. "Isn't it always? Are you a stockholder?"

"No."

"Press?"

"I'm investigating the circumstances, Melinda. You are Melinda, right? One of the partners is Edward Oz, correct?"

The receptionist batted her eyes while grabbing a pen. She twisted the instrument back and forth with both hands. "Yes, Mr. Oz is a named partner. Who did you say you were with?"

"Does that mean he works here all the time?"

She stood, her shoulders stiff, her demeanor curt. "If you're not a stockholder, I'm going to have to ask you to leave."

Melinda wore a black V-neck sweater that hugged her curves when she stood. Her dark green skirt came to about two inches above her knees, her nails were painted blood red and she wore a pair of take-me-now stilettos. No wedding ring, either. The full ensemble, combined with just a hint of cleavage, was what he'd heard Roxy call "slightly slutty." What would she do to climb the corporate ladder? He looked straight into Melinda's eyes. "How long ago did your affair with Edward Oz end? Or has it?"

"I—I think you should leave." The receptionist's voice was no more than a hoarse whisper.

Skip was amazed. The Hail Mary had paid off. "This will go much quicker if you just answer a couple of questions. What does Edward Oz do here?"

She crossed her arms over her chest; her brow furrowed into something resembling a grimace. "Not much. He's a venture capitalist. He and the Barracuda—sorry, Mrs. Welton. She's the one who put up half the money to get the business going."

"Mrs. Welton is tough?"

"Please, leave me alone," she begged.

"Your boyfriend put up the other half?"

"Ozzie?" She looked indignant. "He's not my boyfriend, he's my fiancé."

"You're not wearing a ring."

"We're keeping it quiet. Office politics."

She looked cold when she rubbed her arms with her hands, but Skip knew the real reason—nerves—and he doubted it had anything to do with an affair. He guessed Melinda was committing a cardinal sin by talking to a stranger. Why would she take that chance? He said, "The company went public last year. Why, exactly, is the stock tanking? It's not because your boss died. Companies survive that kind of hit all the time."

Melinda's ragged breath cut the air. "Screw it." She watched the door intently while she spoke. "You didn't hear this from me, but we're getting calls from clients this morning telling us about an email they got last night. It sounds like Jack was running a scam. Our investors are selling their holdings along with our stock. It's like being on the Titanic. At the end."

"Have the police been here yet?"

She shook her head before slumping back into her chair and nervously pulling her hair back.

"If I were you," said Skip, "I'd start looking for another job."

The side door burst open again. A young woman, a female clone of the man who'd been out before, rushed to the desk. "I need this done yesterday!" She dropped her stack, which was even larger than the previous one, and rushed out.

Melinda waited. When they were alone, she displayed a fire Skip hadn't seen before. She muttered, "Ozzie will fix your ass, bitch."

Skip stood outside of Welton's office, confident that he was a step ahead of the cops. Maybe now he could give Baldorf something solid to look for. He thought about Melinda's spunkiness. How did she really feel about Oz? He shook his head, wondering what she'd do if she knew her lover was seeing "the Barracuda."

Skip dialed Baldorf, who answered the phone with a somber, "Dude, we need to talk."

"I just left Welton's business. The place is in a panic over some email that went out this morning or last night. There's something about a scam. They've got clients selling off their holdings and stock like crazy."

"Hey, man, the market's an apocalyptic mess. Any news can cause trauma. I've got a dilemma we should talk through."

"Let me finish. I need you to see if you can work any magic to uncover some sort of scam that Welton might have been running. I was going to have you look for Anita, but I suspect she's somehow secondary in this."

"They're selling their company stock and their investments? Sounds like he was inflating stock values based on false recommendations. Pump and dump, dude."

"That would track with what I just heard."

"It's consistent with what's happening in the market. Stock values for their largest holdings are dropping. Those companies were just penny stocks before Welton's clients started accumulating them. Now, they're huge. Any paper trail is probably being destroyed as we speak."

Skip heard a distant rumble that grew louder by the second. A garbage truck, its iron arms extended, closed in on a giant Dumpster. The arms lifted the container, raised it in a wide arc, eventually upending it. An army of plump plastic bags fell into the waiting cavern at the back of the truck. He watched, transfixed, until the mechanical arms returned the giant can to its upright position. When the lid clanged back into place, he shuddered, unsure if his reaction was from the mini-thunderclap caused by the falling lid or his memory of the dark alley. He said, "What did you say?"

"The paper trail, someone's got to be in charge of shredding. Dude, I wanted to ask you something else."

"Shit!" Skip slammed his hand against the steering wheel. He'd just witnessed the very act and missed it. "I have to go!" He jumped out of the car and ran back to Welton's office.

CHAPTER 47

R O X Y

Standing between Shaina and Baldorf was creepy. Her anger, or whatever it was, ran just beneath the surface. So far, I had no idea why she was so pissed. On the flip side, I hadn't seen Baldorf, who was your basic introverted geek, this intimidated since the day we'd met. Whatever the interpersonal dynamics, my main goal right now was to get us out of here.

We still didn't know who was after Shaina or if they even were. To keep her safe, we needed a location that couldn't be easily tracked back to me. That left just one person. I hated to involve anyone else in this mess, but saw no other options.

I dialed Marjorie's phone number, part of me wishing she wouldn't answer. Barging in on her seemed like grounds for friendship-divorce from the one person in the world who accepted me at face value. We went through the pleasantries, but it was obvious she suspected something when she prodded me for an answer. After a few seconds, I caved.

"Skip is up in L.A. looking for Anita because she's disappeared. Do you have any idea where she might have gone?"

"I'll have to think about that." Only a few seconds passed, but they felt like minutes. "You tried her cell?"

"She doesn't want to talk to me."

"I'll see what I can find out."

The easy question was out of the way, now it was time for the deal breaker. "Um, look, I have another favor—this one could be huge. There's this mother—she's got a little girl—they need a place to stay for a couple of days while Skip and I sort out a few things."

"What kinds of things?"

"She's the girlfriend of the guy who tried to kill Skip. The little girl is their daughter." I paused while I took a deep breath. What the hell, I thought. Tell her everything. "Worst case, there might be a drug dealer trying to kill them."

CHAPTER 48

S K I P

Inside the elevator, Skip pressed the button for the 17th floor, then immediately jabbed the "Close Door" button several times. He ignored the two men in suits who were approaching from across the lobby calling for him to hold the car. He heard the words "rude" and "asshole" as the doors came together.

Less than a minute later, he entered Welton Investments through the impeccably clean glass doors. Melinda was gone, but in her place was a stack of papers much like the ones he'd seen this morning. He read the note affixed to the top document. "ASAP. Oz says you know what to do with these. Late for my OBGYN. Wish me luck! Bets."

Skip rotated the stack in his direction. He pulled off the note, then flipped through the stack, quickly counting twenty or more sheets. All were titled, "Welton Investments - Buy/Sell Worksheet." The pattern became obvious almost immediately. Each form was for the purchase of one of a half dozen different securities. He'd taken pictures of a dozen of the orders when Melinda burst in from the hallway.

"What the hell do you think you're doing?" She strode across the room, scooped up the papers as though she could undo what had already been done. "These are confidential!"

"You're pretty young to be spending time in prison for securities fraud."

She shook her head. "I don't know what you're talking about—I'm just doing my job."

"Right," said Skip. "Destruction of evidence. Your boss, oh no—your fiancé—must be giving you a substantial bonus."

"Two people being in love isn't a crime. I'm calling security."

"Where was he last night?"

Melinda pulled her hand back from the receiver, her previously buried caution and self-doubt showing through. "He had—business. He's going to rip you to shreds when he hears about this."

Skip leaned forward on the desk. "Who do you think he's going to blame for destroying documents, Melinda? All that note says is that you know what to do. He'll just say you misunderstood him. By the way, last night he was with Frederica Gurney-Welton."

Melinda's lower lip trembled with the effort to fight back tears as she shook her head. "No. He said he was out of town. He had to rush back because of all this mess." She cocked her head at the side door. "In there, it's a madhouse. Jack hired a bunch of morons. Ozzie told me that."

"Remember what I said earlier about looking for a new job? You'd better start with a good attorney. When your boyfriend dumps you, you'll be the scapegoat for everything."

Her skin color turned ashen. She whispered, "I don't believe you. Ozzie wouldn't do that."

"I know, I know. He loves you and wants to marry you. Believe me, he loves money and power more." Skip extended his hand for the documents.

Melinda shook her head. "Ozzie would kill me."

"Ozzie will send you to jail for a very, very long time. Be smart, Melinda, save yourself. Don't get taken under because you didn't have a plan."

Melinda kept her bear hug on the stack of orders. "I know what I'm doing. Get out!"

Rubbing the back of his neck to erase the growing tension, Skip wondered if she really thought those orders would protect her.

"You're going to regret this. I'm sorry for what's going to happen to you." He left Melinda standing alone behind her desk, papers in her arms, chewing on her lower lip.

By the time he reached his car, Skip resolved to spend the rest of the day in L.A. He'd have to stay overnight, but this situation was ready to blow sky high. Staking out the Welton's home seemed like the logical next step. Before he did that, he had another stop to make.

CHAPTER 49

R O X Y

Shaina, the girls, and I were just climbing into the car when my cell bleeped with a text message. While everyone else got settled in, I read what Baldorf had sent me. "Watch your back. Something not right with her."

No shit. Thanks, Baldorf. I deleted the text as a precaution.

"What was that?" asked Shaina, her bitchiness still seeping through.

The two would probably never meet again, but Baldorf already had enough problems with Shaina and sharing his thoughts would only make things worse. "Marjorie confirming that she's ready for us. She's a real stickler for a clean house. Not my forte." I flipped on my blinker and pulled away. A block later, I caught a glimpse in the rearview mirror of Lily playing with Tina. Just two kids. Neither of them had done anything to warrant having their lives endangered. A lump filled my throat at the unfairness of it all. But, life was never fair. I looked away before Lily sensed my attention.

Next to me, Shaina sat in the passenger's seat fuming. Personally, her anger meant nothing. I was supposed to keep her safe despite her lack of street smarts, which could easily get in the way of that job. Amateurs. They did stupid things like use credit cards or call their relatives. She'd be dead in a day.

I pulled into traffic on the Coast Highway, wishing I could shove away the mental darkness that closed in around me. I couldn't help but steal another glance in the mirror—how closely Lily's life paralleled mine.

Without going completely off the grid or into an underworld where thieves ruled and nice guys finished dead, I was certain that the only person I could trust was Marjorie. I desperately wanted to call my parents with a strong suggestion that they take a trip, but one of the most basic rules of disappearing is no contact with loved ones. I'd practiced that rule with my business dealings my entire life and I'd still put my dad's life in jeopardy because I'd trusted one person. I suddenly felt more sympathetic toward Shaina's emotional state. No contact could be nothing less than a brutal policy.

Tina squealed with laughter as Lily tickled her. Shaina whirled in her seat. "Keep it down!" Her bark seemed to surprise even her. Maybe that's why she added, "You okay, baby?"

"They're fine," I said, wondering how long it would be before Lily tired of her new playmate. "Look," I added, "Fu Zhang won't know about Marjorie. She'll help, but you'll need to keep your temper under control. I know this isn't what you had planned, but we need to work together."

"It ain't that."

"Then what?"

She pondered something of major significance out the side window. After a moment, without looking at me, she said, "I missed my period."

I licked my lips, unable to come up with anything positive to say. Obviously, "congratulations" wasn't the word she was looking for. "Why tell me?" seemed too callous—so did a "who's the father" comment or a lecture on conjugal visits for inmates. Maybe it was time for a little gal-pal commiseration. "Well, that sucks."

For the first time since we'd met, Shaina almost laughed. "Yeah, it does."

We drove the rest of the way in silence with Shaina staring off into space while the girls played in the back seat and I calculated the odds of Joey Santino being the father of Shaina's next kid.

The off-street parking at Marjorie's apartment building was blocked by a moving van and unanticipated events like that leave me feeling exposed. Call paranoia an occupational hazard for me— it comes with the territory. The number of close friends I have had in my life can be counted on one hand without even bringing the opposable thumb into the calculations. Most people, even those from that dark underworld where honest folks shouldn't go, met me only once. Until Skip, my life's mantra had always been, never trust a soul.

After I'd parked, I said to Shaina, "Fog's lifting. Maybe that's a good sign."

"I hate the fog," she said. "I hate my fricking life."

Okay, so much for a good sign. Forget the gal-pal option, too. I opened my door. "Everyone out."

Lily helped Tina to the sidewalk and took her hand. I realized she'd done a magnificent job of winning over the younger girl. It doesn't take a con artist to know the best way to get to a parent is through their child.

I pointed in the direction of Marjorie's apartment. "It's that way."

Lily led the away. "Let's go, Squirt."

Shaina started to reach for her daughter; she stopped when Tina threw back her little shoulders and said, "I can do it, Mommy."

Tina puffed up her little chest, then skipped ahead to catch up with Lily.

I leaned over to Shaina and whispered, "Five going on fifteen." I'd hoped that my comment would relax her, instead she bristled more. I said, "Lily, stay close."

She gave me a thumbs up, a gesture that Tina mimicked a second later. The two girls chatted in a conversation peppered with "likes," "you knows," and other staples of kid-speak.

I gave Shaina my best reassuring smile. "We all did it, you know."

"Did what?" Her anger was back—or maybe it never left.

"Grew up."

Shaina looked me up and down, a smirk on her lips. "You must have grown up early. You're pretty young to have a teenager."

Ouch, talk about sharp claws. "Lily's twelve." I ignored the barb and spoke to the girls. "It's the apartment on your left."

Before I could knock, the door flew open. Marjorie's eyes widened at the sight of our little band. In seconds, I was forgotten while she gushed over the girls. Ignored, it was my turn to bristle. "Oh, you two are just adorable!" She gave each of them one of her squishy hugs. Lily rolled her eyes, while Tina welcomed the attention, melting into Marjorie's ample bosom. The contrast nearly gave me the giggles.

Marjorie introduced herself to Shaina. To my surprise, Shaina politely extended her hand. No bitchiness. No anger. Marjorie ignored the gesture, wrapping Shaina in another of her cream-puff hugs. I heard a little "oof," probably Shaina struggling to regain her composure. The group was herded into the apartment, leaving me standing on the doorstep.

When I didn't follow, Marjorie turned to face me, tears welling in her eyes. Just like the others, she took me in her arms. "You look like you need a hug, honey. C'mon in."

I slipped into her outstretched arms, whispering so only she could hear. "Thank you." My face burned with the emotions I tried to bury in the wool of her fluffy sweater. "I need help."

She held me at arms length, her eyes glistening. "Thank you for trusting me, honey. I can't tell you how much this means."

I stood, unable to think or move while she left me alone in the entry to her apartment. A moment later, she was back. "What's wrong?"

I wasn't sure. No one had ever thanked me for burdening them with my problems before. I followed her into her home, unable to fathom how someone could trust me enough to take me and three strangers in without even a question.

Marjorie, the consummate hostess, moved the girls to her dining table. "Shaina, would you like something? Some tea? What about the girls?"

It took only a moment for the shit to hit the fan. Shaina said, "Tina's mine. She shouldn't have anything other than a little milk. She's already filled up on cookies." Her eyes were cold.

I started to say something to head off what I knew was coming next, but was too late. Marjorie asked Shaina, "Lily's not your daughter?"

Shaina shook her head. "She's Roxy's."

Marjorie blinked. In my mind, I said a quick "ah shit."

Lily, bless her heart, tried to rescue me. She looked straight at me and said, "Mom? Can I, like, have a soda?"

Until that moment, I might have had a chance to rescue the situation. Now, I had three pairs of eyes fixed on me, with Tina being the only one who seemed indifferent to my situation.

Marjorie glanced at Lily, then me. "What the hell?"

"Marjorie, I can explain."

"You have a daughter? What were you? Ten?"

"Marjorie! Stop. Lily's not my daughter."

Lily's face fell. I think she realized she'd only made things worse.

I pulled her close to hug her and whispered in her ear. "Thanks for trying, sweetheart. You've got good instincts; you came so close to pulling it off." She hugged me back, but it was time to face the inquisition. "Marjorie, Shaina, let's go sit down. This is kind of a long story."

I condensed the past two days into a few minutes. When I finished, Marjorie beamed at me while she patted my hand, a small smile on her lips. What was that all about? I didn't have a clue.

"I get it," said Shaina. "I'm sorry I was so bitchy before. I didn't know if you was on the level or not. This maybe being—damn that man."

Somehow, she couldn't bring herself to say the word, so I interjected for her. "Shaina thinks she might be pregnant."

Marjorie peered at Shaina with one raised eyebrow. "You haven't told anyone?"

Shaina shook her head. "I ain't even sure yet."

"We need to keep you safe while Skip, Baldorf, and I find out what's up with Joey. We still don't know if we can trust him or if he's being held captive or is on the run. He did try to kill Skip—twice."

"The guy put him in jail. If it wasn't for your boyfriend, Joey and me might have had a chance."

"Shaina? Really? What would you and Joey have done? Reconciled? Raised a passel of kids in the burbs while he robbed convenience stores at night?"

"He was drunk!" she blurted. Her brow furrowed by thoughts off in that place they go when difficult problems face us. Was she thinking about Joey? Or how to get away?

Marjorie started to say something, but I shook my head. We both waited for Shaina to reach a decision. At last, she said, "Whatever Joey's done, he ain't never hurt a kid. Anybody's kid. He had it rough when he was growing up and he took an oath with God that he'd never hurt a kid no matter what. That's what he swore to me! I believe him, which is more than I can say about you."

Before I could respond, Marjorie jumped in. "Shaina, by the time this thing is over, you'll see Roxy for what she really is, your best friend right now." She turned her attention to me just as the girls walked into the room. "Honey, do you need me to take care of Lily for a while?"

Shaina avoided my gaze by watching Tina. "Hey, baby girl. You doing okay?"

I could feel, but not see Lily behind me.

Tina stood close to Shaina. "Mommy, can Lily, like, stay with us? She ain't got no place and Roxy's gonna kick her out."

Is that what Lily really thought? I wanted to run to her and explain, but Marjorie's strong grip on my arm stopped me. "I'm okay," I said. But, I wasn't. Lily was gone.

Marjorie nodded toward the hallway. "Check the bathroom."

An image of the first time I'd met Lily, her breaking and entering through a window, flashed into my mind. No, not the bath, I thought, a bedroom. I found her in the first one on the left, but was shocked to see her sitting on the edge of the bed. She had her elbows on her knees, her face buried in her hands. When I approached, she looked straight at me. "I, like, never should'a trusted her. She so blew it."

"You put her up to that."

"Kinda. She, like—whatever."

"She went off the script?"

Lily nodded. "So, like, when you gonna take me back to—them?"

The art of the con prepares you for almost anything—except honesty. "Is that what you want?" My voice cracked. "In your heart, Lily, tell me what you'd have me do."

CHAPTER 50

S K I P

Skip found Jack Welton's condo complex without difficulty despite the growing rush-hour traffic. A doorman greeted him just inside the entrance. It was a tactic Skip recognized, one designed to serve two functions—welcome residents and friends while keeping out intruders. He went on the offensive with a question almost guaranteed to get him an affirmative answer. "Good afternoon, is there a manager for the building?"

"Indeed, sir, Mrs. Montgomery."

One "yes" down, time for another, he thought. "I wonder if it would be possible for me to see her, I have some urgent business that concerns one of the tenants."

The doorman wore a crisply pressed gray jacket, white shirt and hat. His tone was cordial, professional, yet sly like the fox he resembled. He said, "Certainly, sir. May I give Mrs. Montgomery your name and business?"

"Skip Cosgrove. I'm here about Jack Welton."

The man's hazel eyes narrowed; he reached for the telephone. "Very good, sir."

Skip stepped away from the station to wander around the lobby while the other man spoke on the phone. With each turn of his "aimless" wandering, he scanned another section of the lobby for cameras—there were two. He approached the doorman again. "I'll bet no one gets in here without getting a pass or going through you. Am I correct?"

"Yes, sir. Our security is excellent. Why do you ask?"

"Well, with the recent suicide of Mr. Welton, I just wondered."

"Terrible situation, that. Terrible."

"Is this station manned all the time?"

"Oh, no, sir. The station is manned each weeknight until ten o'clock. On weekends there is a man on duty until 1:00 a.m. After that, the doors are locked. Entrance is limited to those with a pass— or by calling Mrs. Montgomery. That is a step which I would not advise unless the situation were, shall we say, dire."

"That night, was there a call?" Skip mirrored the doorman's posture.

The man's brow creased as he thought for a moment. He licked the tip of his finger, then purposefully flicked back the top sheet on his clipboard.

"Looks like a log," said Skip.

"Indeed, sir. It's a record of the phone calls we receive here at the front. I check each morning to see how busy it was the previous night. One must ensure that they are not, dare I say, slacking on the night shift. I am the shift supervisor. I do take my position quite seriously. It was quite odd when I read the log on the morning after Mr. Welton met his demise." He ran his finger down the entries, stopping midway on the page. "Here it is. Mrs. Welton called."

Skip strained, unsuccessfully, to read the log upside down. Behind him, he heard the ping of the elevator bell. Quickly, he asked, "Why's that unusual?"

The doorman dropped the top sheet back into place when a heavyset woman in a blue suit approached. "Here's Mrs. Montgomery now, sir. Perhaps she'll be able to shed some light on that." He smiled at Mrs. Montgomery.

Mrs. Montgomery's suit was a conservative cut with a hemline a full two inches below the knee. A white blouse with a frilly, but high, collar, offset the sky blue jacket. She crossed the lobby, all the time eyeing Skip suspiciously. "Henson said you had questions about Mr. Welton."

Skip wondered why her greeting was so cold—no handshake, no openness. Like Henson, Mrs. Montgomery also had a British accent. Her erect posture was, if possible, even more rigid than Henson's. Skip surmised that this had been, or was still, a woman of means.

"I've already spoken to the police and told them everything I know." The woman folded her arms across her chest.

The words "family friend" popped into Skip's mind. Maybe this was a misunderstanding? Did Mrs. Montgomery want to protect Frederica? He smiled, "I'm here on behalf of Mrs. Welton—Freddie."

The manager raised an eyebrow. "Ah, poor woman. Losing her husband like that. Has she changed her mind?"

Skip tilted his head from side to side and shrugged. He feigned a mild reluctance to reveal too much detail to mask the fact that he had no idea what they'd discussed. "She may be reconsidering." He smiled at the doorman and Mrs. Montgomery in succession.

The sly old fox guarding the front door nodded approvingly, as did Mrs. Montgomery. Her stiff veneer melted as she gloated at Henson. "I told you she'd come around."

"Indeed, madam. So you did."

Mrs. Montgomery took Skip's arm. "Why don't you come upstairs? I'll make some tea." She guided Skip across the lobby, their footsteps in sync on the polished floor. "Freddie and I have gotten close over the past few months. It would be dreadful to see her sell the unit in this market."

They walked away from the doorman's station, Skip well aware of the greeter's watchful eye. When he looked in that direction, the doorman gave him a deferential nod and a wink.

Skip waited until after the manager had pressed the button for the third floor. "Mrs. Montgomery," he said, "I think you're going to be a lifesaver."

CHAPTER 51

R O X Y

My heart thumped in my chest as I waited for Lily to answer my question. She showed the classic signs of someone having been pushed too far—swallowing hard, watery eyes, drawing herself into a tight ball with her knees to her chest and her arms wrapped around her legs. She searched the carpet for solutions instead of my face, which scared the hell out of me. What if she said yes? Would it be worse if she said no? I was the last person on earth who should be interfering in this girl's life. I had no job. No scruples.

I put my arm around her and felt her lean into me. Her thin body shook almost imperceptibly, her breathing came in halting bursts. My vision blurred—I should let this kid go. Get her away from my bad influence, but then I was kneeling before her, desperate for a sign of hope. "Do you want to stay with me?"

She shrugged. "It ain't my decision."

"The hell it's not!" I blurted. Anger, frustration and fear all surged through me. I put my hand under her chin, lifting gently until her gaze locked with mine. "Don't you ever let anyone tell you that you don't have a say in your life! You always have a choice."

Her lower lip trembled until I thought she might explode from her pent-up emotion. When she threw her arms around me, I tightened our embrace, holding her while she cried into my shirt. When her shuddering lessened, she said, "I wanna stay."

I swallowed hard. "You and me, sweetheart. We'll find a way out of this mess. Together."

Those arms around my neck just drew me in. The tighter she held on, the stronger my determination. I knew nothing about what I was getting into other than I would protect Lily—from her own mother, if necessary. A gentle knock on the door jarred me back to reality. Was I serious about what I'd just promised? How could I protect her if I went to jail for what I'd done in L.A.?

The door opened just enough for Marjorie to poke her head in and stare at us. "Are you two okay?" Her voice was tentative.

We sat on the floor, our backs to the bed. "Never better." I sniffled, then took a deep breath. Lily's hand found mine. I returned her gentle pressure. "We've got a plan."

"We do?" Lily blinked.

I laughed between the tears. "We have to fill in a few of the blank spots, but we know where we're headed, right sweetheart?"

Lily leaned her head against my shoulder. "Yeah, we've like, got a plan."

Marjorie beamed at me from the doorway. "Anything you need from me?"

"Could you take Lily out to the living room. I have a phone call I need to make."

Lily jerked away, gaping at me. I reached up and stroked her brow. "It's okay. There's nothing to worry about. It's you and me, but this call is totally on me."

"For real?"

I kissed her on the forehead and stood, raising my right hand like a good Girl Scout. "For real, scout's honor, whatever you want. This is just one of those fill-in-the-blank places where I have to do something and you have to trust me."

Momentary panic seemed to wash over her, but Lily recovered a few seconds later. "I . . . trust . . . you."

My eyes stung; the pressure behind them, intense. Nobody, including Skip, had ever said those words to me before. With good reason, I thought. I'd never even trusted myself.

When the door closed, I plopped down onto the bed. There were four little bars on my phone's display. Good signal strength; I was alone. I started the browser on my phone. It took less than a minute to get to the bank's website, log in to the account I'd set up for Anita, and check the balance. Holy crap. Two point five million and change. Why hadn't I thought to change the password before? Why hadn't Anita?

"Sorry guys," I said. "I'm not in the mood to share."

Amateur hour was over. It was time for me to take control of my life.

CHAPTER 52

S K I P

Mrs. Montgomery's condo reminded Skip of a private art gallery. On a wall opposite the entryway hung a modern oil painting consisting of bold strokes in blue, red, and jet black. Skip had seen a similar painting, but a much larger version, at Frederica's. He stopped to examine the piece. The name wasn't familiar—and art was not his area of expertise—but he recognized the style.

"Beautiful painting. Very bold."

"I'm usually more interested in the Old Masters, but this one was a gift—a very generous one I might add—from a friend. It's an original by a young up-and-coming local artist."

"I've seen one similar to this recently . . ." He rubbed his face and neck, pretending to search for a memory while he kept an eye on his host. Mrs. Montgomery took his arm to lead him into the condo. "I'm sure you'll think of it," she declared in a remarkably cheery tone. She pointed at a painting on the wall behind the sofa. "My late husband and I bought the Matisse when he was stationed in London." She nodded at another painting, beaming. "The little Renoir was handed down from my father."

"Quite the collection." Skip surveyed the room. He counted another half dozen oils on the walls. "You've been very fortunate."

She gazed around the room, smiling wistfully. "Mr. Montgomery did quite well in business after he left the State Department. He left a rather sizable estate when he passed, with which I have been able to do good things for the less fortunate—in addition to living comfortably, of course."

"Of course," said Skip. Was that how she'd met Frederica? Through charity work? "Mrs. Montgomery, can I share a little secret with you?" The woman's eyes widened and Skip could see she was hooked. It was a universal truth that no matter how pretentious or rich people were, everyone loved good gossip.

"Why not?" she gestured toward a glass-topped dining table. "Do sit. Tea?"

"I would love some." He wondered how well he could pull off the old fortune teller's trick as he tossed out the first morsel. "This is actually somewhat embarrassing . . ."

The woman crossed the room to a hutch, pulled out a fine bone china setting for two and carefully placed the cups and saucers on the table. Her eyes sparkled with anticipation. "Go on."

"You run in some exclusive social circles, I gather?"

Mrs. Montgomery straightened up, which made Skip wonder if he'd gotten too personal. These Brits and their social mores, he thought. Instead of rebuking him, Mrs. Montgomery went to the stove to heat water in a kettle. She turned back to Skip. "I had an in-home filtering system installed. It makes this atrocious-tasting water far easier to tolerate. The best water Mr. Montgomery and I ever had was—I'm avoiding your question, aren't I?" She cleared her throat. "Well, you are correct, Mr. Cosgrove, this is somewhat embarrassing because, like our dear friend Freddie, I try to work, as you Americans call it, 'behind the scenes.' Why do you ask?"

"I knew we'd have something in common! I, too, am embarrassed. The reason is that Freddie didn't share with me what she wanted to do, only that she was reconsidering and wanted to request your forbearance for a few more days. I volunteered to talk to you because she felt that she may have been a bit . . ."

"Abrupt?"

"Indeed, abrupt, the last time you two spoke."

Mrs. Montgomery poured water from the kettle into a tea pot that matched the delicate cups. "I love this pattern, the gold filigree, the dusty-rose colored petals—such elegance. How do you like your tea?" She placed a metal ball into the pot, then replaced the lid. "Dear Lord, the woman had every right to be abrupt after her husband died that way." She sighed. "I have only known her for a short time—we met at a fundraiser for the arts last Spring, you know—and she has always been friendly."

"I'm not a great tea connoisseur, so however you take yours is fine." He nodded toward the front door. "She's the one who gave you that painting?"

Mrs. Montgomery flushed again. "Well, obviously you have seen the other piece she has from this artist. There is a third, you know. She commissioned three oils from this young man shortly after we met. She kept one for home, gave one to her husband for his office and gave the third to me. I was shocked to learn that her despicable husband had the gall to bring his piece to the condominium, where it still hangs. She was going to send her husband a message by destroying the one in the unit when she learned what her husband was doing in there, but I convinced her she should use it as a reminder of his infidelity. I advised her of what actions would be appropriate."

"What actions were those?"

"To rid herself of that man," she snapped, but immediately turned friendly again. "Of course, I meant divorce. I was not advocating murder."

"Surely you don't think she killed her husband?"

She ran her finger around the rim of her teacup several times, her expression thoughtful. "I hope not Mr. Cosgrove. Freddie is normally a very kind person."

"Unless she's angered?"

"She does have a temper." Mrs. Montgomery took a sip from her cup, all the while holding Skip's gaze. "That, she does."

Skip wondered if the cops knew Frederica had a temper. He also wanted to know why she really gave Mrs. Montgomery the artwork. Was it payment? Was Mrs. Montgomery lying to him? One thing was for sure, Frederica Gurney-Welton had the money to ensure she never saw the inside of a jail cell unless she suffered a meltdown around the cops.

Unfortunately for Frederica, it appeared that Mrs. Montgomery might be in a talking mood. Skip said, "Mrs. Montgomery, were you reporting back to Freddie about her husband?"

She closed her eyes and took a deep breath. "Indeed, I did. Given what has happened, I wish I hadn't."

CHAPTER 53

R O X Y

By 3 p.m., we were all showing signs of cabin fever. Five people in a small apartment got old very fast. For some reason, Shaina seemed to still be in love with Joey despite everything he'd done. Lily tried to be a help, but the more she interacted with Tina, the more Shaina resented her. What? She was afraid Lily would corrupt her perfect child? Turn her into a hip-hopping teenager through a version of kid osmosis? Whatever her reasons, Shaina's focus on her daughter gave me exactly the opening I needed to corner Marjorie about where Skip might find Anita.

Marjorie and I sat at the dining room table chit chatting. We each had a cup of the sludge she calls coffee. Personally, I think I'd do better with tequila shots than shots of Marjorie's coffee—I'd also prefer the tequila buzz over the acid churning in my stomach. The good news was that I had time to maneuver the conversation around to the subject of Anita. "So do you know where she might have gone? How I could reach her?"

She blinked several times, as though doing some sort of mental search through an imaginary filing cabinet or address book. After a few seconds of card flipping, or whatever she was doing, she looked me in the eye. "Roxy, do you think I failed Anita in some way?"

The sorrow on her face touched me deeply. Had I hurt my parents that much? I reached out to caress her hand. "I doubt that you failed her for one second. Whatever she's done, whatever she's become, it was her choice, not yours." It was the same thing I'd told my parents just a couple of months ago. They, just like Marjorie, hadn't believed me either.

"Thanks, honey, I'm one of those nurture, not nature, people. I raised her, so I feel responsible."

Call it a desire to spare her, or just a way to avoid my own reality, but there was no way I could reveal to Marjorie all the things I'd done or the mistakes I'd made. Without going into the details of my life, I had to try and ease Marjorie's burden. "Marjorie, greed makes people do really awful things. I don't think you raised Anita to be greedy." I stroked the back of her hand. "Who knows why she got involved with Welton? Why does any woman have an affair with a married man?"

Marjorie shrugged, but didn't turn away.

"Look, they don't start out wanting to break up a marriage. I guess they just don't see the long-term repercussions. In Anita's case, she truly felt wronged and wanted revenge on Jack for what she perceived to be lies—his lies. Were they? I don't know. What I do know is that your niece made her choices based on a broken heart, not broken values. You didn't do this, she did. Do you think you can help me find her?"

She nodded absently as she rattled off a phone number.

"What? Wait, write that down!"

"It's Dom's clinic. I called her cell, but she wouldn't tell me where she'd gone. I heard dogs barking in the background. The thing is, she went to the clinic at least once a week despite all her complaints about the smell and the noise from the caged animals. I think she really liked being around them. If she's trying to hide out, she's probably there."

CHAPTER **54**

S K I P

"Hey." There was a breezy quality to Roxy's voice—one that might throw a stranger off but raised Skip's suspicions about her hiding something.

He took a cautious breath, then did his best to counter her. "What's up, Hot Rox?"

After a short pause her tone turned serious. "Why don't we just level with each other? The trouble with this relationship is that neither of us can hide anything from the other. We're playing that stupid 'I know that you know that I know game' again—and it really sucks. I'm tired of lying, Skip."

Was she? Or was she setting him up for something else? "Let's give it a try," he said. "I just finished talking to the manager at Welton's condo and learned a few things. Your turn."

She laughed. "Baby steps? Are you kidding me? Fine. Marjorie gave me an address where you can find Anita. Back to you."

"Point taken," he said sheepishly. "That was childish on my part. Here's the deal. Freddie Welton knew about Jack's condo. The manager was keeping her in the loop. She probably knew about every woman who was ever in that place. That could include you. One positive development is that Freddie has moved to the top of my suspect list. I'm on my way to her place for a little surveillance. I can give you the deets later."

"The deets? Serious? You and Freddie are BFF's already? A day in la-la land does not a slang talker make. I like your style the way it is. Don't go making a lot of drastic changes. Okay?"

"Don't worry, nothing's changed."

There was silence on the line, then Roxy said, "We'd best stick to business. You're saying the wife knew and she never let on? Awesome. Have you got time to check on Anita? She may be at Dom's. I can text you the address."

"Something tells me I need to stay on Mrs. Welton for a while, but later tonight I can swing by Dom's. Wait, is that the clinic?"

"Yeah, Anita liked to spend time there."

"Baldorf told me Dom shut it down for a few days."

"According to Marjorie, he lives there, too."

"Even better, things are scarier when they go bump in the night instead of broad daylight."

"This bump is going to be very scary. When you see her, give her a message. Tell her that if she wants to see her money, she has to come to Auntie Em's."

"That's it? That's the message?"

"As Baldorf would say, roger that."

One thing he didn't want to do was to sound critical, so he kept his tone light. "So you have it? How much?"

"Two point five million. I'm the gatekeeper. I don't know who deserves that money, but until we figure out who killed Welton, no one gets it."

Skip stared absently at the dashboard clock wondering why she'd told him about this. Was she intending to return that much money or was this just a ploy to bring Anita in? He almost jumped when he heard her voice in his ear.

"Hey, you still there?"

"Sorry, guess I'm in shock that you told me. Thanks for giving me your trust. Okay, I'm in. I'll give her the message. What else do you need?"

"Are you sure you should be up there? It's a dangerous game you're playing."

"Only if I get sloppy," said Skip. "Besides, you can't be mucking around in L.A. without implicating yourself."

"What do you need me to do?"

"Get us a start on Joey's situation. Do what Baldorf normally does. You know, research things from your end. See if you can come up with something that ties Fu Zhang and Joey together. That way, when I get back in a day or so we can jump right on it."

"Have you talked to him? Baldorf, I mean."

"It was pretty one-sided. I'd just figured out what was going on at Welton Investments."

"No rush, but call him tonight. I think he needs some guy time."

"I'll do it, but I can't be worried about you while I'm a hundred miles away. It's too delicate of a situation and if I mess this up, it'll make things worse. So let's get your problems fixed first." When he heard no resistance, Skip continued. "Then we can worry about Joey, Shaina, Tina . . ." With his voice soft, he added, "When this is over, I want to go away. Just the two of us. Somewhere private."

There was another long pause. When she spoke he almost didn't recognize her voice. "I promised Lily she could stay with me. I won't go back on my word. That girl has been through so much."

Skip swallowed hard—she was changing. "Wow, so this is what grown up Roxy sounds like."

"Marjorie says I'm maturing." She snickered. "I never thought of myself as a late bloomer before."

"I think she's right. We'll work through it."

"Thanks. Skip, I . . ."

Someday, hopefully, she'd be able to say those three little words. "I know, me too."

When the call was done, Skip tossed the phone onto the passenger's seat and leaned back to clear his head. The reality was, with Roxy, nothing was clearcut. He said, "Goddamn I love her. I just wish I could trust her."

CHAPTER 55

R O X Y

At best, all I'd done with Skip was buy a little time. Sooner or later, I'd have to either give up the money or break everyone's heart—mine included. That wasn't a decision I was prepared to make right now. If anything, I wasn't even prepared to think about how I might make that kind of choice. Not now, maybe never.

When I returned to the living room, Lily approached with a pad of paper in her hand. It was the one Marjorie had given her earlier to keep her entertained. Lily wasn't exactly the artsy type in my opinion. I doubted that she'd ever had an art class, so I resolved to be supportive—no matter how bad her drawing skills might be. "Hey, sweetheart, what've you got there?"

Lily showed me the top sheet. "You, like, wanted to know about the morons that sell drugs, right?"

I was having a hard time focusing on her words because of the detailed sketch. The man had long, scraggly hair with a scruffy beard. Deep lines on his face gave him a weathered appearance that said he'd seen many hard days. I stammered, "You—you drew that?"

Lily rolled her eyes. "Duh. Like, yeah, it's Maniac. You don't recognize him?"

"I do, it's just, well, I was shocked because you're such an amazing artist. I had no idea."

Marjorie inspected the drawing. "That's fantastic. Look at the eyes. You can—you can see they're just, well, vacant."

"Sweetheart, you are an amazing artist."

"Whatever." Lily shrugged. "Do you wanna, like, know about this guy or not?"

This kid belonged in a school for art prodigies. Her talent was better than some of the artists who displayed at the street fair twice a year. Hell, it was better than some of the work in the local galleries. "What about him?"

"He, like, knows everything about the streets."

"Really. Everything? Why didn't we just ask him while we were at lunch?"

She rolled her eyes. "Seriously? You didn't even, like, know these guys had two places."

"You're right. He knows a lot?"

"He's awesome. He's got, like, all this random knowledge in his head. You just gotta catch him when he's straight."

"Got it," I said. "Marjorie, we need to get going. We've got to find this Maniac guy before he gets too wasted."

We made a quick exit. I felt guilty leaving Marjorie alone with Shaina and Tina, but nothing else could be done. Skip had asked me to do research, just not this kind. Next time he might be more specific—not that it would matter. It took us thirty minutes to get to Oceanside, only a few more minutes to find Maniac. He was a creature of habit—habits Lily knew almost to the minute. We were close enough to hear him talking to himself when Lily said, "Just, like, be cool. I got this. Hang back."

Great, my life was in the hands of a twelve-year-old.

The guy from the fast food joint sat on a bus bench in front of his favorite liquor store. I felt as though the sketch were coming to life before me. His lifeless eyes watched some unseen event off in space. Even though the day was warm, he wore a jacket and shivered as he hugged himself. I wondered if the drugs had completely destroyed his circulation. How did he live this way?

Lily slouched into a nonthreatening posture with her hands buried in her pockets. "Hey, George."

The guy she called Maniac barely reacted. Behind those dull eyes there had once been a human being. Now, this creature lived only for his next fix. Even though there was a spark of recognition when he peered at her, it seemed fleeting.

"This is a friend of mine. Her name's Roxy."

"Hey, George." I extended my hand.

He watched me, looked down at my hand for only a moment. No recognition. Nothing.

Lily motioned at the bench. "Can I, like, sit? Got a question."

George shifted position on the bench, he blinked a few times, apparently trying to focus on Lily. "Free country, Squirt."

The response was more than I'd expected. It led me to believe there might even be a person inside that shell. I also recognized the nickname Lily had used on Tina.

Lily plopped down on the bench, seemingly unbothered by George's odor, a cross between unwashed skin, accumulated urine, and vomit. I was happy to hang back a short distance as Lily had suggested. It put the bench between us, but George was in no condition to make any sudden moves. "You, like, know the name of the head dealer here?"

It took a moment for George to process the question. When he did, he shook his head. "You don't wanna get messed up with that shit, Squirt." He turned on me, his anger sending a chill through my spine. "She puttin' you up to this?"

"Dude? Seriously? You, like, know me. I don't do that shit. You always told me you, like, wanted to get some payback."

George's cheeks twitched, but otherwise, he didn't move—with the exception of wiping his nose on his sleeve while he watched her face. "You shittin' me, Squirt? I always liked you. You on the level?"

"I ain't lyin'." Lily extended her fist. "She's cool. She can, like, make it happen."

George exchanged fist bumps with Lily. He straightened his posture, but Lily appeared not to notice the exchange was draining her friend.

"Mexicans running it now. Word is some Asians want to take over."

"I thought Fu Zhang ran it all," I said.

George pointed his thumb north. "Nah, him and Jackie was second in command for Boss Guito, then the shit hit the fan when someone took out Boss. Fu Zhang's gang is stronger a couple of blocks that way now. But they're losing ground to the Mexicans over there." He jerked his thumb in the opposite direction. "Gonna be a goddamn war between them."

"Who's in charge?" I asked.

A shiver ran through George; he seemed not to notice my question. "I ain't got no way out, Squirt. Don't be doin' this for me. I ain't worth savin' no more." He leaned away, his hand on the back of the bench for support. The strain on his face gave him away—he wanted to leave, but didn't have the energy.

Lily grabbed his arm. "George! C'mon, like, don't give up. Who is this moron?"

He slumped down into the bench. Air, heavy with the effort to even breathe, escaped his lungs. "Ain't got nothin' left." His left cheek twitched a couple of times; his face and eyes went blank. A moment later, he returned from wherever he'd been during that short mental lapse. "Jacinto Fontanal. His friends call him Jackie."

George peered past Lily at the line of cars accelerating from the stop light a block away. A dark blue Chevy pickup that had been the lead car in the left lane roared away from the light, then switched lanes abruptly. George glared at me, a sudden fire in his eyes. "You bitch! Goddamn bitch! You're with them!" He lunged at me, but the back of the bench caught him waist high. He tumbled forward over the obstacle with his legs flailing in the air in a desperate attempt to gain traction.

I had no idea why, but suspected the blue pickup spelled danger. "Lily! We have to go. Something's wrong."

Lily scrambled around the bench to kneel next to Maniac. She shook him, but he didn't respond. "George!"

I pulled her away by the arm, but she jerked free and rushed back to her friend. The blue pickup skidded to a stop around the corner.

The driver, a wiry guy, was already out of the truck, glaring at all of us. A snake tattoo twisted down the length of his left arm. The fangs of the snake's mouth had been tattooed onto his fingers, which were clamped around the butt of a gun.

I tried to grab Lily again, but she drove me away with a wild swing. "We have to go!" I yelled.

"No! I ain't leaving him."

The driver stopped a few feet away, no longer brandishing the gun like a club. He kept it aimed squarely at me as he reached for Lily, but she lashed out, fists and arms flailing at him and empty air. My heart nearly seized when he raised the gun high in the air to pistol whip Lily.

I leapt at him, seized his wrist, and twisted. The move caught him off guard, driving his arm down and his body with it. His back slammed hard into the concrete. I smashed the wrist of his gun hand with my foot. He howled in anger as the gun clattered to the sidewalk, then reached for my ankle with his free hand.

An uncontrollable rage surged through me. I dropped. Square onto his chest. Knee into solar plexus. The impact drove out his last bit of fight. He doubled up and rolled to his side, spewing vomit onto the sidewalk. I kicked the gun away. It skidded into the street, then tumbled down the storm drain. The guy struggled to his knees with one hand planted on the concrete.

I landed a kick on the side of his head. For a second, I thought I broke his neck. He went down, his blood splattering the sidewalk. "You're done!" A red trickle from his jaw formed a growing puddle on the sidewalk.

Lily's voice cracked. "Is he—like—dead?"

George sat on the sidewalk. He, too, seemed uncertain of what to say or do.

Through the hammering in my chest, I heard a voice that sounded much like mine. I took a couple of deep breaths. "He'll live. But, we might be dead if he has any friends around here. Sirens are approaching. We've got to go."

"What about George?"

George gave Lily a weak wave. "It's okay, Squirt. Cops'll take care of me."

I pointed at the street. "Tell them the gun is in the storm drain."

He nodded. Would he remember? I wasn't sure.

The sirens drew closer. "Lily, we've got to move."

George raised a weak hand and one finger. "Lady, whoever you are, get outta here. That was one of Jackie's muscle."

"Do you know anything else?"

He shook his head. "Not me, but the man who knows everything is Buzz. She knows him." He nodded at Lily.

Oceanside PD squad cars were three blocks away. I shook Lily, but she still looked dazed. "We have go. Now!"

She started to run, but I reeled her in with a firm arm around her shoulders. "Walk, don't run. Otherwise, you look guilty."

CHAPTER 56

S K I P

Skip parked two blocks away from Frederica's house. He watched the house, patiently waiting for Edward Oz to show. When Oz wasn't there by 4:30 p.m., Skip began wondering if his hunch had been wrong. He was about to give up when a Mercedes with the license plate MNY MGR drove past. The car parked midway up the next block.

The Mercedes had gone by too quickly to get a look at the driver, but the MNY MGR license plate made perfect sense to Skip—if the car belonged to Oz. There was only one way to be sure, get a closer look. Skip walked to where the car had parked. The black E-550 coupe had a panorama roof. Bells and whistles galore. Lots of bucks. Skip barely slowed his pace until he reached the next corner, where he saw an alleyway midway down the side street. He walked to the alley, turned right, and realized what was missing from the front of the homes—driveways. Judging by the line of cars he'd passed on his walk, all visitors, including a number of the residents, parked along the main street. Here, however, "No Parking" signs confined the cars to the opposite side of the street.

Skip surveyed the area in search of security cameras. There were none. The small white sign with red lettering indicating the alley was to be kept clear on Thursdays made him laugh. Who were these people kidding? There was nothing here to disturb the "perfect neighborhood" image. No trash, no BarcaLoungers—not even an old toaster set out for scavengers. He backtracked along the alley toward the Welton's house, walking by garages and stuccoed back walls with iron gates. He didn't know whether the Welton place was the third or fourth from the corner. "Damn," he said.

At the iron gate of the third home, he snuck a peek. Not it. He'd never seen this backyard before. Gurgling noises from a nearby yard caught his attention. He remembered the fountain he'd seen through the glass slider on his previous visit. He knew if he got a look, he'd recognize the yard, so he peeked through the next gate. It was the same fountain and hot tub he'd seen earlier. This time, Frederica sat in the hot tub, her arms spread to her sides, a glass of wine in one hand. "Come on, Ozzie, stop being a stick in the mud."

Oz wore a perfectly tailored suit and tie, but despite his impeccable appearance, his face was tinged with impatience. "Freddie, we have to lay low for a while."

"I know, but now that Jack's gone, I can't wait. The only good thing Jack ever did for me was hang himself. Now we can be together. Take off that damn suit and get in here."

"Not yet, the cops might be watching. Besides, we shouldn't be having this conversation out here in the open."

Frederica stood to face Oz. Slowly, she untied the black string bikini top, then dropped it into the water. "I know you want it, come on in."

"Freddie, are you nuts? What about the neighbors? We can't be so goddamn blatant."

"Relax, they're all gone. Both sides are on vacation. Why are you so uptight, anyway? You've never minded afternoons before. Here in the tub might be fun. I'll even do that thing you like so much."

Even at this distance, Skip could see Oz wavering. Frederica took a step out of the hot tub. Water streamed off her skin. With her next step, water pooled at Oz's feet. He rubbed the back of his neck and shook his head. "No. Baby, look, I've gotta go. I got a meeting and we need to keep this cool for a little longer."

Frederica reached for Oz. She was either not aware or didn't care about the water splattering Oz's shiny wingtips. He tried to sidestep the drops, but was too late. He kissed her hard on the lips while she fumbled with his belt buckle. Seconds later, he pushed her away and left without a word.

"Bastard!" Frederica snatched up her towel before she stormed into the house.

Skip wanted to know what meeting could drag Oz away from his lover. He ran back to the car and was almost there when he saw the Mercedes about a block away. He paused on the far side of a giant King palm to let Oz drive past. The Mercedes had a three-block lead before Skip could follow. He tucked in about a block behind Oz and followed for about 20 minutes. At the outskirts of Century City, Oz turned into a residential neighborhood. The car pulled to a stop in front of a plain single-story home on a street dotted with a hodgepodge of architectural styles ranging from Victorian to Craftsman to 50's cheap to adobe.

The parking spot Skip found a few doors down gave him a perfect view of the house. It was traditional Craftsman construction with perfectly trimmed, sedate blue paint and white accents. The house reminded him of a distinguished gentleman decked out in his finest tux for a grand ball. The landscaping included a small patch of grass accented by a flower bed filled with lavender, pink, and flaming red. The porch spoke of days gone by in a generation where neighbors were friends who knew each others hopes and dreams and sorrows rather than just their street addresses.

Oz climbed the steps with the familiarity of someone who had been here numerous times. A woman met him at the screen door. Though their bodies were shadows through the screen material, their embrace was clearly that of a maturing, yet still blossoming, relationship—one step past the passion of newfound lovers, a few steps shy of the familiarity gained in a long-time marriage.

Skip pulled out his cell phone to use the camera. The figures would be too small to discern, but maybe Baldorf could work some magic. The woman went back inside with Oz right behind. Skip muttered, "How the hell many women are you screwing, Oz?"

CHAPTER 57

ROXY

Lily and I stood amidst a gaggle of spectators watching the spectacle from a block away. Rubberneckers on the road snarled traffic into a line of impatient commuters. An EMT van was trapped in the middle of the pack. The nearest cop cars blasted out short siren bursts, but that only intensified the confusion. Between blaring horns, the accident potential on the Coast Highway, and two guys sprawled out on the sidewalk, the cops had their hands full. One of the first responders scanned the area for witnesses, but no one came forward.

Lily started to turn away, but I held her firmly at my side. When the cop looked directly at us, I spoke quietly. "Don't move. Just . . . watch."

Our cue to leave came when the EMTs finally maneuvered up to the curb and the cop turned to watch them, not us.

We strolled in the opposite direction and were almost to the car when Lily asked, "Will George be okay?"

"He should be fine. The EMTs will get him medical attention. The other guy's probably on his way to jail for the night."

"If he ain't, like, a cripple now." Her face lit up as she gave some imaginary enemy a kick that might have bruised a kneecap but little else.

"Be cool, we don't want to call attention to ourselves."

Lily's grin conveyed the innocent passion of a child. "That was, like, totally awesome."

Now that my heart wasn't beating in double time I was starting to think about the consequences of taking out a drug dealer's muscle. I faked a smile for Lily. "Totally," I said, hiding my bigger concern, which was why had the dealer's guy been after George—or us—at all? Which gang was he working for? "Look, George should get a night in a warm bed, but he'll be back on the streets tomorrow. I need to find this Jackie. How come you called him Maniac anyway?"

"It's, like, his street name. Me and him been tight a few weeks— ever since I, like, helped him out."

"Friends call him by his real name, everyone else uses the street name?"

"Kinda," she shrugged. A moment later, anger tinged her voice. "What're we doin' about Buzz?"

"I need to get you to Marjorie's. I'll come back tonight."

"Nuh-uh. You don't know him!"

"Lily, this isn't a safe place for a kid to be. Especially at night."

"Duh! Where you think I been sleeping? I'm here, like, all the time. It's my territory. You're the one who ain't, like, safe. We gotta find out, like, why that moron was after George."

"Maybe he wasn't." I could have kicked myself for voicing my fears out loud when I saw Lily's reaction. I'd freaked her out, and that had not been my intention at all. To make matters worse, Lily was right. The world she knew—bars, drugs, prostitution—was foreign to me. The drunks didn't care about anything but booze, the addicts only had money for their next fix, and I had no stomach to con a girl who had to make money on her back. My typical client was a wealthy businessman who craved easy money—something I promised him with a coo and a smile. "You're right, this isn't my territory. I wish you'd stop being right so much, it's annoying."

She leaned her head against my shoulder. "I'm sorry." It was a lousy job of faking sympathy beneath her pre-teen self-satisfaction.

"I won't argue that you know the players and the territory, but you have to stay in the background. If anything goes wrong, run like hell. A karate kick can't stop a bullet."

She nodded, her face impassive.

"This isn't a con," I said. "I can't just get someone excited about something and have them throw money at me. This is straight up fact finding where a misstep could be fatal."

"I know."

"So we're good? You'll do what I say?"

She watched my face, that infectious smile of hers reeling me in. "Long as we can get a pizza first."

I pulled her into a hug and kissed the top of her head. "Good grief, I've created a monster."

We returned to our pizza joint, which was almost deserted. Shortly after the magic hour of 5 p.m., however, hungry customers trickled in. It didn't take long for the two of us to start labeling them. We had "Fat Guy," and "Biker Chick," and, Lily's favorite, "Stud." Stud had chiseled arms, looked to be about 17, and Lily wanted to bet me that he could "crack walnuts with his butt." I declined the offer, but worried that she was already starting to notice boys.

We took our time with the pizza, but neither of us had the appetite to finish the last slice. Despite the pizza-and-beer induced euphoria around us, it was time to find out what Lily knew. "George said you know this Buzz?"

She shrugged. "I didn't, like, know who he was before. George said that and I was all, duh—oh, that guy. I only met him, like, a couple of times. He was just, like, another random pervert."

"You thought."

She shrugged. "Whatever."

"I need to find him."

"There's this bar where he like, hangs out. Me and the bouncer are kinda, like, related."

"Related? You? To the bouncer? In a bar?"

Lily stirred her drink with the straw, studying the ice that rattled in the plastic cup. When she looked up, sadness painted her face. She pursed her lips, her eyes glistening in the dim light. "My mom had, like, a good business goin'."

Oh, I thought, good job, Roxy, you just stepped into that one. I reached across the table to take her hand. "It's okay. I didn't realize it was that kind of related. Did he ever make a move on you?"

She recoiled as though she'd just discovered ants crawling on her skin. "Eewww. That's, like, gross. Maxie's cool. You wanna go see him? But you gotta be, like, super careful."

"You just said he was cool."

Lily drummed her fingers on the table, impatiently slurping the last of her drink. "Not, Maxie! Duh, it's Buzz you gotta worry about. I thought he was gonna, like, kill me or something after he gave me a couple of bucks for dinner."

"That doesn't make any sense. Why would he give you money if he didn't like you?"

"He did a deal. Like, right in front of me. I was all, it's okay mister, I won't tell and he was like, you ever do and you won't live to see morning."

I hate dealing with situations where there are lots of wildcards. That's why I hate poker. Unfortunately, I had to play in the game with someone who sounded like a walking deck.

CHAPTER 58

S K I P

Edward Oz had Skip's curiosity in high gear. How the man kept all of his women straight—and apart—was a mystery. No matter how he accomplished that feat, the very fact that he did gave Skip hope that Oz's sexual appetite might be the leverage he'd need to break the Welton murder wide open.

In order to cause that conflict, Skip needed more information about the woman Oz was currently visiting. He was about twenty feet from the mailbox when he realized he was humming. The potential interpersonal conflicts he was about to unleash were what Baldorf would call "epic." In this case, that conflict made Skip very happy.

The address on the mailbox was 1213. Skip texted the information to Baldorf, then returned to his car to wait impatiently for a call with the name of the house owner. The time gave Skip the opportunity to wonder if Oz had other stops to make tonight or if this was his last.

A few minutes later, Baldorf called him back. After exchanging greetings, Skip said, "Roxy told me you might want to talk."

"Well, yeah. Are you familiar with the cause and effect hypothesis in which an unusual combination of circumstances could aggravate a potentially unstable situation?"

"Baldorf, I have no idea what you just said."

"Perfect storm, dude. Perfect storm."

"I assume we're not talking about the movie, are we?"

"No. We're talking about that video surveillance we did on Fu Zhang. I had Roxy pick up Shaina because I thought all the little Chinese guys were assembling to stage a kidnapping. Turns out that wasn't what they were up to at all. There's a huge shipment coming in tomorrow."

"Go on." Skip listened while he bit his tongue. He was unwilling to alienate Baldorf because the kid made a bad choice and things had worked out so far. How long would that last, though? The more he heard, the more certain he was they needed to bring in the cops. How could he do that when he had to keep the surveillance a secret?

When Baldorf finished, Skip said, "I need time to digest this. Plus, I need you to do two more favors for me. The first one is kind of tricky. I need you to do deep background on a cop, Detective Tom Holmes. He's in Homicide in Carlsbad."

"When do you need this?"

"An hour ago."

"Dude? Seriously? Okay, why him?"

"Because he's an abrasive son-of-a-bitch who doesn't trust anyone. He's the only other one who was at Joey Santino's trial every day. He never testified, but I always had the impression he wanted to nail Joey for something more serious than armed robbery."

"A couple of hours be okay?"

"That should work. I'll also need you to tell me who owns this place. It appears Oz is playing both sides of the fence. He's got another girlfriend."

"Wait! You mean in addition to his wife's partner?"

"Plus his fiancé."

"Holy shit. That bugger gets around."

Skip kept a watchful eye on the front door of the house. "This adds a new dimension to everything. This afternoon, I was sure Frederica was the killer. Now, with a love triangle, there's a whole new angle."

"This would probably be a quadrangle . . . or a pentangle if you can—"

"Just tell me who she is before you count to twenty in Latin or Greek or whatever language you geeks speak when you're talking math. The point is that Oz was not only screwing his partner, but maybe Frederica—in more ways than one."

"It's classic, dude. My money's on the double-cross. He uses her to get to Welton, then turns on her."

"If he did have something to do with the murder—I can expose him to Frederica. She'll rat him out in a heartbeat."

"I thought you sounded pretty chipper. You're going to play the scorned woman card? I'm sure you know how effective—not as in having suffered it personally—uh, I mean—I'm not calling you . . . you know."

"Focus, Baldorf. It's fine, I knew what you meant. What about the house?"

"It belongs to an Andria Comadran. Today's her birthday. She's an Account Executive with a bank. The girl's in a relationship with a guy that she's been seeing. She thinks they're headed for marriage. Dude, I'd guess she has no clue about your boy's extracurricular activities. By the way, her car broke down yesterday. That really pissed her off because it cost her over $400 in repairs."

"Baldorf, quit jerking my chain. I know you're good, but no one is that good."

"I am."

"How the hell did you learn about her car breaking down yesterday?"

"She's an FB Blabber, dude."

"Do you expect me to understand what you just said?"

"She's a Facebook junkie. I just did a little speed reading on her posts. She probably has no clue that what she says can be seen by everyone. It's all there, except for the house ownership part. I had to get that from public records."

Skip sat in silence for a moment. "Sounds like I have another playing card. I wonder how many secrets she knows."

"Dead on, dude."

"So, did she, um, say what she was doing on Sunday night and Monday morning?"

A few seconds later, Baldorf said, "There's a big post on that one. She made spaghetti and meatballs for dinner Sunday night because her boyfriend said he was coming over. He bailed for a big fundraiser thing before dinner. He told her he'd come back later, but never did. That one pissed her off pretty good, too. She had quite a rant."

"When I get back, remind me to close my Facebook account. Anything else?"

"Yeah, she's pregnant."

CHAPTER 59

R O X Y

The bouncer at the door was the size of a minivan. He'd pulled his hair back in a ponytail and sported enough body art to be an exhibition piece in a gallery. I might have a red belt in karate, but this was the kind of guy who could make me cross the street just to get further away. Despite his appearance, Lily's confidence came through in her street swagger.

"Hey, Maxie."

"Hey, Lil."

"Buzz inside?"

With zero head movement in any direction, his eyes flicked from Lily to me, then back again. "Get outta here, kid. Take your junkie friend with you."

"She's not messing with anything." I placed a protective hand on Lily's shoulder. "And I'm not a junkie. We just need some information."

"Who's we, lady?" The guy resembled a robot with limited flexibility, but power to spare.

"She's cool, Maxie. She's, like, helping me out with the foster care thing."

This time, the bouncer's head rotated my way; his expression softened, but he still eyed me up and down. When the visual inspection was complete, he cocked his head at the door. "Be cool, lady, Lily's got a lot of friends."

Inside, I said to Lily, "You're a regular Godfather."

She rolled her eyes, let me give her a hug. "Whatever." A fraction of a second later, she pulled away.

Despite our surroundings, a cross between early-American shipwreck and junkyard throwaway, I felt a glow inside because Lily had leaned into me just a second longer than necessary. She might have friends here, she might have a persona to maintain, but she wasn't ashamed of me. Dingy overhead lighting cast the mismatched tables and chairs into a gray haze dotted with seedy inhabitants, raucous laughter, and a brag fest in full swing.

Any semblance of self-satisfaction I might have had evaporated the moment I took my first drag of stale air. How could I use a child to find a drug dealer? In a place like this. At night. I'd reached a new low in my life. "Stinks in here," I said.

Lily ignored me as she scanned the room. "That's him." She tilted her head at the opposite side of the room.

My throat tightened. Two men stood by the restroom door. Their roles couldn't be more plain. Buzz was stuffing an envelope in his black leather jacket; the other guy looked fearful and strung out. He practically had the word junkie stamped on his forehead.

Watching Buzz move sent my self-defense meter into overload. Besides the fact that his baggy jeans and jacket gave him a half dozen places to hide any number of lethal weapons, his every move projected a fluidity and confidence that said he wouldn't need a weapon to do the job.

One of the few empty tables in the place wasn't that far away, so I motioned at Lily to sit. "Stay here," I cautioned. "I don't want you involved in this."

To my surprise, she didn't resist, but just nodded. "I'm cool."

The junkie who had been with Buzz scurried past me, hunched over and breathing hard—probably at the anticipation of getting his next fix. When I turned back to look for Buzz, he was standing next to an empty stool at the bar. He downed the contents of a waiting shot glass in one smooth movement, tossed a bill on the counter and headed for the door.

Clearly, it was now or never. Unless I intercepted him, our meeting would take place outside—a thought that chilled me to my core. "Are you Buzz?"

He looked right past me, gestured at someone he knew, then started to go around. I sidestepped with him. "Who wants to know?" He stuffed his hands in his pockets. His eyes flicked from me to the surrounding tables.

"Someone who's got some valuable information for your boss about Fu Zhang."

At the mention of Fu Zhang's name, Buzz's eyes bored into mine. "Bitch. You ain't got a clue who you're messing with. Move."

"I know what I'm doing. Your boss has a long-standing rivalry with Fu Zhang. I know how he can eliminate that competition."

Buzz's jaw muscles tightened, causing the scar beneath his right cheek to crinkle. Had I hit a nerve? He'd gone from being on alert to suspicious as all hell. "You a cop?"

I shook my head. "I help people with their investments."

He snorted, then slowly surveyed the room. When he was done, he turned his attention back to me. "Not seeing a lot of investment types in this place. Maybe you got the wrong address." His eyes went cold again as he took a step to the right. Again, I countered to block his way. He snarled, "You've got 30 seconds, bitch, what's your play?"

"I know of a sure-fire way to get rid of Fu Zhang."

"You think I'm nuts or something? Trust a scammer? Get out of my way."

I locked my gaze onto his. "I've still got time left."

"Fine, fifteen seconds. Make it good."

"I understand you know a guy named Joey Santino."

"Ten seconds."

"Joey tried to murder a friend of mine twice and I want him to pay for that. Bring him to me so I can turn him over to the cops. In exchange you get information about Fu Zhang's next drug shipment."

A scruffy man approached from behind. He stood on his tiptoes to whisper into Buzz's ear. Buzz listened until the man walked away. When he spoke, his voice held a chill. "You expect me to believe that you're doing this 'cause you got an itch to see justice served? Ain't happening."

"Joey's got a cute little girl he may never see again because he pissed off his ex. Whether he gets to see the kid or not, I don't care. I only want to make sure the kid sees her next birthday."

There was a flicker of recognition, something buried faint and deep, in Buzz's eyes. To my surprise, his hard exterior softened for a split second, but before I knew it he was all business again. "You went over your time, bitch. I ain't seeing nothing in this for me. We're done."

A short man with a pencil-thin mustache pushed past two drunks. His movements were confident, bordering on arrogant. He had the confidence of a much larger man, which he demonstrated when he double-tapped Buzz on the shoulder, clearly indicating who was in charge.

"Boss? You need something?"

"Me and this lady got some business to take care of."

"Uh—sure. You want me to stick around?"

"Since you thought so little of me being able to get rid of my competition, no. Here's the thing Buzz. I ever hear about you doing that again without telling me, you'll be out—understand?"

Though the threat was directed at Buzz and not me, I felt a quavering in my stomach. I was pretty sure this guy had the money and muscle to take out whoever he wanted. My guess was that in this organization you got one verbal reprimand. After that, you most likely turned up dead in an alley.

"Got it, Boss. Sorry."

"Make the rest of your rounds. Don't forget what I said."

Buzz nodded, turned, and fled the bar, obviously interested in staying alive.

The small man's red-tinged eyes followed Buzz's retreat. Too many late nights? Too much time spent in smoke-filled rooms. "Lily tells me you got important information for me. What've you got?"

I whirled around. The table where Lily had been was now occupied by an amorous couple engaged in a game of "I can swallow your tongue."

Behind me, I heard, "She's fine."

I turned back to the short man in time to see him cock his head toward the end of the bar. There was Lily, perched on a stool, sipping a golden liquid that was either ginger ale or beer. I took a deep breath, hoping it was the former.

"I like that kid," he said. "She's gutsy."

"Who are you? How do you know her?"

He seemed not to hear me. Instead, his eyes roamed my body. My skin crawled at the thought of letting this slime even think of touching me, but I waited, a hopelessly outnumbered prisoner in his camp. When he was done, he smiled to himself.

I realized Lily was watching him visually undress me. Even though I'm not a lip reader, it was easy to read her reaction. "Moron."

The pervert, as Lily would call him, finally spoke. "Jacinto Fontanal. Call me Jackie. Follow me." He led me to a vacant table near the rear of the bar. I went deeper into Jackie's lair because there was nothing else to do but play this one out. I fought back my fears and sat. "You didn't answer my question. How do you know Lily?"

"Fair enough. She asked the right person real nice about me. The kid and me kinda go back a ways."

"That's pretty dodgy. Be more specific."

"Her mother worked for me. I promised her nothing would happen to the kid while she was doing her time. Our agreement was that I always stayed in the background. I got worried when she disappeared from the streets. Where you been keeping her?"

A drunk in rumpled clothes with a hat pulled down stumbled out of the restroom behind Jackie. He staggered past our table, bumping my chair in the process. I turned, but he was already in the crowd, only part of his back visible. Was this a ploy to throw me off my game? One of Jackie's cohorts messing with me? Jackie motioned at a man who had been watching us. He got a nod in return. When he looked back at me he said, "It won't happen again."

"Aren't you just the benevolent protector? How sweet. What strings were attached with Lily?"

He smiled. "Know what, I kind of like you, too. Gutsy, just like the kid. I wouldn't call them strings—more like mutual favors."

Good God, no, I thought, not that kind of favor. "Lily didn't talk about you, she didn't even know who you were."

"Her mom wanted it that way. Let's just say she's under my wing for a couple more months."

Is that what had happened at the bus stop today? Jackie's guy? The rock in my stomach had me wanting to run to the curb so I could throw up in the gutter. "Stay away from her."

"Or?"

"Just stay away from her. She's a good kid."

He pursed his lips. "Relax lady, I ain't got any interest in the kid. When she introduced herself, she told me she was gettin' off the streets. She vouched for you, said you was gonna take her in. That true?"

"I want to help her. That's it. Period. I understand you run things around here, so I think you know how to find Joey Santino. Am I right?"

"All I hear so far is me, me, me. You'd better have something good. Get to it."

Behind me, chairs scraped on the floor. Two men staggered away, weaving between tables toward the front door. "I have information about Fu Zhang's next drug shipment. I'm willing to turn what I know over to you in exchange for a favor."

"Joey Santino's hide?"

"Something like that. I just want to send him back to prison where he belongs. I've heard he's friends with Fu Zhang. I suspect Joey killed your former boss and helped your competitor execute a power grab."

"Interesting theory. Why would Joey want to do that?" Jackie looked almost amused. "I don't see why Joey would turn on a guy who'd been his friend since they were kids."

"What?" I blurted. His reaction was off—he should have been surprised, not entertained. "I heard they went back a ways. I didn't realize they went back that far."

Jackie's impatience was starting to show. "Lady, I don't want to conduct history class here, but they grew up in the same neighborhood. They're both half and half."

"They came from mixed marriages?"

"Happened a lot in that neighborhood. The marriage thing didn't matter so much. They were outcasts 'cause they couldn't get along. Neither one. Got it?"

"All the more reason they could have been working together."

"The boss got bumped off and the cops never figured out who did it. Funny thing is, his money disappeared. Where'd that go? Fu Zhang sure as hell didn't get it."

"So that's why he was at Joey's trial every day. Trying to figure out where that money was? You weren't there."

"I didn't get nothing out of that but trouble. You still haven't given me a reason to be wasting my time with you."

I caught a glimpse of Lily; she was still at the bar, talking and laughing with the bartender. Maybe it was the dim lighting, or maybe it was just the dinginess, but something about this place was throwing me off. Usually, I was the one who was so confident. Here, it was Jackie. All my senses told me this guy already knew where that money had gone. How did he know so much about Joey? It was time to play one last card—call it desperation. "I can give you details about the shipment. Time and place."

Jackie's tongue flicked over his lips. I could see I'd finally gotten his attention. "How the hell did you find that out?"

"That's not part of the deal. You get the time and location, I get Joey."

"So, why should I believe you? Joey's always been a wannabe—big dreams, but no juice."

"Sounds to me like you're just making excuses."

He threw up one hand in a dismissive gesture. "So I should just, what? Go blast my way in? Why would I want to mess with Fu Zhang? I'm a businessman."

I was unwilling to let this drug dealer best me. "I must have had bad intel. I thought you were a man of action. A take charge kind of guy. I heard there's a showdown coming."

"Lady, Fu Zhang's been trying to move us out for a couple of years."

"I know."

Ice crept into his voice. "It ain't gonna happen."

"It will unless you do something to demonstrate you control the game."

The intensity in his eyes was almost frightening; he planted both elbows on the table. "Like?"

"Like cut off the head of the snake. The organization will go into free fall with a move that bold—same as last time."

"When and where? That's what you're bringing to the table. If your info is wrong, lady, you'll wish you were never born. Lily, too."

"Leave her out of this."

"She brought you to me. You willing to risk her life, too?"

I stood and put my hands on the table, leaning forward so I towered over Jackie. "No."

"Yes." Lily stood to one side, her face calm, composed.

"Lily!" I shook my head. "No! I won't allow this."

"I trust you Roxy. Anyway, if Jackie, like, sends a couple of his morons after me, you'll, like, kick their butts." She smiled. "Just like that one this afternoon."

Jackie leaned back in his chair, laughing. "You two make quite a pair. Fine, you got yourselves a deal." He handed me a business card with embossed lettering. It read, Jacinto (Jackie) Fontanal, Imports/Exports. "I wondered if that might have been you."

"Was that your idea of protection? Pistol whipping a kid?"

"Jose got caught up in the moment. I didn't realize he was so bad with kids. Anyway, I had Buzz visit him in the hospital—just to explain how disappointed I was. That's how it goes sometimes—you've got to send best wishes, you know, for a recovery." He winked at me. "You ever need a job, lady, you come see me. I'll be needing a new enforcer."

The rock in my stomach was back, bigger and heavier than ever. I wanted to smack Lily for revealing what I'd done, but felt a sense of satisfaction knowing that she was proud of me. I also wanted to get the hell away from this place. "No thanks, I'm looking for something with more job security." I put the piece of paper Baldorf had given me on the table in front of Jackie. For the first time since we'd met, he looked surprised. Maybe even happy. I could only hope that he'd follow through on his end of the deal.

CHAPTER 60

S K I P

Skip parked two houses away from the veterinarian clinic to wait for Dom's return. The most likely scenario was that Anita had run to Dom for help and the two were together. Since she wasn't at her place, they must be here—or on the run. He reclined his seat to conserve his energy. An hour later, there was still no sign of Dom or Anita. Most of the open parking spaces on the street had been taken by people returning home from work. Fortunately, his Kia blended in with the conglomeration of old and new pickups and sedans. The neighborhood, located on the outskirts of Glendale, contained a mix of older homes interspersed with small commercial buildings. All were connected by a spiderweb of overhead power lines.

The streets, which the city must have paved during the era when concrete was king, were lined with cracks large enough to throw a bicyclist or a skateboarder off balance. He passed the time watching young daredevils cut switchbacks down the street, hopping the cracks like seasoned pros.

The differences between this area and where Jack Welton lived couldn't be more stark. Even the neighborhood where Oz's girlfriend lived wore its age better. Unfortunately, Skip doubted that her loser boyfriend intended to be a father or a husband—let alone a good one. In Skip's mind, she was just one more young woman destined for heartbreak saddled with a child who would never know both parents.

In the distance, another siren pierced the otherwise steady drone of city background noise. The siren faded, again leaving only the normal sounds of city life—and still no sign of Dom or Anita. He waited, trying to formulate a plan, something to help Roxy out of the mess that she'd gotten into. Even if he wasn't a killer, Oz had laid the groundwork to ruin at least two women's lives. Skip cursed himself for wanting to don a white hat and save the day, but that was him. He knew it. He couldn't stop it. The big question was how could he use what he knew to bring down Oz? He had to find the silver bullet.

He reached for his phone to call Frederica Gurney-Welton, then thought about how many questions still remained to be answered. What if she'd killed her husband? She couldn't have done it alone—not a hanging. Would Oz have helped? How could he get all of the players together?

During the next hour, Skip lost track of how many times he concluded this was a wild goose chase. He promised himself that if nothing happened by 9:30, he'd call Roxy and tell her she'd been wrong. At sundown, with no streetlights to illuminate the darkness filling in, the last of the skateboarding daredevils went in for the night. The deserted streets took on the unnatural quiet of a ghost town, prompting Skip to retrieve his Sig .357 and tactical flashlight from the trunk. He continued the surveillance, flashlight next to his hip, gun resting on his lap.

It was 9:10 when a pair of headlights turned the corner. The car entered the clinic parking lot, its doors opened and the interior glow illuminated a man and a woman. Skip got out of his car, slipped the gun into the waistband of his jeans, then grabbed the flashlight. With luck, it would be all he'd need.

The woman slammed her door. The edge in her voice made her words unnecessary. "Goddammit, Dom, I'm tired of this. We can't keep running!"

Dom's voice was conciliatory, but insistent. "Sis, we have to get out of town. It's the only way. We talked about this."

Their bickering continued from the time they left the car to the front door of the clinic. Both were so engrossed in their conversation that neither noticed the approaching silent figure. Dom was still trying to get his key into the lock in the darkness when Skip flipped the flashlight switch to low. "Dom and Anita Hewson?"

Both jumped, shielding their eyes against the beam's glare. It was Dom who stepped forward. "What the hell? Who are you?"

Skip stayed about ten feet away, knowing from the ache at the back of his head he'd been up far too long. All he wanted to do was leave Roxy's message, then return to his room for some sleep. "Skip Cosgrove."

Dom glared at Anita when she seized his arm. "What's wrong with you?"

She pointed at Skip. "That's him, Roxy's boyfriend. I remember the name."

"My reputation precedes me." After he said it, Skip realized the words sounded stupid, nothing like the clever quip he'd played in his mind.

"What are you doing here?" asked Anita. "How'd you find me?"

"Roxy remembered you talking about this place."

"I—I mentioned it maybe once."

"She's good at that sort of thing. I came here to give you a message only because she hasn't been able to reach you by phone. It seems you two are planning on, what, leaving town?"

Dom eased Anita out of the way, then stepped forward.

"I don't think you want to do that," said Skip.

It took a second for Dom to react, but he inched closer to Skip. "I don't much like having strangers accost me and my sister on my property in the middle of the night."

Skip winced at a hot flash shooting through his head and neck. He held up a hand in hopes of shutting down the other man's anger. "I'm not here to cause any trouble."

"He's dangerous, Dom."

Anita's brother stopped, then glanced over his shoulder at Anita.

"Roxy told me," she said.

Dom retreated a half step, his tone tinged with venom as he spoke. "What do you want? Leave us alone."

"Anita, Roxy said you should meet her at Marjorie's tomorrow afternoon. Two o'clock." Not exactly true, thought Skip, but it might give him enough time to get back to Carlsbad. Assuming he could pull off a miracle with the murder case and get out of L.A. before noon.

"We're not going there," said Dom.

"Roxy didn't say anything about you. It's Anita she wants to see."

Dom glared at Skip while he pointed at Anita. "She makes her own decisions. Neither of us are going to kowtow to that scammer girlfriend of yours!"

"I was trying to play nice, but you're not making this easy. I'll rephrase that." Skip turned off the beam. He took a few steps forward, but remained just out of Dom's reach. His voice turned sinister. "Roxy changed the password on the account. Be at your aunt's tomorrow at two p.m. or you'll never see your money again."

Even in the darkness, Skip saw Dom's stance change—he planted one foot forward while leaning back to take a swing. Skip countered by aiming the light directly at Dom's face. He flipped the switch to its highest setting.

"Shit! Shit!" Dom shielded his eyes as he staggered away. "Son of a bitch!" His ankle buckled on the edge of the sidewalk, but Anita caught him before he went down.

The short confrontation had Skip's adrenaline pumping—now he was wired and no longer in a hurry. Screw it. These two had pissed him off. He wanted answers. "We're going to talk for a few minutes," he said. "I have questions about what really happened after Roxy left that condo." He gestured at the front door with the tactical beam, then turned it off.

CHAPTER 61

ROXY

Making someone paranoid is easy once you know their hot buttons. If they don't like snakes, a trip to the pet store can give you everything you need. If, like Buzz, they're afraid of screwing up in front of their boss, you give them the opportunity to do exactly that. The only question in my mind was what steps I'd need to take.

Lily and I were on our way back to the car when I spotted the outline of a large man hanging out in the shadows behind us. Lily must have seen him also, because she grabbed my hand. She whispered, "Roxy? Is that Big & Ugly?"

"I think he's been behind us since we left the bar." I squeezed her hand in return, not wanting to admit we could be in trouble, but also unwilling to take a chance with her life. I tried not to sound worried as I added, "He seems to be following us."

Lily sucked in a breath; she looked at me. "He was, like, in the light for a second."

"You saw his face?"

She nodded, but didn't say a word. The tightness in her body telegraphed itself through her grip. This girl was scared to death.

"It's him, isn't it?" I asked.

"Yeah. Like, what're we gonna do?"

"You're going to run like hell when I tell you to. You remember where we parked?"

"Next corner, halfway up the block. But I can't leave you."

Two marines in full uniform exited a bar directly ahead of us; we were no more than 10 steps behind them. Both were big strapping young men ready to help their country. I wondered what they would do for a damsel in distress?

"Maybe you won't have to." I straightened up, doing my best to look prim and insecure.

The shorter marine looked at us before saying something to the other. The taller one, who reminded me of a bean pole, peeked next—he did a double take when I smiled at him. Someday, maybe I'd lose my touch, but tonight I was hot and helpless, even with a twelve-year-old companion. They both stepped to one side.

I put my free hand to my neck, dropped my gaze to the sidewalk and gave our soon-to-be bodyguards an innocent, but friendly opening. "Thanks. You two look like you've been partying."

"Yes, ma'am. Shipping out tomorrow."

The four of us staked out a little section of the sidewalk. Lily and I stayed just behind the marines. I wet my lips. With just a hint of hesitation in my voice, I said, "Look, um, I hate asking strangers for favors, but do you see that man behind us in the shadows?"

Beanpole's eyes flicked up, then returned to meet my gaze. "Yes, ma'am. Is he bothering you?"

"I think he's following us."

The glint from the shorter one's name tag glistened in the storefront light. His name was Gonzales, but I still couldn't read Beanpole's name tag without being obvious. Gonzales was still several inches taller than me, probably weighing in around 180. He edged closer to Lily, his watchful eyes focusing on our stalker. "Got him."

Lily put her arm around my waist. "He's, like, so creepy."

They flanked us, Beanpole on my left, Gonzales to Lily's right. Beanpole spoke in soothing tones. "Ma'am, we don't want any trouble, but can we walk you to your car?" Despite his words, their body language conveyed clearly that they were ready for action.

"That would be wonderful. I'd feel so much better if you did. You two get gold stars in my book."

When we got to the corner, we all turned right and they escorted us all the way to my Toyota. Lily even gave Gonzales a big hug when he opened her door. I thanked both men before locking the doors. We made a U-turn back to the Coast Highway. On the opposite side of the street we spotted the man who'd been in the shadows. It was definitely Big & Ugly. Again.

"Holy shit!" Lily said.

"Yeah." This time, our tail was no longer alone. Instead, he was engaged in a heated argument with another man—Buzz.

CHAPTER 62

S K I P

It had taken more coaxing, but after a few minutes, Dom and Anita realized they no longer controlled the game. Skip sat with the brother and sister around an old dining room table Dom had pulled out from the corner. Skip's chair reminded him of the wobbly one he always got when he was growing up—annoyingly unpredictable. The walls of Dom's kitchen, along with the chipped and faded Canary yellow 50's cabinets, needed a good paint job.

Skip wasted no time asking his first question. "Anita, tell me what happened after Roxy left Welton's place."

Dom started to speak, but Skip silenced him. "I want to hear from her first, then you can talk."

At first, Anita seemed lost for words. When they came, they tumbled out like a rushing stream. "It's . . . it's all . . . just a blur. We weren't there for more than another fifteen minutes after Roxy left. I was so shocked about the money that I couldn't function. So I had Dom come over and he did the transfer."

"I just did what you told me to!"

"Quiet!" Skip held up his hand. "I want to hear more from Anita. So Roxy left first?"

"Yeah, she left when someone called to tell her you were—well, she was freaking out. I said she should go. You know, there was no reason we couldn't finish up."

Skip felt sadness and warmth at the same time—no wonder she'd been so uncertain in the hospital. "Did you hang Jack?"

Anita's eyes filled with tears; her lower lip trembled. She shook her head. "God, no! I still loved him!"

"Tell them about the call," said Dom.

"What call?"

"The phone rang just before we were getting ready to leave. I think it was from Jack's business partner. That guy is such a sleaze." The look on her face went from disgust to fear. Panic entered her voice. "Look, I'm so afraid. If the cops find out about me being at Jack's that night, they might arrest me."

"The call?" Skip interrupted.

"He left a message as we were walking out. What was it he said, Dom?"

"He wanted to meet in the morning. Can I say something?"

Skip nodded.

"When we left, Welton was out cold. I drugged him and, yeah, I would have been happy to hang the son-of-a-bitch myself after he dumped Anita, but I didn't. I'm telling you, someone else did it. Not us."

Anita swallowed hard. Splotchy gray patches filled in between what had been a healthy complexion just moments before. "Sure!" she exploded. "I took the money! I—we—did. But, we were out of his condo right after midnight."

"Can anyone corroborate that?" asked Skip.

Anita shook her head. "Just me and Dom. I still have the code for the parking garage and the key, so no—unless there's security video."

Thanks to Mrs. Montgomery and the doorman, he already knew there was video and a log entry by the doorman they'd kept on late that night. The log said the doorman had hailed a cab for "Mr. Welton's guest" at 12:07 a.m. There was no record of these two leaving, but now Skip knew why.

"Video will put your girlfriend there, too," sneered Dom.

"Is that a threat?"

"I'm just saying," said Dom. "She's the one the cops will want to find. They don't know anything about you, Sis."

Skip silenced Anita with a wave of his hand, then leaned in closer to Dom. "You're trying awfully hard to set Roxy up as the scapegoat. How about if we look elsewhere?"

Dom snorted. "Where? A crystal ball?"

"Instead of fighting amongst ourselves, we need answers. Let's try and focus on who might have come in after you left. Anita, who else would have a key to the condo?"

"Supposedly Jack loaned the place out for visiting guests. I suspect all those guests were female. I can't go to jail. I just can't."

Skip gave Anita's arm a reassuring squeeze. "If you didn't hang him, we ought to be able to figure out who did. What happened to your key?"

"Jack never gave me one."

"Roxy said you gave one to her."

Anita dismissed that with a wave of her hand. "I know, but that's one I had made from the one he kept at work."

"Welton kept a key to the condo at work?"

"It was on a special ring. He was always worried that his wife would figure out he was using the place, so he left it in the receptionist's desk. He'd take the whole thing. When he was done, he'd return it. He never told Frederica about the condo. Even if she got suspicious—he said she'd never find a thing unless she went there."

Obviously, Anita didn't realize how much Frederica knew, thought Skip. "Is it possible anyone else made a copy of the key?"

"I never thought about it before, but anyone could have."

"So any woman who worked for Welton could be a suspect?" asked Dom.

"It would have to be a man," said Skip. "Frederica couldn't do it on her own. It could have been a couple of women, but it's not very likely two girlfriends decided to cooperatively kill a guy because he dumped one of them. So we're back to it being a man."

"Jack wasn't in the habit of screwing men," Anita grumbled.

"Don't be so sure about that," said Skip. Right now, he wasn't thinking in the sexual sense, but if Jack was running a scam on clients, what might he have done to his partner?

Anger flared in Anita's eyes. "What the hell's that mean?"

"What about Edward Oz?"

Anita rubbed her arms as if she were fending off a chill. "Like I said, the guy's a creep, he'll screw anything in a skirt." Her voice hardened when she looked at her brother. "Go to hell, Dom. I know what you're thinking. Don't think he didn't try, but the guy's got slime written on his forehead."

"Whatever you say, Sis." Dom shrugged while he drummed his fingers on the thin tabletop, sending a hollow echo throughout the room. "Anyway, Welton was alive when we left. Are we done here?"

Suddenly, Anita cocked her head to one side; her eye movements told Skip she was accessing a visual memory. "No. He was alive when I left." She looked at Dom. "You were up there alone with him for about five minutes."

"You two didn't leave together?"

"Dom thought it would be better if we went down one at a time. You know, just in case security was watching or something."

"Exactly how long were you alone in the condo?" Skip noticed that Dom stopped his drumming and had thrust his hands into his armpits.

"Minute or two."

Anita pressed her lips together tightly, the frown on her brow deepening. A moment later, her voice was firm. "More like five to ten."

"No way. You're off by a mile."

"Nuh-uh, I remember because I kept looking at my watch. You came into the parking garage at 12:27. It was eight minutes after I got downstairs."

Instead of saying what he was thinking—that was plenty of time to hang a man—Skip said, "Eight minutes isn't very long."

"So you think I'm innocent?"

"Of course, man. I get it. It's a timing thing. No worries. Let's walk through it so we can prove you didn't do this. Give me the details of what happened after Anita left."

Without hesitation, Dom began rambling. "Anita was all freaked out. She had no idea Welton had so much money. Her head was still spinning. I rechecked my bag to make sure I hadn't left anything behind and . . . and . . ." He paused for a moment, but it was obvious he knew he couldn't change the situation. "I spent the time looking out the window."

"Great view from up there I'll bet?"

Dom hesitated. "I don't remember. I wasn't paying attention. You know? I was just kind of . . . worried." The little lines around the corners of his eyes crinkled. His tone of voice spoke to his fear.

Skip was almost sure he was telling the truth. At least, in part. "When you left, where was Welton?"

"On the couch where we'd put him. I wasn't about to move him. No way I wanted him waking up with me alone."

"Did you want to see him dead?"

"Who wouldn't after what he did to her?" He cocked his head at Anita. "But you've got to believe me, I didn't do this."

"It was my choice to get involved with him, not yours."

"You have to agree, Dom, this looks bad. You're the last guy in the room with the victim. How light was the tranquilizer? What would have happened if you had moved him?"

"I'm used to dealing with dogs and cats, not people. I was scared shitless he might wake up. I also didn't want to raise the dose for fear I might kill him. Basically, I didn't want to touch the guy. I sure as hell wasn't going to drag him around his goddamn house."

Skip still wasn't satisfied; he watched the rise and fall of Dom's chest closely, took in the speed of Dom's breathing. "The papers said he hanged himself in the bedroom. How far was that from the couch?"

"I don't know. It would be at least ten feet to the door. Bedroom was pretty big, too."

No change in breathing, thought Skip, but he'd glanced away for a fraction of a second. "So you did some exploring while you were there?"

"Uh, yeah. I wandered around a bit."

Anita gasped. "You what?"

Skip ignored her. "What else, Dom? I can't help you without all the details."

"I, um, had been drinking a lot of coffee while we were waiting." Dom's face flushed. "I took a leak."

"I told you to lay off that stuff." Through clenched teeth, she said, "Men!" Anita stomped out without looking back.

Skip waited until she was out of the room. When he spoke, he kept his tone measured. "You do realize that you might have left DNA behind."

"My nerves got the better of me. I knew I should hold it, but—urine doesn't contain DNA, anyway."

"Let's just hope LAPD doesn't decide to do a full sweep on that bathroom. Otherwise they might pick up other sources that you left behind when you unzipped your pants."

Dom cleared his throat. "Would they put that kind of effort into this?"

The possibility of the police obtaining a successful DNA match based on a single hair or a few epithelial cells was remote at best because the cops probably wouldn't go to that extent. The science was there, but not the money. Still, Skip had no desire for Dom to know that. Apparently, Dom took the bait because the signs of recognition came quickly. He tugged on his ear, clasped his neck, swallowed hard—no longer was he cocky—he'd turned contrite. Skip was thankful Dom had been brainwashed into believing every crime scene was combed, vacuumed, and analyzed with unlimited resources and almost immediate results. Perception was a playing card he could work with.

He asked, "If the cops come calling, what are you going to say? You need to think this through."

"I know what to do."

"You're going to put this on Anita?"

"She's my sister."

"Doesn't answer my question. Try again."

"Forget it. I don't answer to you."

"I'm not trying to be antagonistic, Dom. I want to help you out. If you didn't kill Welton, tell me exactly what happened so we can structure your response for the police."

Dom sat back in his chair with exaggerated casualness. A moment later, he said, "I told Anita to split because I needed to use the john. I knew she'd freak out if I said anything, so I just told her I'd tidy up. She left. I did my business. I made sure to give the condo a quick once over. I got curious about how this guy lived. I've never seen a place so . . ."

"What?"

He shrugged. "Spacious. Immaculate. I don't even know why I did it, but the next thing you know I was checking out this jewelry drawer. The guy had diamond rings—for a man. The bastard had a diamond-encrusted Rolex."

Skip saw Dom's eyes dart up at the mention of the watch. What had he done? "Go on."

"Huh? What do you mean?"

"I mean, what about the Rolex? Something about it's bugging you."

"No. There's nothing. You're just fishing."

"Nuh-uh. I can see it in your eyes, you took it. Didn't you? You got your own little bit of revenge on Welton for dumping your sister."

Dom slammed his fist onto the tabletop. "Go to hell! It was just waiting for someone to take it. I knew Welton wouldn't—couldn't—say anything about what happened, so I figured I'd help myself. Made me happy to know it would stick in his craw. You can't prove I took it."

"Where is it now?"

"Screw you."

If it wasn't for greed, thought Skip, the cops would have almost nothing to do. "You realize how stupid that was, right? Sorry, I shouldn't be judgmental, but it was. If someone finds that watch, you're going to jail for a long time."

"It won't turn up."

Skip shook his head. "Things like that have a tendency to get found at the worst possible moment. We need to keep it under lock and key where no one will find it—and you won't be tempted to wear it. I have a friend who's an attorney. He's got a safe deposit box. I can ask him to store it for me. I won't tell him where it came from. He won't ask."

"No. I'm keeping it."

"Don't be stupid."

Dom jabbed a finger in Skips direction. "So, the truth about you comes out."

"What I meant was—"

"No! You meant what you said. You think I'm stupid. We'll go see your girlfriend tomorrow afternoon. After that, we disappear."

CHAPTER 63

R O X Y

Big & Ugly and Buzz were in cahoots?

Almost to the second, Lily and I said, "Shit."

"Roxy, now what? That was Buzz. He's gonna, like, so double-cross Jackie."

"He's not going to have time. I'm not giving up yet." I wanted to double back to a half block from where we'd seen the two men, so I took the next right. Tail-light reflectors from cars parked along the street winked at us each time my headlights passed over them. "What's with all these cars? Every space is taken, dammit!"

"It's so like this all the time at night. Sometimes I can, like, make good money with all these dudes walking around. They, like, feel all guilty cause I'm a kid."

"How much do you make in a night?"

I caught her shrug out of the corner of my eye. "Like, twenty, thirty bucks."

My eyes were on the road, but my thoughts flooded with anger. I jerked the steering wheel too hard when I made the right onto Seagaze.

"I don't, like, come down this street much. The primo spot's a couple of blocks over."

"It pisses me off that you have to beg for money. Twenty bucks? Are you frigging kidding me?"

Lily pointed at the opposite side of the street. "That's, like, bad over there."

It irritated me that Lily accepted her lot in life, but maybe the truth was I didn't understand what she had to do to stay alive. As we approached the back side of the cinema complex, it reminded me of one of those streets where someone had drawn a line down the middle. The north side of the street was new stucco and tile with ample lighting provided by the complex, exactly the opposite of the southern side with its one lone streetlight, old buildings, and dark alley.

"It's cool." Lily placed her hand on my leg. "It's like, better than Old Man Tucker's."

Despite her words, I felt the desperation in her voice. I gritted my teeth, intent on being strong for her. If this kid could make the best of her situation, I could suck it up, too. Even though we were on the back side of the theater, empty parking spots were almost nonexistent. The street's north side would be a "no man's land" for a panhandler. Even I could see that. "Not much business there, huh."

She rolled her eyes. "Everybody's, like, afraid of the dark over there. They don't got no time for a homeless kid."

Another surge of anger swelled inside me—it pissed me off that people, including me, didn't care. Ahead of us, a man staggered along the sidewalk until he reached an old beat-to-crap pickup truck. I grabbed his parking spot, thankful for good timing. Lily shivered as she faced me in her seat. She clutched her sides with both hands; her eye glistened with tears. "Like, what're you gonna do?"

"Are you cold?" Who was I kidding? That wasn't the problem. She knew what was coming.

She threw her arms around me. "He's, like, dangerous!"

A moment later, I eased her back into her own seat. "I have to make some things happen, sweetheart. I won't be long." Damn, I hated it when Skip used that on me. Here I was, doing the same thing to Lily. I got out of the car to get the black Taser case out of the trunk, then returned to the driver's seat.

When I sat next to Lily, she pointed at the case. "What's that?"

"A Taser. It's less lethal than a gun. It shoots two little darts."

"I, like, know what they do, I just ain't never seen one up close before." Her face lit up for a moment, morbid curiosity replacing her fear. "Can I, like, hold it?"

I jerked it out of her reach, suddenly ashamed of myself for even letting her see it. "We don't need your prints on this just in case things go bad."

"I, like, should'a known that. Now what?"

With the vision of Jack Welton still vivid in my memory, I reloaded the Taser. "Crap."

"What's the matter?"

"Nothing, everything's cool." I'd only bought one set of the untraceable darts. "I need to find Buzz."

She pointed toward the opposite side of the street. "That ain't hard. He's, like, comin' this way."

I looked at where she pointed. Sure enough, there he was, coming into the streetlight halo. In half a minute, he'd be in front of the alley. If he ducked into that shadowy hole, my edge would disappear. He knew these streets, I didn't.

I handed Lily my keys. "If this goes bad, get the hell out of here."

"Hello? I can't drive."

"Right." Talk about feeling stupid. "Then lock the doors and call Marjorie. Her number is in my phone. Also, call 9-1-1. Tell them I'm being attacked."

On the opposite side of the street, Buzz passed through the lighted halo. He became just another shadow within the shadows. Had he seen me?

I ran across the street. When I reached my destination, the gravity of my mistake hit me full on. Tattoo Boy stood on the corner half a block away, watching. I suddenly had a thousand questions running through my head with no time to even think about answers.

A shadow moved. Shit.

This was exactly what had happened to Skip.

Panic set in. One Taser. Two targets. No way.

Tattoo Boy edged in my direction. Should I run? We'd never escape in time.

Before I knew what had happened, Buzz charged. I raised my weapon. Fired. Confetti spewed into the air. A car horn echoed off the buildings. The probes reached their full range, then fell to the ground without touching Buzz. He tucked and rolled. One now-dead line caught on his pant leg.

He came up, the line wrapped around his leg. Buzz knew what to do. Like a fool, I dropped the Taser. Lily slammed on the horn again. The noise sent Tattoo Boy back to the corner, but unless I got lucky, I was about to die at the hands of a drug dealer.

Buzz faced off against me. "Lady, who the hell are you?"

The scent of my own fear engulfed me. Where were the cops? "I told you in the bar; I'm after Joey Santino."

Sirens wailed a couple of blocks away; they were so close.

Two derelicts staggered out of the alley, one held a bottle in his hand. He yelled, "Hey! Knock it off!"

The other took an unsteady step in the opposite direction. "C'mom, Fred, let's find someplace quiet."

Headlights lit us up as the first Oceanside PD car rounded the corner. Buzz made the mistake of glancing in that direction.

I delivered a roundhouse kick. He pulled back. My foot grazed his chin. To my surprise, he went down in a heap.

I stayed in the ready position, unable to believe a superficial hit would take a guy that size out of commission. He'd seen it coming. He'd made the perfect avoidance move. My heart hammered against my chest; the cops were here. The two drunks, their movements now jerky in the riot of blue and red flashing lights, gawked at us sideways while they slipped away.

The one with the bottle said, "Shit, man, I ain't never seen a broad do that before!"

"Goddamn, I need another drink. C'mon, Fred, I ain't messing with her."

The cops took forever to get out of the damned car. By the time they approached, the two drunks were halfway down the block. The cops circled around us from different directions.

"You, okay, ma'am?"

"I'm fine." I pointed at Buzz, who lay prone, but opened one eye as the officer moved closer. "This man is a drug dealer. He attacked me."

My Taser rested on the ground near Buzz, one lead still wrapped around his left leg. When the officer knelt over him, Buzz opened both eyes. The cop's partner stood nearby with his gun pointed at the ground.

"Don't move," he said.

Buzz rolled onto his stomach. The process of cuffing him took only seconds—everything went way too smoothly in my opinion. On the other hand, if I had two guys pointing guns at me I might be docile, too. The cop picked up the Taser. He inspected it for a moment, then looked at me. "This yours?"

His partner approached. "Ma'am, you're going to have to come with us to swear out a complaint."

Across the street, the glow of the cell phone cast Lily's face into weird colors, but she gave me a thumbs up. A split second later, she ducked down. Everything was happening so fast. What was wrong here? The entire arrest had been way too simple. The cops had let the witnesses go and Buzz had been almost—cooperative.

"Ma'am?"

I hate being ma'am'd, especially by some guy older than me. I started to walk away, but his partner grabbed my arm. "You should come with us. What's your name?"

"Am I under arrest? He's the attacker, not me."

"You're the one who had him on the ground. You need to swear out a complaint." He gestured at Buzz. "Give us a statement. Or we'll have to release him. You don't want that."

While we were debating my involvement, the one who had arrested Buzz picked up some of the confetti.

"Fine. I'll meet you there," I said.

My guy wasn't buying that line for a second. He shook his head. "First, I need to see your identification. Please."

"Look, Officer . . ." I peered at his chest, but still couldn't read the name tag in the darkness.

His tone became more impatient. "McGinnis, ma'am. Your ID?"

The other one took Buzz to a marked car that had just arrived. What the hell? The way he'd gone—so willing, the way these guys were acting—it was all far too scripted. Were these guys on Jackie's payroll? What was I caught up in? Leaving Lily here was out of the question. I knew if I said anything about her, she'd be taken in. It would take them only minutes to discover her identity. Then what? I had to stall to make sure Lily wasn't alone for long. "Can I call my boyfriend? He expects me home and this sounds like it could take a while."

"Sure. Go ahead. I'm also going to need your ID."

I craned my neck forward, my eyebrows raised in expectation.

Officer McGinnis nodded. "Oh." He reached for his utility belt. Even in the darkness, the black leather shined. He handed me his cell phone.

I dialed my number. When Lily answered, I said, "Hi, sweetheart, I had a problem on Seagaze Drive in Oceanside, right near the backside of the theater. The cops want me to swear out a complaint against the guy who attacked me. Can you call Auntie Em and have her bring Lily in? You were going to call her anyway, right?"

"What am I, like, a dog?"

McGinnis watched me with piercing eyes that took in my every move. I gave him an innocent smile and winked to make nice while I held the phone away. I whispered, "Puppies are such a hassle." He grimaced—maybe he didn't like dogs, or maybe he didn't want my germs on his cell—either way, I didn't care. I returned to my conversation with Lily. "How long will it take her to get to my place?"

"Like, maybe fifteen to twenty."

"So Auntie Em will take care of that?"

"This is, like, so messed up. Morons. Yeah, it's cool."

We disconnected and I handed the phone back to its owner. "I just got a new puppy and—well, you know." I also had a plan for the ID. It was time for the ditzy blonde to make her appearance.

Officer McGinnis holstered his phone. His patience was obviously wearing thin, exactly what I wanted. Though his words were cordial, his tone of voice already gave away his desire to end this interaction. "No problem, ma'am. Your ID? I'll also need you to tell me what happened."

The car with a sullen-looking Buzz in the back seat pulled away. Time was not on my side, at least, not yet. Maybe I could change that with the bimbo act.

It was the officer's turn to give me the expectant look. I started to ramble. "Oh, right. ID. When I saw him coming, I pulled the Taser from my purse. I guess I threw it—the purse, not the Taser, right? I mean, I had that in my hand, but the bag should be over here somewhere—in all the commotion—where is it?"

Behind me, McGinnis followed obediently, exactly what I wanted.

I pointed to a spot against the building just below the storefront window. "Can you shine your light thingy over here?"

His club-sized flashlight lit up the area.

"Wow, that's bright!" I threw my hands in the air, then pointed in a different direction. "Maybe over here?"

The light went right to where I pointed, the only thing there was a crumpled up scrap of paper. His impatience deepened. "Are you sure you had it with you?"

"My purse? Of course! That's where I keep everything! You men just don't understand anything. Where is it? Dammit!"

"What color is it, ma'am?"

I glared at him with my hands planted on my hips. "Would you stop calling me that? It's, like, totally unnerving. My name is Roxy Tanner. You can call me Miss Tanner, Ms. Tanner, or even just Roxy. But, please, don't ma'am me again."

"Sorry, ma—Miss Tanner. So what color is your purse?"

"It's one of those shopping-bag sized thingies with little compartments inside. The Taser has its own pouch to make it easy to get to. It's really a very nice bag. You don't suppose someone stole it, do you? It was on sale at Macy's—or was it—no, it was last Christmas because the big sale was going on—oh, God, there were two guys who came out of the alley. What if they took my purse? It's got my ID and my keys and—"

"It's not here. You're sure you had it?"

"Well, I can't go anywhere until I find it! It's got my address book and pictures of Lily. You know, the puppy." I buried my face in my hands. "What am I going to do?"

"Do you have a phone, Miss Tanner?"

"Duh, who doesn't?" Across the street, the car was dark. It needed to stay that way because if Lily used my phone and lit up the interior again McGinnis might get suspicious. I cleared my throat. "Well, more like had. My boyfriend put it on lockdown." I made quotation marks in the air with both hands. "He says I'm in the 'penalty box' because I went over my data limit. Asshole! Sorry, I guess I shouldn't swear around you guys."

McGinnis placed his hand over his mouth. His mouth moved, but the words weren't for my ears.

I rambled on. "He says he'll give it back when I can pay the data charges myself. Like that's gonna happen. Where the hell is my purse?" I began circling frantically.

"Did you see someone grab it?"

"Everything happened so fast. No. I'm not sure what happened. The two guys . . . maybe it was one of them? What do I do? Do I need to report that, too?"

Apparently, Officer McGinnis couldn't take any more of this ditzy woman. "Sure, we can handle it at the same time. Just tell me what happened. Please?"

CHAPTER 64

S K I P

Shortly after 9 a.m. on Wednesday morning Skip waited in the lobby of Welton's office building. Around him, impeccably dressed employees entered through the glass entryway, exchanged waves with the security guard and friends, then drifted off to other parts of the building. From his position behind a tropical indoor planter, complete with palms and a small waterfall, he watched a parade he'd never seen up close before. Most men wore traditional dark suits, white shirts, conservative ties. Women matched those choices, but opted for decorative blouses instead of ties. Occasionally, a renegade sported something casual.

At 9:20, Baldorf's prediction came true. Andria hurried around the corner from the parking garage. She searched the lobby for a second, then fixed her attention on the elevators. She never saw Skip until he punched the elevator button a second before her. They exchanged a smile, hers more forced than his, then she avoided his gaze by watching the floor indicator over the elevator. At most, he probably had thirty seconds to gain her trust. He jabbed the button a few times, wondering if the simple act of matching her mood, a mirroring technique, would be enough to establish rapport right away. "You look pretty upset. Bad news?"

The doors opened; Skip gestured for her to enter first. She grimaced, but stepped into the waiting car. "Thanks."

Inside, Skip took a position in front of the buttons; Andria retreated to the back corner. He looked her in the eye. "What floor?"

"Seventeen."

He pressed the number 15. "Oops. Sorry about that. I'm going to 17, too. Guess my brain took a vacation." She smoothed the material of her blue-and-white flowered dress. Skip nodded at her stomach. "Boy or girl?"

She smiled for the first time. "A girl."

"How far along are you?"

"Six months."

Her jaw tightened. Was that anger or frustration? "A pretty young woman like you with that look? It can only mean man troubles."

"He texted me that he needed to see me right away. It's always been a rule, never come here. Ever."

"Guess he changed his mind. Maybe it's serious."

"It better be." Her face flushed bright pink when the doors opened for the 15th floor.

"Are you going to Welton Investments by any chance?" asked Skip.

"How'd you know?"

The doors to the 17th floor slid open seconds later. Skip did his best to look sheepish. "Look, the receptionist is a real busybody. You probably won't want to deal with her, so I'll distract her while you head back to see your boyfriend. Have you been to his office before?"

"Once, when we first met. I think he wanted to impress me." She gritted her teeth. "After that, he said to never come here again."

"Follow me." Skip flung the heavy glass door wide enough to allow Andria easy entry. He lowered his right arm to his side, waving her forward with his hand while making sure to shield his signal from the receptionist. To Andria, Skip whispered, "Go for it."

Melinda grimaced at Skip, but eyed Andria as she waddled past. Skip planted both hands on the desk. "I'm running late for my appointment with Oz."

When Andria reached the side door to the bullpen, Melinda's jaw fell. "What's she doing?" She jumped up, slamming her thigh into the top desk drawer. "Son-of-bitch!"

Andria stopped, but Skip waved her on. To Melinda, he said, "That must be painful."

Melinda gritted her teeth and fell back into the chair. "Was she with you? You were supposed to be here twenty minutes ago. I don't think he can still see you. Wait here while I go after her!" She punched a number into her phone. "Harriet, take my desk for a few minutes. Some woman just blew me off and walked on through. I have to find her." She hung up without waiting for an answer, winced as she rose, then marched toward the door Andria had used.

Skip followed the moment the door closed behind Melinda. He found himself at the outskirts of the bullpen, about ten steps behind his unwitting leader, when a short woman who was swearing under her breath approached. She opened her mouth to speak, but he cut her off. "You must be Harriet, I'm with Melinda."

The woman fixed Skip with fiery eyes. "Of course you are," she said as she moved to one side. "You better hurry." Her squeaky voice was almost lost in the din.

Melinda took a winding path through the cubicles. Skip followed her with his eyes, noting the leers and sneers she received. It reminded Skip of an office version of the wave. Obviously, Melinda had a reputation.

He followed her, taking the same jigsaw path. All they needed was one final player, the one he hoped Baldorf could deliver. Near the rear of the bullpen, the sounds of a raging argument overpowered the background hum. Andria was unloading on Oz when Skip entered the room. "You texted me, goddammit! You said to get down here right away. Life and death is what you said. What the hell's going on?"

"I told you never to come here!"

"Get your shit together, Ozzie! What's with the damn games? You texted me!" She pulled her phone from her purse.

Oz bellowed, "Melinda, get her the hell out of here! Why's she back here, anyway?"

Skip stepped away from his spot in the doorway and into the fray. "Tough spot to be in, Oz."

Of the three who stared at him, it was Melinda who caught on first. "You! You set this up!"

In the daylight coming through the floor-to-ceiling windows the attractive blonde took on an almost haggard appearance. The reaction to her passing through the bullpen now made more sense. Too much makeup, not enough soul. Skip raised his hands in a gesture of surrender. "I might have had something to do with it."

Andria still looked confused, but recognition dawned on Oz's face.

Melinda jabbed an accusatory finger at Skip. "You bastard!"

Oz started around the desk, but Andria cut him off. She shoved the screen of her cell phone at his face. "There's your text. Goddammit, I want an explanation!"

"That's easy," said Skip. "Mistress 1, meet Mistress 2. Ozzie has been, quite literally, screwing both of you."

"So you don't know everything," said Skip as he watched Melinda gawk, open-mouthed, at Andria's swollen abdomen.

An instant later, Melinda stepped deliberately in Oz's direction, crimson veins standing out on her cheeks. Her voice was stone cold. "You're gonna have a kid?"

Andria's attention bounced between the two a few times before she inched closer to Oz and planted a hand on his chest. "Ozzie, this is a mistake. Tell me this is a mistake."

Oz grabbed her by the shoulders, his face ribboned by bands of angry red. "Shut up and go home, Andria. Don't say another word."

Andria's face turned ashen, her jaw fell. Skip caught Melinda smirking to one side. She crossed the room to stand before Skip. "You really know how to stir up a shit storm, don't you?"

There was a certain amount of satisfaction with knowing he was on track, but Skip kept his emotions to himself. He stayed silent, waiting for the next visitor.

"I never saw this coming. How could I have been so stupid?" She stormed back to where Oz and Andria stood. This time, she got right in Oz's face, practically spitting out her anger. "How the hell many others are there?"

Oz pushed Melinda away. "Shut up!" He seized the phone, dialed, and said, "Call the cops, Harriet. I want an intruder arrested."

While Oz hurried back to Andria, Skip listened to the low hum of voices and keyboard clacking in the bullpen. The hum level was dying with every passing minute. Oz was losing ground in his attempt to keep his women apart. The storm was just beginning.

"I don't know who the hell you think you are, Cosgrove, but you're going to be sorry you screwed with me."

A movement at the door caught Skip's attention. He smiled at Oz. "I don't think so. Everyone, meet Mistress 3, Frederica Gurney-Welton."

CHAPTER 65

ROXY

Sleep didn't come until near dawn. Of course, this had to be the one morning this week when the sun was shining like it didn't know what a cloud was. Talk about a pain in the ass.

A shower and two cups of coffee later, my nerves were frazzled and my thoughts a jumble when there was a knock on the door. Crap! My hair was still wet, my face, plain Jane. I dashed across the room and flung the door open, oblivious to what I should have realized—Skip was still in L.A.

The man standing there jolted me into full alert mode. It was Buzz.

I pressed against the door to slam it shut, but he easily blocked it with one hand and a foot. What had I done? Always check your door, I knew that. Adrenaline raced through my system. Little movie clips of ways to die played in my mind. Then the questions began. Why hadn't he killed me already? What was he waiting for?

I stared at him. "What the hell?"

"Miss Tanner, I'm an undercover cop. Will you let me in before one of your neighbors calls the police. I don't want my cover endangered again."

"How'd you find me?"

"You gave your name and address to the officers last night."

How could I forget those two? My suspicions about them resurfaced. Were these guys all in Jackie's pocket? "Who do you work for?" The demand sounded preposterous. Why would he tell me anything?

"I'll tell you everything, just not out here."

I remembered how cooperative Buzz had been when the cops took him away. A distant observer wouldn't have noticed, but I'd been standing over him. Right now, my choices were to have Lily call 9-1-1 or—or what? Trust him? Talk about not liking my options.

He held up both hands, the badge in one, no gun in the other. He removed his size 12 from the doorway. "Truce? While I explain?"

I still hated my choices. "Why are you here?"

He stood patiently. "I still need to be careful. That paper you gave to Jackie last night triggered events that are just now breaking."

That told me nothing, however, my curiosity had gotten the better of me. "What's your real name?"

"You can call Detective Holmes, he briefed Skip early this morning."

My heart skipped a beat at the mention of Skip's name. Had I missed a text from him? The longer I stood face-to-face with this guy—on my doorstep, no less—the more idiotic I felt. The bedroom door creaked open behind me.

"Roxy? Who are you talking to? Holy shit!" Lily slammed the bedroom door.

"Dammit!" I ran across the room, but she'd already locked it. "It's okay, Lily!" Behind me, I heard Buzz's voice. Crap! I couldn't be everywhere.

"My name is Jason Killian," he said. "I work for an interagency drug task force. This morning we took down both Jacinto Fontanal and Fu Zhang. This Joey Santino, he's disappeared."

I turned to face Jason. "What did you say?"

"Santino is missing. We think he might be after you next."

CHAPTER 66

S K I P

Frederica Gurney-Welton slammed the door to Oz's office, sending a shudder through the walls and windows. She did a double take when she saw Skip. The veins on her forehead mapped out her anger along with something else—suspicion.

Across the room, Oz still stood next to Andria, his face now buried in his hands.

Melinda was off to one side, bathed in the harsh daylight from the window, that sinister smile still on her face. She was the first to break the silence. "You warned me."

"I tried, but you weren't listening."

"I'm listening now, what do you want to know?"

Frederica's icy tone cut in. "Enough of this bullshit chit chat." She glared at Skip. "What do you mean, Mistress 3?"

Skip figured Oz would try to lie his way out of this mess, so he wasn't surprised when the man left Andria to approach Frederica. When his expression turned to one of shame and remorse, Skip wasn't sure what would happen next.

"Honey, I've made a terrible mistake. I was unfaithful to you and I'm sorry."

Skip cursed under his breath. Now he was going to tell the truth? Oz was a wily son-of-bitch, no doubt about it. Skip watched Frederica's tough veneer crack.

Melinda arched her back, gazing calmly at Frederica while Andria stroked her stomach and bit her lip—the worry on her face unmistakeable.

Frederica swallowed hard. Oz stood no more than a couple of feet from her. "With both of them?"

Andria slumped into a chair near the window, tears streaming down her cheeks. She sobbed quietly, stroking her stomach while she muttered to herself. "What am I going to do? My sponsor warned me about you." She shook her head in disbelief, her eyes pleading with Oz.

For the first time, Melinda showed a softer side. She approached Andria, knelt next to her and put a consoling hand on her arm. "Don't feel bad, honey, he fooled me too. At least he's a good liar." She craned her neck in Oz's direction.

Any strength Andria might have had appeared shattered. She gripped the material of her shirt in a fist and jerked her arm away from Melinda. Her cheeks were ringed in black, her voice shaky, when she looked up at Oz. This time, defiance rose from beneath her anguish. "How could you do this? You said you loved me."

"Honey, he'll say anything to get you into bed." Melinda made another attempt to console Andria, but the sisterly approach appeared to be a wasted effort.

Frederica shook with rage. "You're finished here!" She slapped Oz with a blow that turned his head sideways.

Through the glass wall, Skip saw the final players approaching. Frederica turned to walk away, but Skip blocked her exit. "You need to stick around, the best is yet to come." He motioned at the four men who stood outside the door to enter. Frederica's eyes widened. Two detectives and two uniformed LAPD officers distributed themselves throughout the room.

She glared at Oz, who was still rubbing his cheek. "What have you done?"

Skip recognized Buddy, his friend from LAPD, but not the second detective. It was Buddy who took the lead. "Mr. Oz, you called about a disturbance?"

Oz pointed a finger at Skip, his teeth bared as he sneered. "Arrest him! He's trespassing."

Buddy regarded Skip with pursed lips. "I'd love to, but did you, by any chance, have an appointment with him?"

"No! The son-of-a-bitch barged in here without authorization."

Melinda said, "He was late, but he had an appointment with Mr. Oz."

"Goddammit Melinda! What the hell are you doing?"

"What I should have done the first time you asked me to destroy documents you lying snake."

"Shut up!" Oz started in her direction, but stopped when Buddy clamped a hand on his arm. When Buddy released his grip, Oz muttered, "Stupid bitch."

Melinda distanced herself from the fallout by drifting to one side. "Detective . . ." She paused, watching Buddy expectantly.

"Winestock."

Skip admired the move; it was one Roxy might have used to make nice with the man. It also made him wonder if this girl might be more dangerous than he'd calculated.

"Detective Winestock," said Melinda, "Someone has been stealing from the firm."

Oz lowered his voice—his tone still seethed. "If any documents have been destroyed, it was her idea. I was getting ready to fire her anyway because she's incompetent."

"You don't have the authority to fire anybody in this company," Frederica said.

Buddy ignored the exchange. Instead, he focused his attention on Melinda. "You have any proof of this, Miss?"

"I have some documents in my car that Mr. Oz asked me to shred. I've got a few other batches at home. Plus, I have his email that I must have forgotten to destroy."

"So you did listen to me," said Skip. "Smart girl."

Oz dabbed at the beads of sweat on his forehead. His complexion blanched.

"You've been stealing from me? And Jack? Tell me you didn't," said Frederica.

"Oh, he did," countered Melinda.

Oz searched the room as though he might find an excuse propped up against the wall or perched on top of his credenza, but there was nothing. "Why would I do that? Jack was my partner."

Frederica grunted. "Did you kill him?"

He crossed the room to stand next to Andria. He placed a hand under her chin. His smile was confident, even sincere. "No, we were together that night. Weren't we, honey?"

Ouch, thought Skip, using one mistress in front of the others. Talk about desperate. All eyes in the room settled on Andria, who sat, apparently disconnected from the events around her. When she looked up, Skip wondered if she realized that she now held all the power. Would this give her the leverage she needed to corral Oz into marriage? She sat up straight, braced herself on the chair, then rose to face him.

"You two-timing son-of-a-bitch, I won't lie for you." She turned to Buddy. "He slipped out right after he got there."

Oz stammered. "No. You're not remembering correctly."

Her voice was confident with a hint of satisfaction around the edges. "I'm not mistaken. He left my place after he told me he was going to some swanky party. I remember it clearly."

"Andria, baby, what are you doing?"

"He went to see you?" Melinda crossed her arms over her chest. She planted one foot in front of the other while she looked Oz up and down. "You blew me off to be with her? And then you went to a party?" Melinda's face softened as she looked at Andria. "He is a son-of-a-bitch, honey. He told me he had an early meeting. How long have you two—been together?"

"Eight months."

"Shut up, Andria!"

"No, Oz, you shut up!" Frederica strode to within inches of Oz and jabbed him in the chest with an accusing finger. "You were screwing me for money?"

It sounded more like an accusation, but Skip supposed it might have been a question. In any case, Buddy was doing his damnedest not to smile while he wrote furiously.

Oz grabbed Frederica's arm, but the fire in her eyes said the game was over. He released her arm. "No, Freddie, it wasn't like that."

"Then how was it?"

"I'll tell you how it was." Andria's voice faltered. "This guy's a sex addict. That's how we met. At first, he was all, let's take it slow. He's so smooth. Even though it was against the rules, he got me to sleep with him. Next thing I know, he wants it all night long and I'm right back where I was. When he wasn't around, he said he was either out of town or remorseful for having dragged me back into 'the game.' He doesn't have a remorseful bone in his body."

Frederica shook her arm free, backed away and sneered at Oz. "So that's what I was? A game?"

Oz waved his hands back and forth. "No, no. You don't understand, Freddie, she was the game. I was only using her for sex."

Andria muttered, "Bastard!"

"So you got her pregnant?" Frederica sneered at Oz. "So that makes me what?"

Skip searched her eyes, now brimming with tears, for anything other than hatred. He saw nothing. Quietly, he said, "A widow."

Frederica slapped Skip. When she reached back to slap him again, he clamped a hand on her wrist. She crumpled into his arms, sobs wracking her body. "You killed my husband because of what? Money? This?" She waved a hand in the air.

"I'm not taking the fall for her. She's the one that wanted Jack out of the picture."

"Oh no you don't." Frederica's voice sounded ragged. "You're not pinning that on me. I said it would be nice if he would go away."

Oz pointed at Frederica. "You're one hell of an actress, Freddie." He looked at Buddy. "That's not what she said at all. Two weeks before Jack died she said she wanted to have him killed. She begged me to kill him."

Skip helped Frederica into the nearest chair, her face was now pale, her entire body sagged. "That night he got me drunk, that's when we—I—started fantasizing about what it would be like to be rid of Jack. I was being stupid. Now I can see that this one's worse than my husband."

"Sounds like he took you seriously," said Buddy.

"Bullshit!" shouted Oz. "She wasn't drunk and I can prove it. I've got it all on video at my apartment." He closed his eyes when Buddy turned suddenly to face him. "I want my lawyer. Now."

Buddy nodded. "Yeah, you might want to quit while you're ahead. I think, what, maybe twenty people just heard that."

"Oh my God." Frederica's breathing was fast and ragged. The blood had drained from her face. "You videotaped us? Me? Doing— I'll be ruined."

Oz snarled, "This is entrapment."

"You were the one who called the cops, remember?" said Skip.

Buddy gave Skip a thumbs up before motioning to the other detective, who stepped forward along with one of the officers.

They read Oz his rights before leading him from the room, but Buddy watched Frederica expectantly. "Mrs. Welton?"

"I'm not saying a word."

"Yes, ma'am."

Melinda, still off by herself, fidgeted with her left earring. "What about me?"

"You'll need to show me those files. I've also got questions about your involvement."

"What about her?" Melinda cocked her head in Andria's direction.

Andria stared absently out the window. Skip felt sorry for the torture she would be forced to endure. He hoped it would make her stronger in the end.

Buddy said, "She may be the only one in this room who is innocent."

CHAPTER 67

R O X Y

Lily opened the bedroom door. She stood, waving my Taser in the general direction of our intruder—or me—depending on how far her arm wavered. Buzz or Jason or whatever his name was held his badge high in the air. I went to Lily, took the weapon from her hand and aimed it at our visitor.

"Holmes told me you were trouble," Jason said.

"Holmes? Why'd my name come up? What's this got to do with me?"

"Relax. Your boyfriend was busy last night. He sent some video surveillance to Detective Holmes. Holmes and I worked a couple of cases together a long time back. He did a brief stint in vice. Later, he jumped ship to work Homicide. Anyway, the video told us all about a delivery this morning. Holmes said Skip was going to contact you about me."

Sure enough, a text from Skip in my messages vouched for Jason. "It's okay, Lily. Buzz—I mean, Jason is really an undercover cop. What should I call you, anyway?"

"Jason's my real name."

"Fine. Jason it is. Coffee?"

Lily looked conflicted. First, she eyed me, then the Taser, then Jason, who still stood uneasy in the corner.

I gestured at the table. "You can both stop worrying about this thing, I'm out of cartridges. Right now, it's dead. Speaking of that, why did you come after me last night?"

"When I saw you on the street, Tank and I were just finishing up. He'd gotten orders from Jackie to kill you, so I pulled a knife and told him Jackie wanted me to take you out personally—and quietly. I planned on making a show of a struggle so I could get you to safety, but you surprised me." He nodded at the table. "If you'd have gotten me with that thing, he would have shot you. Lucky for you, he panicked when he heard sirens."

"So I didn't connect with that kick."

He smiled sheepishly. "You were a tad slow."

"That's it," I said, "I'm going back into training tomorrow." I poured two cups and gave one to Jason. Lily's face was still clouded over. "What's up, sweetheart?"

"I don't, like, trust him." Her eyes flicked in Jason's direction.

"Skip vouched for this guy. Apparently, he knows Detective Holmes, who's a real thorn in his side, but Skip thinks he's trustworthy."

"He's, like, a cop."

"You don't trust the cops because of your mom?"

She took the chair opposite Jason. It looked to me like she was ready for a confrontation, but no sooner had her butt landed in her seat than her eyes lit up. "Could I, like, have some hot chocolate?"

"You bet." I turned to Jason. "While I start on that, tell me why you were with Big & Ugly and Tattoo Boy—I mean, Tank—in the first place. What were you finishing up?"

"Big & Ugly? We'd better keep that one quiet. But, it's pretty close to true. Cho's a smart guy—not a bad sort—for a psychopath."

"You still haven't told me why you were talking to him on the streets. Or this guy Tank."

Jason leaned back in his chair. "Are you familiar with how spies work?"

I chuckled. "Can't say that I ever got an offer from the CIA. How about you, Lily?"

She shook her head, still watching Jason suspiciously.

"Fair enough," said Jason. "Most people don't know there's a back channel. We need info, so do they. You don't share everything, just enough to maintain equilibrium. A few months ago, the equilibrium started to break down, but Cho and I kept the channel open anyway. We were exchanging information and debating the merits of killing off Joey Santino when you went by. He thinks the guy's a shit, I said Santino had some value."

"As what? A killer?"

"You've spent too much time looking at this from the wrong angle." He went on to describe how Joey had worked for Jackie Fontanal.

I was halfway to the table with Lily's hot chocolate when he dropped the bombshell.

"All three were in Boss Guito's gang. They were really tight for the longest time."

"What?" I stopped in my tracks, the drink almost spilling on the floor. "All three of them were friends?"

"Gimme that!" Lily reached up to snatch the mug from my hands. "What's the big deal? Them being, like, friends ain't no different than in school."

Jason ignored Lily's statement. "They grew up together. Nobody ever trusted Joey except for Jackie, so Fu Zhang and Jackie rose up through the ranks as equals, but Joey was always the third wheel. Anyway, it was a big, happy family until the boss started suspecting he had a snitch in the ranks."

I burst out laughing.

"What's so funny?" Jason asked.

"You don't get it. Another piece of the puzzle just fell into place." They both gave me blank stares, but the con artist in me got it. I now understood Joey. "Last night when I was talking to Jackie, I kept having the feeling that he was holding something back. You know, like he had a big secret."

"Like I said, it ain't no different than school." Lily glowered over her mug. "That's why I hate it."

"You're going through a tough time sweetheart."

She licked her lips, but looked me in the eye. "The bullies, like, tell lots of stories about the other kids. Jackie, he ain't no different. He's just, like, better at it."

Jason nodded. "She's right. My girls have the same problems at their school. You know, that's exactly what Joey did, tell stories to the boss. According to Tank, Joey's the one who asked Jackie to eliminate you last night."

"Wait a minute! Joey was at the bar last night?"

"The weasel is there a lot. I think he had a meeting with Jackie just before you showed up. Why?"

"Some guy bumped into me when I was talking to Jackie. I only caught a glimpse of him, but he seemed somehow familiar."

"Probably Joey," said Jason. "He's always scheming in one way or another."

Lily's eyes went wide. "Creepy? That's your dude? The one who bumped you?"

"What do you mean creepy?"

"I ain't never, like, heard a name. That's what I call him. Creepy, like, talks to Jackie all the time."

"Since when?"

She shrugged as her tongue massaged her upper lip. "Since, like, a week ago?"

I nearly spit out my coffee. The solution had been right before me all along. "No wonder Jackie looked so amused last night when I told him about Joey. He's not a third wheel anymore, he's the one orchestrating everything."

"He never had that kind of power."

"Not power, Jason—influence. He had Jackie's ear. I'll bet he had Guito's at one point."

Jason had a "what the hell" look on his face. He said, "How did you make that leap? There's no evidence Joey had some master plan."

I smiled. "People are my business."

All I got was a scowl in return. "I have to work from facts, not wild guesses. From what I hear, you and Skip operate on your 'experience' a lot."

Ouch, talk about snippy. "Skip's a bit more traditional than I am, but think about it for a minute. Joey lies to the boss about Jackie. Since he's Jackie's best friend and he's ratting him out, the boss buys the story. He tells Fu Zhang to take out Jackie. He probably ordered Joey to be the one to pull the trigger, but Fu Zhang is the insurance policy. In the boss's mind, he's got two guys watching each other. As far as he knew, he had a redundancy built in; nothing could fail."

"So why didn't Fu Zhang take out Joey and Jackie?"

"I have new respect for Joey. He must have been working Fu Zhang at the same time, dropping hints every once in a while about who was next. When the two of them got their assignment, Fu figured Joey knew what he was talking about. Joey brokered a deal between the two lieutenants and the three agreed to take out the boss."

Jason looked lost in thought—he did a little nose scratching, a bit of head tilting from side-to-side. It must have been one hell of an argument going on behind those rough features of his. He punched a number into his phone, then waited.

"Yeah." No hello. No introductions. Obviously, these two knew each other well. Jason said, "You wanted me to call if Tanner came up with a theory. It's just crazy enough to be true."

He went on to describe what we'd discussed, grunted some sort of agreement and disconnected. He looked me in the eye when he spoke. "Holmes thinks you might be right."

"That was Holmes? What did he have to do with this case?"

"Holmes got the Guito homicide. He always liked Joey as the killer, but Santino was legally drunk when they arrested him for the robbery. The only thing Joey said was that he did the holdup and wanted a lawyer. The only reason I can think of that a guy might confess to armed robbery is if he's trying to hide something bigger."

"Like murder."

"We had two witnesses, the video and a confession. The ME couldn't narrow down the time of Guito's death so it didn't seem likely we could convince a jury some drunk murdered the biggest drug dealer in town then ran down the street to hold up a liquor store for a few hundred bucks. I like your theory. Trouble is, it's not possible. Joey couldn't pull it off alone."

"Shaina?"

"Too straight."

"Fu Zhang? Jackie?"

"Both had alibis."

I remembered Baldorf telling me how he'd found Shaina through a relative. "What about family? She's been staying with a cousin."

"Maybe. So, you think Joey enlisted the help of a cousin to kill his boss and hold up a liquor store? Santino's always been nothing more than a two-bit drug hustler. Why would he want to do hard time for armed robbery? That's pretty farfetched for a couple of hundred bucks."

Oh. My. God. He didn't do all this for a few hundred bucks, I thought, he did it for a score. How stupid could I have been? This was my business—no, my life—and even I hadn't seen it. I'd conned some very wealthy people out of nearly $5 million a few months ago and returned the money only because Mr. Right wouldn't let me do wrong. In some ways, it still pissed me off that Skip had put me in a position where I had to choose between destroying his life or living mine. The difference was that Joey didn't have someone like Skip trying to make him go straight. "Was there a safe at the homicide scene?"

"Yeah, Guito had a few grand in there, but the safe was locked."

"It was locked when you found it, not necessarily when he was killed."

Jason's eyes defocused as he pondered what I'd said.

When he looked back at me, I said, "So with the boss dead, the gang split?"

"Down racial lines."

"You also said you thought Joey had value—why?"

"He's an opportunist. He also knows how to exploit weaknesses. That's what Skip called him at the trial. He said Joey was the kind of guy who would turn on anyone if he had a chance to gain. He testified that he was convinced Joey committed the robbery, but the motive had nothing to do with getting money from the store. He always thought there was something bigger. With the right inducement, that kind of guy could be turned into a valuable asset."

"I should have seen this long ago. The more you talk, the more I realize how well I know Joey's next move. While you're setting him up to snitch, he'll be playing you. Believe me, I get this guy."

"If Joey stole all this cash, why didn't he spend it on an attorney? It was a public defender all the way."

"I suspect Joey conned everybody, including his two best friends. He planned a robbery he knew would fail so he'd get busted."

"That's what Skip said. So you both think he benched himself?"

"That's messed up."

"You've got that right, kid," said Jason. "None of this has made any sense from the beginning."

Quite the contrary, I thought. If you understood the lure of the con, it all made perfect sense. Joey had patience and cunning. That made him exceptionally dangerous. "Let's change our focus." I had a mental picture of me watching Joey topple a line of huge dominoes with one push of his hand. In the picture, I acknowledged his skill with a quick thumb's up. Now that I understood him, it was time to rein him in. "Who got what? Who had what to gain?"

Jason laughed. "Everybody got screwed. The boss got killed, the gangs had to rebuild. Even Joey went off to prison with nothing. Sounds like a bad plan."

"Maybe not, Jason. If Joey did get a bundle out of Guito's safe, he might think a few years locked up was a small price to pay for permanent retirement. Maybe he didn't know about the camera in the store or thought he could skate on that charge, too."

"We may never know. Problem is, Joey has disappeared. Holmes wanted me to warn you and see if you had any theories about him."

"I didn't think Holmes was part of the Roxy Tanner Fan Club."

"He's not." Jason said.

Message received, I thought. You don't like me, but you need my expertise. This street went two ways. "So Skip sent Holmes that video last night?"

"We can't use it in court. However, we did use it as background to line up the bust. It got us a whole bunch of bad guys. Fortunately, these guys have gotten so arrogant that they were conducting their business in plain sight, so the DA will be happy. Jackie's gang was well represented, also. It was quite a party. It could take a couple of days to bring in all of the players, but we've caught a major break thanks to that video. Anyway, let's go back to the reason I came here—Joey's missing. We think he'll be after you and Skip."

In the pit of my stomach, I had a sick feeling, the one that accompanies news of a disaster. "We're right back where this all started."

"Sure looks that way to me."

CHAPTER 68

S K I P

The morning sky was the coastal equivalent of blue, with bright sun and water vapor saturating the air to create a distant silver haze. The constant pressure since Joey's attack had drained most of Skip's energy. On top of that, the close-knit, fast-paced traffic from L.A. had sapped his last ounce of strength.

At the rest stop north of Oceanside, he pulled in for a short break, parked in the first available spot, reclined his seat all the way, and was asleep within seconds. The sounds of nearby car doors slamming jarred him awake twenty minutes later. After walking to the restroom to splash water on his face, he felt refreshed enough to finish the drive. Soon, however, he was going to need some serious downtime. He called Roxy to tell her that Anita and Dom would be at Marjorie's at 2 p.m. Instead of relieved, she sounded hesitant. "What's bothering you?" he asked.

"Jason just told me that Joey's gone missing. Skip, you were right about him from the get go. He's out to kill both of us—maybe he thinks you'll figure out his plan."

"That's ridiculous, I have no idea what his plan is."

"Actually, you did. You said Joey had a different motive for holding up that convenience store. Holmes thinks Joey killed Guito in some sort of deal with Fu Zhang and Jackie Fontanal."

"Who's this Jackie? I've never heard of him. Did the cops find Joey?"

"He disappeared. I'll fill you in when you get here."

Joey on the loose was the worst possible scenario. Skip wondered where he would turn up. When? "Goddamn he's slippery."

"More than you know. Hang on, my other line's ringing."

CHAPTER 69

R O X Y

The caller on the other line was Marjorie. With Jason gone and Lily in the shower, I felt this might be a perfect time to get a few pointers on how to deal with a twelve-year-old girl. After all, Marjorie had been through the whole routine with Anita in a parenting role. I had zero experience with that phase of life other than what I'd been through myself.

"Anita and Dom are here," said Marjorie. "She's demanding that you show up right away."

Already? Something was wrong. I guess the parenting tips would have to wait. "She's there? Now? Skip told her two."

"Sorry, honey."

"Okay, twenty minutes." I disconnected Marjorie's call. Damn, we needed to be ready to roll in five minutes. Talk about a challenge. I hurried to the bathroom to alert Lily, who was just finishing up her shower and wasn't at all happy with the news.

"Serious?" she said.

"Serious."

"That sucks."

"Tell me about it." Now we'd both look like we'd just rolled out of bed. I returned to Skip's line. "Anita's at Marjorie's. How far away are you?"

"Not that far," said Skip. "I'm at the rest stop. What do you think she's up to?"

"That was going to be my question. You're the one who saw her last."

"She wants Welton's money. Bad."

"I'm counting on it. Meet me at Marjorie's, okay?"

"Will do. One more thing. Be careful. She's on the edge."

Half an hour later, an unusually subdued Marjorie greeted Lily and me at her door. She pointed back into the room with a nod of her head. "I've never seen her this mad."

Anita and Shaina huddled together in the living room with Anita perched on the end of Marjorie's couch, Shaina in the chair immediately to her right. Dom was nowhere in sight. Before I could say a word, Anita jumped up and stormed across the room. Given what she was wearing, a pair of painted-on designer-knockoff jeans and imitation Lucchese cowboy boots, I was surprised she could move so quickly. The outfit made her look like a two-bit hooker on the hunt.

"There you are! Where's my money?"

"Anita, technically, it's not yours." I watched her closely. Her normally blue eyes were pale gray. Her anger, I could manage. Dom, however, I wasn't so sure. Time to divide and conquer. "What do you two plan to do next?"

"I don't know. I—I'm not sure."

"Running may not be your best choice."

"Roxy's right," said Marjorie. "Leaving now won't solve your problems. They'll only get worse."

From the couch, Shaina added her two-bits. "You can't trust no one, girlfriend."

"I trust Dom, he's my brother. He won't betray me."

"C'mon girl, you think he's gonna put your interests before his own? Push comes to shove, your brother's gonna roll over on you without thinking twice."

Great, Anita's new BFF was a deadbeat mom with a healthy distrust of the world. How perfect. "Who's idea was it to run? Dom's?"

Anita stared absently at a spot on the floor; even her voice sounded disconnected. "When Dom heard about Jack, he said we needed to get out of town. You know, before the cops started putting the pieces together."

It made no sense to me that Dom would want to give up his business . . . unless. "You sure that wasn't the money talking? Is he in some sort of financial trouble? Why would he abandon his clients?"

"Business hasn't been the best lately. People are getting tired of huge vet bills when they can't afford to feed their kids. Dom's suffering. We told all this to your boyfriend last night."

"Anita, Dom didn't work for that money," I said. "For that matter, neither did you."

"Well, isn't that just the pot calling the kettle black? You can sit there and lecture me after I hired you to steal in the first place?" Gazing into Marjorie's eyes, Anita reached out to take her aunt's hand. "Sorry, Auntie Em I haven't made the best choices. I know I've disappointed you, but I never stole anything before. Not like her."

Despite the two bitches with attitude wanting to tear me down, I pressed on. "That's precisely why I can say that. Believe me, I know what it's like to run. Who knows, maybe you'd be happy with that life." I glanced over at Lily for a split second before looking back at Anita. "It's taken its toll on me."

Shaina pulled back her dark hair, the smirk on her face growing by the second. "You told me you were trying to save me from those dealers. You're a thief?"

"She did step in to save you," said Marjorie. "Roxy's no crook."

I wanted to crawl into a hole. How could Marjorie not know what I did for a living? She couldn't be that naive. Well, now she'd know and she would hate me, too. "That's fine, Marjorie. I deserve it. Since we're all being honest, I can't even tell you how many cons I've pulled. Just remember that if it wasn't for me—and Lily—right now you'd be strapped to a chair next to Joey while some goon stuck needles under your nails. Or maybe they'd just shoot you up to get you—or, better yet, Tina—high in front of Joey. I'm pretty sure he'd tell them anything they wanted to know at that point." I watched the color in her face drain. "Yeah, I thought you might not have thought that far ahead. Right now, Shaina, this crook saved your ass—and your daughter's."

"She risked her life to save two people she didn't even know," said Marjorie.

Anita leaned forward, dismissing her aunt's statement with a derisive laugh, then glared at me. "What's your price for that?"

"Anita! Shame on you!"

I could almost feel the color draining from my cheeks—Lily would know what I was. This could go no further, whatever the consequences. "Marjorie! Why are you defending me?" I swallowed hard. "She's right, I'm a crook."

Lily's face fell.

Marjorie shook her head at me. "No, Roxy, Anita's not right." Anita's smile disappeared when Marjorie faced her. "You're the one who contacted Roxy about stealing from your ex-boyfriend. Now you're upset because she wants a percentage?" Marjorie burst out laughing. "I can't believe I just defended a criminal enterprise."

A child's cries drifted into the room; Shaina stormed out without another word.

I started to reach for Marjorie, but she waved me away. "Are you okay?" I asked.

"I can't believe I raised this girl. When did you become so obsessed with money, Anita?"

"Since your friend here stole two million dollars from me!"

"So you'd throw your life away for money? That's all you care about now? Two million dollars?"

"That's right!" It was Dom, rushing into the room. "She changed the password on our account so we can't access it."

The shock I'd seen earlier on Lily's face had been replaced by a smile. She whispered, "Sweet."

Marjorie turned on her with a look that plainly said, don't you get started.

"Sorry, Auntie Em." Lily glanced down.

Talk about sweet—I had to admire the kid's quick comeback. Anita, however, wasn't impressed.

"Auntie Em? You two aren't related, you little brat! You're nothing but a—"

I clamped a firm hand on her arm. "Stop right there." Anita's skin was cold to the touch. She might be petrified by this confrontation, but whatever she felt, she wasn't doing a hit-and-run on Lily while I was around.

Marjorie stepped between us. "I've got this Roxy. Anita, I didn't raise you to be rude, but you've turned out that way. I didn't raise you to steal money, but you've done that, too. Now you're picking on a child? I have no idea how you could do that. Maybe you should leave."

"She's a street kid! She's a nothing! You're my aunt, not hers."

Shaina walked into the room holding Tina, who had both gangly arms and legs wrapped around her mother. "Jeez, can you guys hold it down? You woke Tina with all this yelling. It's got her freaked out."

Lily moved in next to me; she put her arm around my waist. "Should we, like, go?"

I watched Marjorie, amazed at the change in her posture and facial expression. Her normally hunched frame became erect, her saggy jaw tightened. In the few months since I'd met her, not once had I seen her so determined. Until this moment, I never would have guessed she'd fretted over anything in her life. Maybe I'd misjudged her.

"Everybody sit down."

We all gawked, but her determination couldn't have been stronger. With the exception of Dom, we all sat quietly.

Marjorie barked, "Now, Dom!"

Dom was unstable in my opinion, but even he had the good sense to sit. Marjorie stood in the center of the room with her hands raised. The image of her doing this with groups of employees flashed into my head. Maybe she had done this a thousand times.

"I'll get to all of you," said Marjorie. "But, I always liked starting these things with something easy. So, Shaina, how's the room?"

Shaina hesitated, then dragged out her single word response. "Good."

"And?" Marjorie watched her intently. When Shaina didn't speak, Marjorie said, "Just in case you didn't understand, it's your turn. It's my house. My rules. You've had a chip on your shoulder since before you got here. Roxy has done everything she can to save you. If you can't appreciate how much she's risked, you're not welcome here. You can call a cab. Hell, I'll call one for you. Whatever you want."

Marjorie moved closer. "Look, you've gotten some bad breaks. Maybe you had a no good boyfriend." She paused, gazing at Tina for a moment, who tightened her grip on her mother's leg. "But he gave you a beautiful daughter. It's time to choose, Missy. You can either hold that grudge for the rest of your life or you can move on. You and your daughter are welcome here while Roxy helps you out. I sure don't understand why she's doing it; I wouldn't. Anyway, my place is small, but if you want help, I'm willing to lend a hand."

Shaina shifted Tina so that the little girl sat on her mother's lap. "Roxy, I'm sorry for being so hard on you. After you left, Marjorie and me talked some more. I get it, the chances you took."

"That's better," said Marjorie. I swear the look she gave me was the same one my mother used when I was in trouble—which was pretty much all the time after my eighth birthday.

"You're welcome, Shaina." I said a silent thank you to Mom for her years of persistence, but couldn't help suspect that something wasn't quite right with Shaina. She had wheels turning in that head of hers—she was working on a plan—I needed to know what it was. I decided to play one of those hunches Jason hated. "Have you heard from Joey?"

She wrung her hands while she balanced Tina on her knee. "No. You really think he's in trouble?"

It wasn't the response I'd expected; she really seemed concerned. I remembered what Jason had said about Joey, how he'd disappeared. He'd abandoned his girlfriend and child? It was time to fudge the truth. "Nothing's changed. He's still being hunted by Fu Zhang." I blew air out of my cheeks in an exaggerated huff. "He's gone, Shaina."

He's disappeared?" Her complexion went ashen.

Maybe she was starting to realize all might not be what she thought. I asked, "What do you know about him?"

"Not much, Joey always kept me out of it. He said that guy was bad news."

Poker players call it "the tell"—a subtle change in appearance so minor the inexperienced eye will miss it. In Shaina's case, it was how she batted her eyes. She'd never done that before—with those killer lashes, I would have remembered. She'd just lied. But why? I smiled sweetly. "I'll let you know the moment I get any news. Okay?"

"Thanks," she said.

Marjorie was about to say something to Anita when there was a knock on the door. She pointed a finger at Anita and Dom. "Stay put." She crossed the room, opened the door, and said, "Good. You, too. Come in, sit down, and keep quiet until it's your turn."

CHAPTER 70

SKIP

Skip entered the room and pulled out a chair. "Yes, ma'am," he said as he sat, expectant and curious. Even though he didn't know where this was going, Marjorie's tone showed she had a clear picture of where she was headed.

He did a visual sweep. He wasn't surprised to see Dom and Anita huddled next to each other on the couch—they both looked scared and ready to run. On the far end of the couch, he recognized Shaina. He'd seen her at Joey's trial, but had never before seen the little girl on her lap. Skip guessed the girl's age to be about four or five. He recalled Roxy telling him the girl's name was Tina. She appeared bored even though her mother toyed with her hair. Roxy sat in a chair that was kitty-corner to the couch. As unreadable as he'd ever seen her, she did wink when they exchanged a glance. He wondered if she was enjoying this little gathering.

So who was the other girl—long legs and arms and wet hair pulled back. He stood, crossed the room to where the other girl stood next to Roxy, and extended his hand. "I'm Skip."

She giggled as she grinned ear-to-ear. "He's, like, so hot!" She reached out and shook hands.

Roxy gently elbowed Lily's leg. "Yeah. He is."

Skip's embarrassment level was on the rise, but that didn't stop him from letting Roxy know what was coming. "We need to talk."

"I told you, Lily's staying with me."

"This is about L.A."

Marjorie cleared her throat. "Later."

Lily grimaced as she plopped down on the floor next to Roxy. Skip returned to his chair, still wondering how Marjorie had gotten everyone to sit so patiently. This was like a kindergarten class in the middle of a reprimand—with the woman Roxy called a cream puff in charge. He'd never seen Marjorie so—stern.

"Now, where was I?" said Marjorie. "Oh, yes, Shaina. Listen to the voice of experience. You're getting a second chance. Don't blow it." Marjorie turned to Dom. "You, mister."

"Me? What did I do?" He raised a guilty hand to his chest.

"It's more like, what didn't you do? You need to stop controlling Anita. Your sister has had enough difficulty in her life. Stop dragging her into something that will send her to jail."

"That's it!" Dom started to rise, but Marjorie pushed gently against his chest and he fell back onto the couch.

Skip thought he saw a faint smile on Marjorie's face and wondered if she'd been waiting for that moment. He also noticed that Lily, who had been sitting cross-legged on the floor, recoiled at the physical confrontation. She seemed to relax when Roxy gave her shoulder a reassuring squeeze.

"No," said Marjorie. "That's not it. You'll listen to what I have to say. Afterwards, if you still want to leave, you'll be free to do so."

Dom's attempt at speech came out as nothing more than wasted spittle. He closed his mouth and sat quietly as Marjorie spoke to Anita.

"Why did you take this man's money?"

"He wasn't a nice man, Auntie Em. He promised it to me before. When we were sleeping together."

"So you were entitled to it." Marjorie's tone was matter-of-fact.

Anita didn't answer, but Dom did. "Yes."

Marjorie silenced him with an icy stare. She lifted Anita's chin and looked into her eyes. "It sounds like you made all the decisions.

I don't see why you feel so helpless. You chose to sleep with a married man, then you chose to steal his money."

"It's her, dammit!" Anita jabbed a finger at Roxy. "She did it! She said she could get me what I deserved!" Anita leaned into Dom, her face buried in her hands. He seemed not to notice. His exterior had gone stone cold.

Skip caught Roxy watching Dom also. She would be ready if Dom got violent. Skip shifted forward in his chair ever so slightly, his head reminding him that a fight was the last thing he needed.

"I'll get to her, honey." Marjorie continued to watch Anita's face. "But right now, you tell me something. And look me in the eye when you tell me. Did you kill this man?"

"No! I already went through this with him." She pointed at Skip. "Last night, he came by the clinic and made us go through the whole thing. He told us that if we didn't talk to him, he'd—he'd—he threatened us."

Marjorie turned to face Skip. He was exhausted. What he needed was sleep, not childish accusations. He kept his tone even. "That's an exaggeration."

"No! It's not!" yelled Dom. "He's lying. Just like she does." He pointed the same sort of accusing finger that Anita had tried just moments ago.

"You people are freaking insane," said Shaina. She stood, hoisting Tina into her arms. "Me and Tina are going back to our room." Without waiting for an answer, she left.

It was evident to Skip from the way Roxy watched Shaina that the two were at odds. No one else seemed to notice the little rocking hand motion Roxy made. When Lily stood suddenly, Skip wondered if Lily had seen Roxy's gesture or his return thumbs up.

"I'm, like, thirsty. Can I, like, get something to drink?"

Before Marjorie could respond, Roxy also stood. "Sure, sweetheart. I can handle this, Marjorie. I'll be back in a minute."

When Marjorie nodded, Skip did another quick scan of the other participants in this little intervention. He stopped when he got to Anita. The color in her cheeks was bright red; her rapid breathing reinforced the picture of someone ready to explode at any second.

Marjorie cleared her throat. "I always taught you to speak your mind, Anita. Don't hold back now."

"I don't believe how you've been taken in by her! She's nothing but a thief! She lies, she steals, and you just turn the other way! You let her get away with it. You even let her bring in that little street tramp!"

Marjorie shook her head. "Your trouble is that you only see one side of people. For instance, all you see in Dom is good. I, too, see the good. But, I know from personal experience just how deep his anger runs. Don't I, Dom?" She paused, but Dom sat with his jaw clamped shut. It might as well have been locked in a vice. "Never mind, don't answer. Anita, your brother's very good at playing the blame game. I've suspected for some time that Roxy has been a thief most of her life." She laughed. "You may think your aunt is an old fuddy duddy, but I've seen through her from almost the beginning. As for the girl you call a 'little street tramp,' she's just an innocent kid caught in a bad situation. Much like you were once. I think underneath it all she's a good kid."

"I don't care how good Lily is," said Skip, "there are laws we need to follow." He needed to make his point while he could. "Roxy can't afford to draw attention to herself."

"Sorry, I got distracted by backtracking. I was referring to Roxy. To you, she's a grown woman," said Marjorie.

Out of the corner of his eye, Skip saw Roxy and Lily return from the kitchen. They stood side-by-side in the doorway. "Marjorie," he said.

"From the moment I met her I knew she was immature, self-centered and impulsive."

Anita had a self-satisfied smirk on her face Skip wanted to wipe off with the back of his hand.

"Marjorie!" he barked. "She's right there and can hear every word you're saying."

Roxy and Lily stood ramrod straight, Roxy's arm locked around Lily in a desperate embrace. No doubt, she felt betrayed—again.

After a moment, Roxy said, "I think you're right, sweetheart. We'd better go."

Marjorie crossed the room to where the two stood. "You're not going anywhere. You think I didn't know you were there? Hell, that's why I got distracted. I could see your reflection in the glass. You've needed to hear that, but I haven't been able to say it before because it wouldn't have done any good. It would only have driven you away."

This was only making things worse, thought Skip. He rose from his chair, unsure how to mend the fence of broken trust. "Marjorie. I don't—"

She raised her hand. "Be quiet!" With her voice still firm, she said, "I'll come back to you in a minute." Marjorie stood before Roxy.

Skip saw the torment on Roxy's face. Would she stay? Or run? He couldn't predict what was about to happen. All he knew was that the next few minutes could cause irreparable damage to their relationship.

"I said I knew those things the moment I met you." Marjorie's voice became soft and soothing. "You should also know I saw beyond that tough persona of yours. I knew someone would eventually get through to you." She reached out and stroked Lily's cheek. "And here she is. This little girl is teaching you how to grow up." She looked straight at Lily, tears welling in her eyes. "What a teacher you must be, to do so much in such a short period of time."

Lily's eyes were wide with surprise. She gulped so loud Skip heard it from across the room.

Marjorie turned her full attention back to Roxy. "You are maturing into a warm, loving, young woman who has the world to give."

Roxy swiped away a tear trickling down her cheek. Skip sat back in his chair, stunned.

"Don't let your head swell too much," Marjorie continued. "In some ways, I wish you were my daughter, but since I can't call you my own, I'm proud to call you my friend."

Anita jumped up from the couch, her arms extended straight down at her sides. "That's it!" she screamed. "I hate you! I hate you! I hate you!" She ran to the front door with Dom scrambling to catch up.

When they were both gone Skip turned his attention back to Roxy, who was now locked in an embrace with Marjorie. "I'm so sorry! I'll go after her." She started to move away, but Marjorie held on.

"She's okay. She's pulled that same crap at least a dozen times. By about the fourth or fifth time, I realized she'd be back."

Lily shifted uncomfortably from side to side. Skip said, "Lily's a runaway. There are laws about harboring a minor."

Roxy snapped, "Lily's staying with me. That's what she wants."

"So there it is," said Marjorie. "You see a runaway child, I see two friends helping each other. Now get your butt over there and work something out with these two young women who need your support, not your criticism."

For once, Skip didn't know what to say.

She winked. "Quit stalling." The old woman with the wild mane cocked her head toward Roxy. "Work it out."

"I'll do anything I can to help," he said. "There's just one thing, what about the money?"

CHAPTER 71

ROXY

If Skip had intended his question to be a cue for me to return it, he might be sorely disappointed. The truth was, I still didn't know what I was going to do. The pull was almost irresistible.

"What happened in L.A.?" I asked. The last thing I wanted to talk about was what I'd done. What had he accomplished?

"Not here," he said, matter-of-factly.

"Marjorie, we're going to go for a walk, can Lily hang out with you until we get back?"

Lily gave me the lost puppy look, but Marjorie seemed delighted at the thought of spoiling her. "Sure, honey. Come with me, young lady. I have some chocolate that I need help with."

She tagged along behind her new best friend for some serious sugar indulgence, the lost puppy forgotten. "Guess I know where I stand." I pouted, but Skip wasn't buying my "poor me" attempt.

"The power of the drug."

When he opened the door for me, I smiled sweetly before giving him a peck on the cheek. I pulled out a long-forgotten skill and curtsied, momentarily a princess in a different land and time. "Why thank you, kind sir."

It didn't take long for our conversation to turn serious. We were barely to the street when Skip said, "The cops have suspicions about Oz and Mrs. Welton. They're sure one or both of them were behind the murder. It's only a matter of time and lawyer fees now. They'll be looking for the money soon. I'm betting Oz did it because it sounds like he was being double-crossed by Welton."

"Let the cops figure it out. Let's go this way." I laced my arm into the crook of his elbow. We strolled along the sidewalk, up Chinquapin, then went left on Adams, neither of us in a hurry to end what we had. We took our time, both of us seemingly lost in a moment when the outside world didn't matter.

It was Skip who broke the silence. "We need to talk about Lily."

"I don't want to talk about her. Or Anita. Or Dom. Or anything. I just want . . . this." I wrapped both arms around him, nestled my ear against his chest and listened to the beating of his heart. He pulled me closer. One beat. Two. Three.

I closed my eyes, breathing in his scent, his warmth, his love. That's all I wanted. No words, no pressures. Just quiet . . . we were enclosed in our own little bubble. Four. Five beats of his heart. Outside our bubble there was traffic—noise, people, problems. I wanted none of that. Six. Seven.

The sound of rolling tires. "Ignore it," I whispered. I felt his hand on the back of my head, stroking my hair. I wished I could snuggle closer.

A few moments later, a horn blared. "Damn cab," he said.

"Who cares?" My voice was barely a whisper. "Maybe you're right about getting out of town." In a way, I hoped he wouldn't hear me, but deep down, I prayed he did. I wanted him to be listening. I wanted—everything I'd never had.

"I guess we could take Lily with us." he said. "It's better than her being on the streets."

Heat rushed into my face. My heart felt like it stopped. I turned my face up to his, but the chirping of his phone burst our little bubble. I was beginning to hate technology.

"Shit," he kept one arm around me while he watched the display. "What the hell?" he said. "It's you." He pushed me away gently, winked and answered. "What's up?"

My phone. I'd left it at Marjorie's. I eavesdropped on his half of the conversation. "Wait, Marjorie, slow down. Say that again. She left?" Skip had other questions, but I lost track of everything. My worst fear about Lily came rushing back. I never should have left her alone with Marjorie. Did she think Skip was a threat? No, it couldn't be. Not again! I searched the street for a sign of her. Where would she go? Skip gripped my arm, but I paid no attention. Tears welled in my eyes. For what seemed like the millionth time in just a few days I wanted to curl up into a ball and die.

Skip shook me back to reality. He mouthed, "Shaina." To Marjorie, he said, "We'll be right there."

I was still in shock when a cab with Shaina and Tina in the back seat rolled by. The yellow vehicle made a left onto Tamarack when the light turned green. "Where the hell is she going?" I asked.

"Damned if I know," Skip said.

CHAPTER 72

S K I P

All the way back to the condo, one question nagged at Skip. Why would Shaina leave now?

Marjorie and Lily greeted them at the door. When Roxy saw Lily, Roxy immediately pulled her into a tight embrace. "I thought you'd run away!"

"Nah, I'm, like, hanging with you now, remember?"

Marjorie pulled Skip to one side. "Shaina just left."

"We saw the cab. I don't know that it's a big deal, the danger's over. Joey's on the run; maybe they're together." He huffed, "Your niece and nephew, too. Who knows where they've gone."

Marjorie grimaced. "Anita called me when Dom stopped for gas." She went to the couch, where she pulled two passports from Anita's purse. "They won't get far."

"All they've got is Dom's drivers license?" I asked.

"Anita said all Dom can talk about is the money. They got along fine when they were kids—unless they had to spend a lot of time together. Dom was always a schemer and Anita—well, she was always eager to please him until he blamed everything on her. Happened every time. I thought she'd gotten past it when she went in the army. I guess the distance made her forget what he's like. Now, she's remembering what trouble her brother is. I told her to get away from him and call the cops if he gives her any problems."

"Will she come back here?"

Marjorie seemed unconcerned. "Anita will be back. Dom will run. It's what he's always done. He ran away right after I took them in, so I never got the chance to raise them both. I never heard anything about him until Anita told me about his business in L.A."

"Marjorie, that place is one step away from foreclosure."

"Maybe he'll hop a freighter and see the world," said Marjorie. "It would do him good. It certainly would be best for Anita."

Skip realized that Roxy and Lily were standing just behind him. He faced them. "Everything okay?"

"Tell him what you told me," said Roxy.

Lily's face screwed up. "I might, like, know somethin' about where Tina's mom went. I didn't, like, think nothin' of it before."

"It's okay, sweetheart, you're not in trouble. You didn't know." Roxy stroked Lily's cheek.

Lily blurted, "She, like, had some hidden cell phone. Tina said her dad told them to keep it secret."

"A burner, you think?" Skip asked.

"Who knows. This doesn't feel right to me. Shaina was in the process of bailing out when we got to her place. Now, she's disappeared again. She had a plan of some sort." I felt deflated by having failed Skip. "Wish I knew what it was."

"Uh oh." Lily raised her hand. Both Skip and Roxy looked at her. "I might, like, have an idea."

"There's more?" asked Roxy.

Lily nodded. "When me and Tina were, like, playing with her dolls, she told me a secret."

"Go on," said Skip.

"Anyways, Tina, like said her mom and dad were messed up. So I was like, grownups screw up a lot and she was all, yeah, but they're gonna be getting back together."

"So Tina told you that her mom and dad were going to reconcile? How would she know that?"

"Cause' they, like, talked all the time on that phone."

"Shit," said Skip. "She wasn't worried about Fu Zhang; she thought Joey had double-crossed her."

Roxy nodded. "Sweetheart, think carefully, did she say anything else?"

"She, like, said they was gonna be rich cause her dad had something hidden back at the house where they was staying."

CHAPTER 73

ROXY

Skip hadn't wanted me to come along, but he relented under my barrage of "what ifs." Lily pulled the same crap on me, so before I knew it, I had also relented. Our ride to Shaina's place was tense, mostly because we all had to struggle against our separate, but combined, stubbornness. When we arrived, all that angst evaporated. Shaina and Tina were in the car alone.

Under threat of death and the determined stares of two adults, Lily reluctantly agreed to wait behind. I dialed 9-1-1 as we approached the car. "There's a man breaking into a house on our street. He's armed and looks dangerous." I gave them the address, making sure they understood this was an emergency before I slipped the cell into my pocket.

The little girl stood on her mother's lap while Shaina tweaked her nose and made funny Mom noises—snorting, oinking—which made the little girl giggle uncontrollably. Their play gave us the opening we needed. Skip went to the driver's side, I took the passenger's door, which she'd left open.

When we were about ten feet away, Tina pointed at me, then began jumping up and down. Shaina was scrambling for her phone when Skip yanked open the driver's door. Tina went into a panic,

Shaina instinctively clutched her daughter to her chest and the phone flew from her hand to land at my feet. I stuffed it into my back pocket.

"You got her?" said Skip.

"No problem. Be careful."

Skip pulled out his Sig, gave me a nod, then went to the front door.

"I told him this would never work. I told him!" Shaina sucked in short bursts of air, then looked up at me with pleading eyes.

"You'd better level with me now before the cops get here, which will probably be in about two minutes. What wouldn't work?"

"Joey double-cross them all."

"Who, dammit!"

"Fu Zhang, Jackie. I don't know anymore. He kept telling me he got away with some big coup thing. He said my cousin stashed a bunch of cash here while the cops were busting him for that stupid robbery. He went in to get a goddamn bottle of booze. 'Cause he was drunk, the owner pulled a gun on him. Joey was only defending himself."

"By holding the place up?"

"I ain't saying nothing more."

"What did your cousin have to do with it?"

"Nothing, he was only driving Joey around."

Already, I was tired of Shaina's bullshit. "Where's your cousin now?" I demanded.

"He left. He was letting me stay here until the end of the month because the landlord raised the rent."

"Where's the money? What room?"

Black smudges of mascara smeared her face and had even transferred onto Tina's. "In the wall. Back bedroom. Joey wanted to get it out before they rented the place, but Jorge said he's done with Joey. Last thing he said was he ain't taking no more chances for him."

It was hard for me to believe that anyone other than Skip would just walk away from a pile of cash. "He left it? Here? In the wall?"

She nodded. "That stupid Joey's always been a dreamer. He was gonna be rich. We was gonna run away together. He wanted his big score. Please—I can't go to jail—I just can't."

I felt sorry for Shaina, but worse for Tina. "You should have thought of that before you got involved in this. It will help if you testify against Joey."

"I can't go against him!"

"Then your daughter's going to grow up without a mother or a father."

CHAPTER 74

S K I P

The front steps to Shaina's house creaked underneath Skip's weight. When he looked back, Roxy had Shaina under control, but Lily had abandoned her post in the car. She was standing next to Roxy. He turned back to the house—now was not the time to think about distractions. He had to take Joey by surprise. Be quiet. Move slowly. No noises whatsoever. Surprise was his friend—the only one he would have once inside.

By rights, now that they had Shaina, the cops should handle the rest. If Joey Santino hadn't tried to kill him twice, if he hadn't threatened Roxy, he might let them do their jobs. This was personal, though. It was time to even the score. To hell with common sense.

Skip released the safety on the Sig .357. He pulled back the slide. The doorknob turned easily. If he had to shoot, he wouldn't hesitate. He gave the door a gentle push; it slipped open, but stopped halfway. He edged into the room.

The house had a small living room with each wall no more than ten to fifteen feet. A couch, a coffee table, and a rickety end table with a lamp were the only pieces of furniture in the room. The couch material was worn, but clean. The walls, bare. Hardwood flooring ran throughout the house. It had once been stylish, now it looked tired and worn. A single piece of artist's paper with a child's finger painting was the only sign of brightness in the otherwise drab room. One room clear, thought Skip.

A loud thud from the back of the house caught Skip's attention. He knew not to rush. The hard floors put him at a disadvantage. Noise would carry. He cleared the area on his left—kitchen and dining rooms—both unoccupied. A couple of seconds later another thud vibrated the walls. This time, a loud crack followed the thud. He heard Joey's voice. "C'mon, you mother. Come to papa."

Skip checked the next room. It was a bath. No towels. No toiletries. Clear. The finger painting had been the only sign that someone lived here. The hammer hit again, followed by more ripping noises. Skip peeked around the corner. Joey stood with his back to the door, bent over, breathing heavily. Skip categorized the weapons—a gun in the back of Joey's waistband, a sledgehammer in his hand, anything else?

A white powdery film covered the floor. A lazy cloud of dust drifted toward the doorway on an almost imperceptible air current. A series of holes across the wall showed that Joey had been busy looking for his prize. In his zeal, he'd pushed the only piece of furniture in the room, a stripped double bed, to one side. The bed stood at an odd angle, which gave Joey room to move. He stood with his hands on his knees, sucking in more deep breaths. He attacked the wall again, ripping off another piece of drywall. He threw it across the room, then glanced back at the opening where the top of a cloth bag was visible. The hole was still too small for the bag to pass through.

"Goddamn son-of-a-bitch, come out of there!" Joey slammed his hammer into the wall. The new opening was just south of the bag. Joey grabbed the bag with one hand while pressing against the wall with his other. The bag looked like it would rip, but then burst free from the wall, sending Joey stumbling backwards with his treasure clutched to his chest. He nearly lost his footing on the slick flooring. After he'd steadied himself, Joey kissed the bag before dropping it on the bed to peer inside. A wide grin spread across his face. He laughed hysterically while shuffling the contents. Skip almost felt sorry for him—Joey's little fairytale world was about to crumble.

"I showed 'em. Every goddamn one."

What was in the bag, thought Skip. Money? Another weapon? His heart pounded, but he concentrated on slowing his breathing. Slower. Slow. Be calm. What better place to hide a weapon used during a murder than with the cash?

Joey lifted a neatly wrapped bundle of money to his lips. Skip raised his gun, bumping against the door by accident. Joey spun on his heel, darkness on his face.

"Hey, Joey. Looks like I was wrong about you."

"How's that, Cosgrove? You thought I was just a dumb ass who did five years for nothing?"

"Something like that. Looks like you had a pension plan set up. A nice stash, I'd say."

"What do you want? How much? I ain't greedy, I'll share."

Skip shook his head. "Let's see, you've tried to kill me twice. I'm afraid you might get lucky on number three. I don't want to worry about you shooting me in the back for the rest of my life. I'll pass."

"In that case, looks like we ain't got nothing else to talk about. Can I at least grab my kid's finger painting on the way out?"

In the distance, Skip heard the warbling of police sirens. How many times in the past week had he heard that sound? "Raise your hands. Put them against the wall. Spread your feet. You know the drill."

Joey did as he'd been told; Skip moved to frisk him. The gun in Joey's waistband caught when Skip pulled on it. In that same second, Joey jammed his elbow into Skip's ribs. Skip caught Joey's jaw with a quick jab.

They both lost their footing on the dusty floor. Joey threw a second punch. It went wild. His third caught Skip's collarbone. A white wave washed over Skip's vision. He struggled for air. Joey almost went down when he moved too quickly. This time, he fell into Skip, still swinging wildly. Another bolt of agony flashed through Skip's neck. Joey hit him again. Then again.

Skip staggered backwards. The gun fell to the floor. Through the haze, he saw Joey grab it. Skip planted his feet wide and smashed his left elbow into the back of Joey's neck. The gun fell from Joey's hand and skittered to one side. Joey fell on top of a small pile of drywall shards and dust. He tried to rise, but collapsed as the snow-white shards slowly turned crimson.

Standing felt like an impossible task, so Skip seized the gun and sat on the edge of the bed. He aimed at Joey's head. "Don't think I'll miss at this range. Right now, I'd be happy to put a bullet in you and call it a day."

CHAPTER 75

R O X Y

Just before the cops arrived, Shaina appeared to give up any thoughts of escape or making a move that might endanger Tina or her own future. A life on the run had obviously lost its allure. I almost laughed when she started talking to me like a longtime friend catching up on old times.

"I don't know what I was thinking getting back together with Joey. Nah, I do. I've been on the run since before the trial. Him and Jackie and Fu Zhang have been friends since they was kids, but if those two found out Joey double-crossed them? Me and Tina would've been dead. When he told me he had enough money so we could all disappear forever, I . . . I said yes. It ain't the first time I said yes to that man and been sorry about it."

"You made a bad choice. My suggestion is that you talk to the DA. Maybe they'll cut you a deal. Your cousin, too, if he turns himself in."

"Jorge's not coming back. All because he drove Joey from some guy's house to that damn liquor store. Jorge didn't know what was gonna happen. We ain't had a life since. Jorge's the smart one, nobody's gonna find him."

Shaina was right about one thing, Jorge was the smart one.

She nodded when an officer ordered her out of the car. Tears streamed down her cheeks the moment he placed handcuffs on her wrists. "What's gonna happen to Tina?"

Shaina was so upset she didn't see the trick question coming. "Could she stay with your cousin?"

"I ought to call him."

So much for not being found, I thought.

The cops relocated me on the opposite side of one of their cars while they prepared for the unknown. Would this turn into a hostage situation? A standoff? I dialed Jason Killian's number on my cell phone using the number on the card in my pocket. He picked up on the first ring.

"Jason, this is Roxy Tanner. Skip found Joey and his stash. There are cops with guns everywhere. I'm afraid something bad is going to happen."

"Ask who's in charge and get me on the line. Now."

I didn't debate. Or question. I just asked the nearest cop. He pointed me in the direction of a man in a suit. I marched straight up to him, handed him the phone, and said, "It's for you."

The man blinked in surprise as he listened. His eyes got wide, then he looked me in the eye as he disconnected. "What the hell are you in the middle of, lady? Never mind." He turned to a uniformed officer, who I assumed might be his second in command. "We got three other agencies want to be at this party before we do anything. Nobody goes near that house until—ah shit."

I turned. Joey stood in the doorway, both hands in the air. Skip was behind him, pain and determination on his face, a gun to the back of Joey's head. The two moved together onto the front porch. Blood dripped from Joey's jaw; when he started to wipe it away, Skip barked at him. "Keep them in the air."

"Jesus," I muttered. All around me, men pointed guns at them— everything from standard-issue sidearms to assault rifles. "It's okay!" I started to rush forward, but a nearby cop forced me to stand by, helpless, as the spectacle unfolded. I realized how much I hated the feeling.

Joey shuffled in front of Skip, his shoulders slumped in defeat. Ten minutes before, he'd had it all—his girlfriend, a daughter, millions of dollars. Now, he had zip.

The man in charge said, "Put down the gun, Mr. Cosgrove."

Skip acknowledged the command. When he bent down to place his weapon on the walkway, Joey glared at him. Skip said, "Don't even try it."

Two cops with their weapons drawn approached. Tensions still ran high and my heart was in my throat. This was the moment when one mistake on anyone's part could trigger a shootout. Bullets would fly. Skip could be shot—it wouldn't matter if it was bad aim or deliberate. Dead was still dead.

Joey studied the odds and the determined faces of the men surrounding him. "Looks like you won, Cosgrove. I should've finished you off in that alley." He shuffled forward, waiting while the cops put him in handcuffs.

I overheard Skip talking to one of the cops. "I cleared the house. There's a bag of money in the back bedroom. It's the missing cash from a homicide about five years ago. You can talk to Holmes or Killian from Carlsbad PD."

The man in charge watched a uniformed officer cuff Joey. "Read him his rights." He nodded at Skip. "He's okay."

We waited, separated, to give our statements. I caught sight of Lily talking to a young officer. She looked frantic, pacing in a tight circle while she waved her hands wildly. She even had tears running down her cheeks. Finally, she gave him a big hug when he escorted her to where I stood.

The guy had one of those baby faces with smooth skin. He didn't even look like he was old enough to shave. "Is this your daughter, Ms. Tanner?"

I hugged Lily and took the moment to whisper in her ear. "Damn, you're good." I looked the young cop in the eye. "Unfortunately, no. She's the daughter of a friend, but with all the troubles her real mother has had—well, you know how kids are." I squeezed Lily's shoulder. "Are we going to be a while with the questions? If so, I should get her over to her Auntie Em's place. If that's okay?" Lily gave me her dejected-puppy look.

The young man said, "We're still waiting on a couple of drug task force guys, but she could come with us while you make a statement."

"I'd rather have her stay with her Auntie Em. Police stations are such a scary place for kids." In a way, I almost felt sorry for the poor guy. A smile, a wink and a kid's tears; he never stood a chance.

Lily gazed up at me with a sweet smile that would soon drive the boys crazy. "Will you, like, come get me later?"

"The moment they say I can go."

"It's cool then."

I called Marjorie to ask her if she could pick up Lily. She said it would be twenty minutes. Twenty minutes. After that, we were home free.

CHAPTER 76

S K I P

Skip was sure of one thing. Now that the headaches had subsided, if Lily wasn't with them, he'd have planned on a much more private activity, something intimate with wine and heavy breathing. Instead, the three of them were walking the beach, admiring the sunset. For now, he had to settle for handholding. Lily seemed fascinated by everything around her. She'd run forward, only to return a minute or two later with a broken shell or a colorful rock.

"Hard to believe she's not here all the time," he said.

"It's not easy for homeless kids to spend quality time beachcombing."

Skip watched Lily for a moment, knowing what he needed to ask next. "What are you going to do about her?"

"I don't know. I can't send her back to the Tuckers. She'll wind up on the streets again." Roxy's eyes misted up, her jaw became tense. "Can Wally help me?"

"A six hundred dollar-an-hour attorney handling a child custody case." Skip laughed. "I love it. I'll ask, but our relationship's been pretty one-sided lately."

"Don't worry, we'll find a way to pay him back."

"I don't want to know what it will cost." He paused, a sudden warmth running through him. "Hey, you said we."

She slipped her arm in his, settling in closer. "I did, didn't I?"

"So you want to keep her until her mother gets out of jail?"

"I've known her less than a week and I love her to death."

"You see yourself in her, don't you? I know what it is, you want to change her life. Roxy, I get the broken-wing syndrome."

Lily ran up to them, the half-opened shell of a mussel in her hand. "Look! It's, like, so cool. Do you, like, come here all the time?"

"I live here," said Skip. "I walk the beach most days."

"That's totally awesome."

Roxy pointed at the shell. "That's a beauty, sweetheart. Look, it's got blue, white, even some black. It's almost perfect."

"Why don't you give that one back to the ocean? Some creature might want a condo."

Lily nodded, waded into the water up to her knees and dropped the shell into the foam of an approaching wave. She high stepped it back to the shore always one step ahead of the foamy surf. "It's, like, freezing out there!" Goosebumps on her arms reinforced the obvious.

Skip nodded. "Imagine what it's like in the winter. See what else you can find."

Lily ran ahead, zigzagging in and out of the water along the shore.

"You're good with her." Roxy smiled.

"So do you want kids someday, Hot Rox?"

She bit her lower lip while she watched the sunset. After a few moments, she spoke. "I don't deserve them. I'd be a bad influence."

Skip put his hands on her shoulders. "Are you kidding me? After what you've done with Lily? You'd be great. Any kid would be lucky to have you as her mother."

She looked into his eyes. "Her? A daughter?" She gulped. "Are you saying you want a daughter?"

Skip felt the heat rising in his cheeks. Did he dare say what he felt? He cleared his throat. "Seems to be a tradition in your family."

Her brow furrowed. He wondered what that expression meant. Afraid to ask, worried that he might apply even one ounce too much pressure, he waited.

After a moment, Roxy said, "So what's this broken-wing syndrome?"

"You know, little birdie's gotten injured and you want to help her out. The thing is, there's no guarantee that the bird won't break her wing all over again." He slipped his arm around her shoulder.

"I know," she said. "But I have to try."

CHAPTER 77

R O X Y

I awoke at 2:17 a.m. with a start. Lily was sleeping beside me, her breathing soft and slow. Even with the blackout drapes, light from the apartment hallway snuck around the edges, casting the room into an ever-present dimness. It was a constant any night, every night.

My heart pounded. Overhead, the light fixture was nothing more than a dark shadow. I rubbed at my eyes. Once again, sleep was a hopeless commodity. The dream. It was always the same—me standing to one side watching a grownup version of Lily sway toward a man wearing a fancy suit. Dream Lily wore a mid-thigh skirt with a skimpy halter that left little to the imagination. She stroked the man's arm. It was the same move I'd used on Jack Welton. The dream Lily gazed at me with cool eyes. She said, "You could have, like, stopped this." She thrust a bare arm at me. Needle tracks. More than I could count. She sneered, "I hate you."

I readjusted the covers after I slipped out of the bed. On my way to the dining room, I eased the door shut. I waited while my laptop booted up, then typed in the address for the bank where I'd transferred Jack's fortune. One point five million. My cut after dictating terms to Anita.

For once in my life, I wanted nothing to do with the poison in that account. It had ruined the lives of investors caught in the pump-and-dump scheme and had, eventually, gotten Welton killed. Skip's friend Buddy claimed the cops were suspicious, but there was nothing to tie me to the theft. They had no leads thanks to a combination of offshore accounts and fake identities I'd set up years ago. I knew a score this big was hard to come by, but Anita, being inexperienced, was clueless. To teach her how naive she was, I collected on my favor from Baldorf. Happy, she wasn't. Compliant, she was after Baldorf hacked her account. He deposited more than a half million dollars without her knowledge. The explanation of how easily the money could go in, or come out, was enough to convince her she'd gotten a good deal.

My biggest concern was what to do about Lily. What would become of her? I stared at the closed bedroom door, chin on my knuckles, elbow propped up on the table. Wavy half shadows cast by the filtered light gave me solace. I needed to consider that little girl's future. What would happen? Every night for a week it had been the same dream, the same pattern. Like clockwork—so the saying went—I was programmed to wake up between 2:10 and 2:25 a.m.

The glow from my laptop screen was a harsh reminder of my impending decision. I remembered my mental image of Joey pushing over the dominoes. His plan had been brilliant, flawed only by his fear of exposure and a desire for revenge. I'd spent my entire life looking for a score like this. Losing three times this amount just a few months ago made the thought of giving this back almost unbearable. Skip was wired that way, not me.

The bedroom door creaked open. I winced. Lily was awake only because I couldn't sleep. She padded toward me, her bare feet making soft noises on the carpet. One of my oversized T's had become her nightgown of choice even though it hung almost to her knees. I closed the browser window, still watching her. So young. So much to learn. All the mistakes she could—no, would—make. Without someone's help, she'd never survive the danger around her.

"I'm sorry I woke you," I said.

"Are you, like, worried about somethin'? You been doing this, like, every night."

She stood next to me; I slipped an arm around her waist. Such broken innocence. "Not worried. I just have grownup stuff on my mind."

"About Skip?"

I shook my head. "A little. Mostly. I don't know, maybe I'm finally thinking about the future."

"Are you gonna, like, marry him?"

"He'd have to ask first and I'm not sure he's ready." I had a sudden flashback about our last walk on the beach. I'd given him an opening to talk about his feelings—he hadn't taken it. Was I wrong about him?

She hung her head. "Oh. You wanna send me back. I get it."

I wrapped my other arm around her and squeezed her tightly. "No sweetheart. That's not what I was thinking at all. I love having you around. You can stay with me until you can get back with your mom."

To me, her smile lit up the room, even in the dimness. "Then, like, you are thinking about Skip."

"Only a little. Right now I have someone else's future to be concerned about."

I closed the lid to my laptop. I stood, my mind made up. This girl was destined to break my heart, but she'd shown me I had one. She'd given me a priceless gift—a life. I had to make sure she got one, too.

"It's time to get some sleep. I know what I need to do."

Lily frowned. "I don't get it. Who's future is, like, so important?"

"Yours."

ABOUT THE AUTHOR

A painting of three mountains inspired Terry Ambrose to write his first short story when he was a child. The painting was titled "The Three Sisters" and the story, which he called, "The Great Spirit," was about how the sisters angered a powerful god, who then transformed them into mountains.

Terry started his business career skip tracing and collecting money from deadbeats. During his first day on the job, he learned that liars come from all walks of life. He never actually stole a car, but sometimes hired big guys with tow trucks and a penchant for working in the dark to "help" when negotiations failed.

Much like his protagonist in the McKenna Mysteries, Terry is a baby boomer, has a quick wit, and likes to follow a hunch. He and his wife live in Southern California where they run their own small business. Terry enjoys walking, swimming, and writing. In addition to working on his next novel, he reports on real-life scams and cons and does profiles of other authors on his website at TerryAmbrose.com.

THANK YOU

I hope you enjoyed reading *Con Game*. One thing readers can do to let an author know they've enjoyed a book is to pass the word along. If you could take a moment to tell your friends what you thought of the book, I'd appreciate it greatly. Whether it's in person or via your favorite social media site, any help you can provide in letting others know about the book will be appreciated. Another great way to help readers find authors is to post a brief review. If you have a minute, I'd appreciate it if you'd go to the site where you bought this book, or any review site such as Goodreads, and let others know you liked it.

Whether it's interviewing the best authors in the business, giving real tips about how to avoid scams and cons, or passing on news about my books, see what I'm up to next on my website at TerryAmbrose.com.

www.ingramcontent.com/pod-product-compliance
Lightning Source LLC
Chambersburg PA
CBHW031547240626
47153CB00002B/407